DOWNFALL

A Matt and Sara Foley novel

Book Three

V. B. TENERY

DEDICATION

To my Savior Jesus Christ.
May all I do honor You.

And

To my beloved grandsons,
Chase, Brandt, and Cole:
You have been the delight of my autumn years.

ISBN 13: 978-1979236102
ISBN 10: 1979236100

Contact Information:
Website: www.vbtenery.com
Blog: www.agatharemembered.blogspot.com
Twitter: @teneryherrin
FB Author Page: www.facebook.com/VBTenery

Scripture quotations, unless otherwise indicated are taken from the King James translation, public domain.

Cover Art by Sharon A. Lavy
Edited by: Barbara Hand
          Kathy McKinsey
Publishing History
First Edition CBC Press, A division of CBC Services April 2015
Published in the United States of America.

A Matt and Sara Foley novel

DOWNFALL

Watch for
MISSING
Book 4
Coming 2017

V. B.
TENERY

CHAPTER 1

The Connelly Home
Twin Falls, Texas

Shannon Connelly stepped out of the shower and slipped into a warm, woolly robe. Toes digging into the carpet's thick pile, she walked across to the bedroom window and opened the drapes. Sleet pinged against the windows and she shivered. Mid-January had arrived with a rare winter storm, the worst in years. She gazed into the distance as large, white flakes almost obscured the second-floor view of the neighborhood.

Almost

Across the street, movement in the near white-out caught her attention. Human or animal? Too tall to be an animal.

Odd.

Most likely her overactive imagination at work. She was nearsighted and her contact lenses still lay in the case on the nightstand. She turned away from the view and punched her feet into furry house slippers.

With a dismissive shrug, she put the scene out of her mind and trailed downstairs.

No work today, thank Heaven. After hearing the weather forecast yesterday, she'd made an executive decision to close the country club. Sundays were usually slow in the winter months anyway. No need to put her staff in danger for the few folks who might show up. As the club's manager, one of her many responsibilities was also the safety of the members. They didn't need to be out on the bad roads.

Spending a rare day off with her husband was an opportunity she intended to take full advantage of. Unlike her, Colin never worked weekends; one of the perks of being president of Twin Falls Bank and Trust.

The aroma of fresh brewed coffee welcomed her into the kitchen. She slid onto a seat at the bar, and Colin handed her a steaming cup of dark French Roast. He leaned over and kissed her brow. "Morning, Love. How about eggs Benedict for breakfast, in honor of my having you all to myself today?"

She sniffed the coffee like a fine wine before taking a sip, and observed her husband. At forty-five, Colin Connelly was twelve years older than she, and two inches taller than her own five-foot-nine-inch height; a little overweight, but firm bodied and very sexy with his shaved head. Not only was he brilliant and an attentive mate, he was also an amazing cook. She took a seat at the bar. "Sounds wonderful. You spoil me."

A scratching sound on the kitchen door drew her attention. "What on earth..." She set her cup on the counter, shuffled her furry slippers across the tile floor, and hoped it wasn't another raccoon. Last summer, when she'd heard a noise outside and opened the door, the masked animal sprinted into the house. It had taken her and a neighbor half a day to trap that sucker.

She peered through the window panel in the door and blinked. A white bulldog whined on the doorstep, almost invisible in the snow except for two pleading obsidian eyes.

"It's Sugar, from across the street," Shannon said and cast a quizzical glance at her husband. "Why would she be outside? The Davenports have a doggie-door."

Sugar's chubby little body hurtled inside when the portal opened. The muscular mutt was too heavy to lift, so Shannon enticed her further into the kitchen with a slice of maple-flavored ham.

Colin removed his oven mitt and knelt to scratch behind the dog's ear. He glanced up at Shannon, his brow wrinkled into a frown. "I think she's hurt. She has blood on her mouth and paws."

"I wonder what she's been into." Shannon said more to herself than to Colin. She stepped into the bathroom off the kitchen and came back with a warm washcloth. With little cooperation from Sugar, she scrubbed the dog's paws and mouth.

"You're just a great big ol' baby, Sugar." Shannon smiled and gave her another treat. Sugar wasted no time making the ham disappear, and then settled on a rug in the living room in front of the fireplace.

"I'll call Kathy and let her know we have Sugar, so she won't worry." Shannon picked up the cordless phone on the breakfast bar and dialed Kathy's number. No answer.

"Guess they're not at home. Maybe at church. After breakfast, while you shower, I'll take Sugar home."

Collin turned from the stove to face his wife. "Maybe Taylor can come and pick up Sugar, or I'll take her after I get dressed," Colin said.

"Taylor isn't at home this weekend. She went on a church retreat with her Sunday school class. Won't be home until tonight. I'll take Sugar. It's not a problem."

Venturing out into the snowstorm wasn't something Shannon looked forward to, but Art and Kathy would be concerned about their pet. They doted on the spoiled mutt.

Shannon swallowed the last delicious bite of breakfast and went upstairs to don Eskimo gear for the trek across the street: a warm, fashionable ski outfit, and boots she'd worn on their last trip to Vail. The belt from her bathrobe made a serviceable leash for the canine house guest.

With a reluctant Sugar in tow, Shannon trudged across the street to the Davenports' front door and rang the bell.

No response.

She rang again. Still nothing.

She looked through the garage window. Both cars were inside.

Funny.

Lights blazed in the entryway. Perhaps the Davenports were ill. Flu season had hit Twin Falls hard. News reports claimed local hospitals were full. She made her way around to the back, admiring the beauty of the white landscape. Cedars, heavy with snow, and bare oak limbs hung with shiny icicles, looked like a scene from a Christmas card.

Sugar's earlier paw prints leading away from the house became a darker red the closer she came to the back door. When Shannon knocked and tried to push Sugar through the doggie-door, the dog whined and balked, staying close to Shannon's side.

Again, the knock went unanswered.

She exhaled an exasperated breath and moved to the back windows, which presented an unobstructed view into the living room.

The sight turned her feet to stone on the hard-packed snow. Bile burned the back of her throat and tears welled in her eyes.

Panic suddenly released her stupor.

She scurried across the street, burst through the front door, and crashed into Colin. He reached out to prevent her falling face-first onto the tile floor.

"Colin, oh, Colin." She took deep gulps of air to slow her heart and quell her trembling hands. "Something terrible has happened to the Davenports."

CHAPTER 2

The Foley Residence,
Twin Falls, Texas

The faint rush of heat surging through the vents woke Matt from a sound sleep. Sara lay curled close against his side. He resisted the urge to disturb her peaceful slumber with a kiss, choosing instead just to watch her sleep.

Looking down at the lovely face of his wife of two weeks, he was filled with tenderness; something he thought he'd never feel again after the death of his first wife three years earlier.

His relationship with Sara had gotten off to a rocky beginning. Although he'd known her for years as his wife's best friend, when Sara's husband had been killed by a hit-and-run driver, she was his number-one suspect. Only after Sara's life had been repeatedly threatened did he learn the truth and come to know the real Sara Bradford.

Fading embers in the bedroom fireplace beckoned. He slipped out of bed and grabbed his robe. He quietly coaxed two logs onto the iron cradle, and then ignited the gas burners underneath. Mission accomplished, he went downstairs for a cup of fresh-roasted caffeine.

He and Sara had cut their honeymoon short by a day to get home before the worst of the snow and ice hit. They'd arrived late last night, just ahead of the storm. He'd dumped the luggage in the foyer, and headed into the kitchen to program the automatic coffeemaker.

He poured an extra cup of steaming black coffee and carried it upstairs. Rowdy, his Yorkie, padded along at his heels. Moving silently across the thick carpet, he set Sara's on the nightstand and watched her face in the flickering glow from the hearth. He sat on the bedside, leaned over, and kissed her lightly on the lips. "Good morning, Mrs. Foley. I brought you something to help you wake up."

Her eyelashes fluttered. She smiled and pushed up to a sitting position against the pillows. "This is cozy. I love your wake-up service. It's much better than a noisy old alarm clock. What time is it?"

"Nine o'clock." He handed her the mug.

"Smells wonderful. This is a habit I could learn to like." She took a tentative sip. "Is it terrible outside?"

"You're really going to miss Hawaii," he said with a laugh. "It's twenty degrees and snowing." He took the last gulp of coffee. "I'm going to jump in the shower then I'll bring up some bagels and more coffee."

One of his brighter ideas when drawing up the plans for this house had been the addition of a small breakfast nook off the bedroom, with a mini-bar and a table for two. Double-paned windows looked out over tall pines. On clear mornings, he could see the lake in the distance.

Sara yawned and stretched. "Give me a few minutes and I'll join you."

"For the bagels or the shower?"

"I meant for the bagels, but I could be enticed into the shower."

"You're much too distracting, and I want to go into the station this morning," he said with a grin. "Finish your coffee. I'll only be a few minutes."

She pushed the covers back, got out of bed, and stepped close to him, slipping both arms around his neck. "Am I distracting?"

He pulled her closer. "You are indeed."

She released a breath, long and slow, then patted his chest and stepped away. "You've been chomping at the bit to get back to work ever since we boarded the plane for home."

He pulled her back into his arms. "We still have one day left of our honeymoon. It wouldn't take a lot of encouragement to get me to stay home."

"Me neither, but I need to check on Danny and Poppy. I've missed them. Maybe we can all build a snowman later." Sara's two adopted kids had stayed with her aunt while she and Matt were on their

10

honeymoon.

"Sounds like a plan." He made his way into the bathroom and called over his shoulder, "You take the Jeep today. It has four-wheel drive and snow tires. The keys are on the hook by the garage door."

After the shower, Matt put thermal underwear on under his jeans and slipped into a turtleneck sweater, then went downstairs.

When he came back with the food and a carafe of coffee, Sara had already showered and changed. She added cream cheese and jelly from the mini-fridge under the bar.

Bagels sliced and slathered with toppings, Matt sipped coffee and took in the vista outside the window. An inch of snow covered the deck, the lawn, and dusted the pine tree limbs.

Near the edge of the woods, a doe, ever diligent, raised her head and glanced around before accompanying her fawn to the corn-filled feeder he kept there. The family appeared most mornings for breakfast around this time.

"This is lovely, Mat, like a picnic in a winter wonderland."

"I enjoy eating out here when I have time." He chuckled. "But usually, I just grab something and run, like now." He gave her arm a squeeze, then leaned in and placed a long kiss on her lips. "I love you, Sara Louise."

He expelled a deep breath. It was go now or never.

Grabbing the keys, he headed for his Escalade.

Twin Falls Police Station
Twin Falls, Texas

Snow followed Matt into the city. The windshield wipers thumped a steady beat as they removed the snow dust, whipped by strong northern winds that blew in from the Oklahoma panhandle.

He pulled into the almost-empty parking lot at eleven o'clock. Squad cars were already on the roads, taking care of accidents and helping stranded motorists. Cops didn't call in sick because of bad weather.

Matt stomped white powder from his feet, must be two inches of snow by now. He stopped at the front desk. "Hi, Chuck, is Davis in?"

A big smile spread across the desk sergeant's face. He stood and gave a hearty hand shake. "Hey, Chief, we weren't expecting you back until tomorrow." The sergeant's uniform seemed a tad too tight. Not surprising, since the sergeant's waistline had been slowly expanding over the years.

"Davis and Turner are upstairs. They're about to head out. Just got a call."

"Serious?"

"Sounded like it," Chuck said.

Upstairs in the detective bureau, Matt ran into Miles Davis and Lucy Turner in the doorway. Miles, ever the classy dresser, was buttoning a gray cashmere overcoat. He wrapped a scarf around his neck and pulled on black leather gloves.

"Welcome back, Chief," Davis said. "How was Hawaii?"

"Much better than here. What's going on?"

"Dispatch received a call about a body in a residence on Glen Haven Court, over on the north side." Davis handed Turner her hooded parka from the coat tree. "A neighbor saw a woman on the floor through a back window."

"Has it been confirmed?" Matt asked.

Lucy shrugged into her coat and nodded. "Yeah, a black and white went by. When they rang the bell and there was no response, the officers figured it might have been a murder, with the husband holed up inside waiting for them. However, upon closer examination, the back door was unlocked. One officer went inside and found a second body, male, just inside the door. He backed out and called it in. They're keeping things locked down until we get there."

"McCulloch left yet?" Matt asked.

"He's loading the mobile crime lab and getting his crew together," Davis said. "You coming?"

"I'll be right behind you."

DOWNFALL

In the gray morning light, Matt watched the two detectives climb into their silver unmarked Charger and leave the parking lot. He congratulated himself. Last year he'd paired Davis and Turner on a temporary basis to handle a major murder case. The switch worked so well, he'd made the change permanent.

Wind caught at the powder-fine snow and whipped it against Matt's face as he hurried back to his car, thankful it was still warm.

Fierce winds gusted down Main Street in front of the station, kicking up a white blizzard. He eased the Escalade onto the snow-covered roadway and past the town square. The old courthouse, now a cultural center, looked like an icy Gothic fortress in the faint light. He punched up the heat and passed under the Highway 75 overpass to the *haves* side of Twin Falls.

'Mansion' was the term most often used to describe the homes in Glen Haven Court, and he had no trouble identifying the right address. Two squad cars, blue and white lights flashing, sat on the street in front of a stately brick Georgian with a slate mansard roof and two-story windows in front; a secluded residence in an elegant neighborhood. Six-foot stone pillars stood on each side of the entrance, with a large mailbox tucked into the one on the right. A black wrought-iron fence the same height ran across the front of the property, the landscaping now covered in a silver-white blanket.

To avoid disturbing any footprints, Matt parked on the street behind the black-and-whites. Matt strode over to an officer leaning against his vehicle, a large Starbucks cup gripped in both hands. He recognized the stocky officer as a former Marine new-hire. "Any tracks in the powder when you arrived?"

The young man shook his head. "Only one set, which appear to be the neighbor's. She checked the front door and then went to the back. That's where she saw the female body through the window. Looks like the folks were murdered before or during the snowstorm. Any prints there might have been were buried by the storm."

"Where's the neighbor?"

"She went home." The officer pointed to the house

directly across the street.

"Do we have an ID on the victims yet?"

With a flip of his notebook the officer read his notes. "The house belongs to Arthur and Kathy Davenport. The neighbor's husband made the identification. He didn't think his wife was up to it."

Matt nodded and pressed his hands into his coat pockets. The wind was bitter cold. He hunched his shoulders against the frosty blast and trudged up the driveway to the back entrance, shivering at the icy wetness that seeped under his collar.

He looked up at the overcast sky and steeled himself before entering the murder scene. Reverence filled him in the presence of violent death. Killers not only robbed their victims of life, but also of their dignity, leaving them vulnerable and exposed in the presence of indifferent strangers. It was an abomination to God.

He and his team were the victims' advocates for justice.

Walking past the front entrance, he entered the residence through the back door. Warmth from the central heating system met him. He unbuttoned his coat and loosened his scarf, then proceeded farther inside.

The officer near the entrance handed him booties and latex gloves. "The sign-in register is on a table by the front door, Chief."

A short hallway branched out into the vestibule and a large, open room. On the left, a wide staircase led to the second floor. The first victim lay face-down in the small corridor. He wore pajamas and a blue plaid robe. One house slipper lay on the marble tile nearby, the other still on his right foot.

The man looked to be in his late fifties or early sixties, Caucasian, about average height, with one bullet hole in the back and one in his left temple. Powder burns surrounded the head wound. The shot had been fired at point blank range, probably after he fell. His position and where he lay suggested he'd attempted to run towards the front when the first bullet struck.

From the angle of the bullet wounds in the man's body, the shots looked to have been fired from the

French doors that led to the patio, but the CSI team would confirm that with exact measurements.

Matt stepped past the body and down the corridor. He met Medical Examiner Lisa Martinez hurrying through the double doors at the front entrance.

"Hey, Matt. You guys just getting here?"

"We arrived about ten minutes ago. We've been waiting for you to come do your thing."

"Yeah, sorry. The roads are a mess. Took me longer than usual. We'll get right on it so your people can get to work."

"Is Joe coming?" Joe Wilson was county sheriff, Lisa's fiancée, and Matt's best friend.

She laughed. "I haven't talked to him, but my guess is he'll be here soon. Just try to keep him away from a major crime in his county." She waved and joined Miles Davis near the male victim.

Matt approached the great room, where several CSU techs stood around waiting for the ME to release the crime scene to them. He stood back to take in the whole picture.

The room was huge, with high ceilings, elaborate crown molding, expensive Persian rugs, and highly-polished Italian Renaissance furnishings.

From his vantage point, a massive stone hearth came into view, embers still glowing in the ashes. A set of iron and brass tools were overturned and scattered on the tiles.

He moved farther into the area. Between a carved mahogany coffee table and plush sofa lay the second body, a woman about the same age and ethnicity as the man, with shoulder-length brown hair. She bore a striking resemblance to actress Sigourney Weaver. She wore navy fleece pajamas, and she, too, had been shot in the temple at close range. Unlike the man, there looked to be knife punctures in her chest. No defensive wounds on her hands.

It was human nature to try to defend the body against attack, even that of knives and bullets.

The stab wounds were most likely inflicted after the fatal shot. That was overkill. And it made the assault personal.

An empty, open briefcase lay on the coffee table, suggesting that the contents had been removed. The initials, AD, were engraved in gold just above the clasp. Had the killer taken everything, or had the owner died in the process of cleaning it out?

Matt left the living room and made his way upstairs to the master bedroom. The Italian Renaissance theme carried into the area, with heavy furniture and rich, dark colors of gold, red, and brown. Swag curtains of Italian silk framed a view of the backyard with an expansive outdoor room, now lost in the snow. The fragrance of sandalwood from a still-burning candle filled the space. He extinguished the flame with two fingers. The last thing they needed was for the crime scene to burn to the ground.

A bronze, enameled jewelry box lay open, its contents scattered on the rumpled duvet.

Expensive diamond bracelets, pins, and a ruby ring glittered in the overhead lighting. Was the killer looking for something in particular? If so, what? Hopefully, the family could tell them if anything was missing.

He stood by and watched the crime scene techs do their job until Davis stepped beside him.

"Mac is finishing up downstairs. Lucy just left to talk to the neighbors, Colin and Shannon Connelly. I'm going to join her. Want to come along?"

Matt glanced over at Davis and raised an eyebrow. Shannon Connelly found the body? The Connellys were good friends, although he'd never been to their home. "I'll tag along, I know the couple. Did our people find any of the casings?"

Davis nodded. "A 9mm shell was lodged in a cushion; probably a missed shot at the woman, from the angle. Looked like she tried to evade the bullet, and it hit the sofa. Now all we need is a gun to match it to."

"Any thoughts on the empty briefcase?"

"Mac found tiny burned pieces of paper in the fireplace. Nothing we could identify. May have been Mr. Davenport or the killer. We need to find out if he was carrying anything important in the case when he died."

They wended their way back downstairs and Davis motioned to the CSU chief, signaling that he and Matt were leaving.

"We have positive ID on the victims as the Davenports?" Matt asked.

Davis wound his scarf around his neck and buttoned his overcoat. "Yeah, Colin Connelly made a visual identification, and the contents of both wallets were dumped on the floor, driver's license, money, and credit cards. It's the Davenports all right."

"Did Lisa give us a window on the time of death?"

Davis nodded. "Tentatively, from four to seven this morning. They hadn't been dead long when the neighbor discovered the body."

Davis turned up his coat collar as they stepped out into the blustery winter wind. "Whatever the motive, it certainly wasn't robbery."

CHAPTER 3

The Connelly Home
Twin Falls, Texas

Glen Haven Court ended in a cul de sac, with four homes on oversized wooded lots. The Connelly residence sat directly across from the Davenports, with the same wrought-iron fence and circular drive, but with Mediterranean architectural arches.

By the time Matt and Davis tramped across the slick street, Shannon Connelly had the door open. She enveloped Matt in a long hug. "Hey, handsome; I didn't know you guys were home. You didn't waste any time getting back into the saddle."

"Unfortunately, murderers don't make appointments." He returned the hug then shrugged out of his coat.

Davis moved farther into the room and closed the door behind him.

Outside of his wife, Shannon Connelly was one of the most attractive women Matt knew. Always fashionably dressed in clothes that flattered her plus-size figure, every strand of her shoulder length, frosted hair in place, and gray eyes that always sparkled with mischief. Today, the sparkle was noticeably diminished.

"I'm sorry you had to come out on this one, Matt," she said. "I'm having trouble accepting they're gone. Art and Kathy were good people, great friends, and hospitable neighbors. They'd planned to retire next year. It's unbelievable that something like this could happen to them. Thank God, Taylor wasn't at home or she . . ."

"Who's Taylor?" Matt asked.

"Their twelve-year-old daughter." Shannon shivered and ushered them into the kitchen.

Detective Turner leaned against the bar, with a steaming cup in her hand, chatting with Colin. He stood at the island in a frilly red apron, his masculinity unthreatened by the feminine garb.

The older man paused from making sandwiches and greeted Matt with a wave. "Grab a bite and a cup of coffee, Matt. Shannon's had me working all morning, thinking you guys could use some food since most restaurants and fast-food joints will be closed."

"Thanks, Colin, maybe later. Right now, we need to talk to you and Shannon, if you can break away."

Matt and the two detectives followed Shannon into the den.

"It'll be quiet in here." She offered them a seat and sat next to the hearth's glowing fire. Colin trekked along behind her, untying the apron as he went, then chose to stand next to her chair.

The two detectives took the sofa across from Shannon; Matt opted to lean against the wall near the doorway.

Turner took the lead, and positioned a recorder on a nearby end table. "Okay if I record this?"

"Sure," Shannon said.

Turner switched on the machine, gave the date, and those present. "Tell us what happened."

Shannon reached for Colin's hand, and then took a deep breath. "The Davenports' dog, Sugar, scratched on our door about eight this morning." She nodded at the white bulldog curled up by the hearth. "We let her in, and Colin noticed she had blood on her paws."

She dropped her hands into her lap and laced her fingers, knuckles white, then ran through the steps that led to the discovery of Kathy Davenport's body.

"Did you see anyone or strange cars in the neighborhood?" Lucy asked.

"No, but that's to be expected in this weather. People stay inside."

"Did you or Colin hear anything unusual last night or this morning?"

Shannon hesitated. "You can take this with a grain of salt, but I thought I saw someone move away from the Davenports' driveway about seven. I dismissed it at the time, since I wasn't wearing my contacts, but I didn't hear anything."

"Any possibility you could identify who you saw?"

Lucy asked.

"No. As I said, I wasn't even sure of what, if anything, I saw. It was snowing heavily and still dark outside."

"How about you, Colin?"

He shook his head. "I didn't see or hear anything until Sugar made her appearance. I called their daughter, Claire; she's a vice president at my bank. I hope that's okay. I thought they should know. Claire's on her way here. The Davenports had three daughters; Claire, Eden, and Taylor. Claire said she'd notify Eden. Taylor won't be home until tonight."

"That's fine; we'll need to talk to them anyway," Lucy said.

As if on cue, the doorbell rang. "That's probably Claire now," Colin said and hurried to answer the summons.

Claire Davenport and her sister, Eden Russell, arrived with Jack McKinnon. Claire looked too young to be a banker, and beautiful enough to star in her own television series. She looked to be in her mid-thirties, tall and slim with blonde hair and dark blue eyes. She wore country-club casual, designer slacks, cashmere layered sweaters, and an expensive overcoat. WASP breeding was etched into her classic profile. She took a seat on the white leather sofa.

Eden Russell was her sister's equal in every way, an outdoorsy type, with a thick blonde mane, the perfect model for a *Town and Country* magazine cover. Eden, obviously the younger, wore jeans, a fleece-lined jacket, and boots. She took a seat in a matching chair across from her sister.

Jack strolled over to Matt and shook his hand. They'd met last year during a murder investigation. Tall and muscular, lean-built rather than bulky, his unruly dark hair was wind-tossed and his square-jawed face wore the slight facial hair favored by young men his age. It gave him a rugged look, reinforced by jeans and a heavy Northface jacket.

Jack nodded at Eden. "She was at my place when Claire called. I came along to offer whatever support I could. The roads are too bad for someone not used to driving in icy weather."

A low moan sounded from Claire Davenport. The banker dropped her head in her hands. "You're sure they're both...dead?"

Matt leaned forward and watched the woman's face. "I'm very sorry. The ID is positive. There's no question."

"How?" Claire asked, a pained grimace on her face.

It bothered Matt that he wasn't watching this daughter with compassion, but as a possible suspect. Over time, he had learned to thrust sympathy aside and observe next of kin with a cop's instinct, watching for false grief and insincerity.

Family members were always suspects until proven otherwise. So far, Claire's grief seemed genuine. "There are things we can't share about the crime scene, but the cause of death appears to be gunshot wounds. The coroner's verdict will be the final word. You can get a copy later in the week if you wish."

"I can't believe this happened to them. I spoke to Mom last night." Claire shook her head repeatedly, tears pooling in her blue eyes.

"What time did you speak to your mother?" Matt asked.

She glanced up at him. "Around nine...nine-thirty. Do you have any idea who—no, of course not. It's too early."

"Do you know of anyone who might want your parents dead?" Matt asked.

"No, no one. This is impossible..." She lowered her head into her hands again.

Matt turned his attention to Eden. "Did you speak to either of them last evening?"

She shook her head, no obvious signs of sorrow, but people handled grief in different ways.

"Can we see them?" Claire asked.

"It's a crime scene. Only police personnel are allowed inside. And I don't think that's how you want to remember your parents. When you feel up to it, we'll need to ask you both some more questions. Someone will call in a day or so to set up and interview."

"Of course," Claire said, and then turned to Colin. "I need to get home and let Win know." She closed her eyes for a moment. "And I'll have to tell Taylor." She sat back down. "I don't know if I can do that."

"Do you want me to tell her? Or call your pastor?" Colin asked, his voice gentle.

"I'll call our pastor. He'll know how to handle it." She gazed up at Colin. "Thanks for the offer, and for calling me."

She rose and gazed at Jack McKinnon, a steely glint in her eyes. The skin tightened around her jaw, and she waited a beat before she spoke. "I'll take Eden home with me, McKinnon. She doesn't need to be alone. And there are family matters—arrangements we have to discuss."

McKinnon, heir to the Grayson fortune, could buy and sell Claire Davenport fifty times over, but he was *nouveau riche*, the son of a gardener. Therefore, apparently in Claire Davenport's mind, socially inferior.

Jack ignored the slur. "Of course. Let me know if there's anything I can do to help."

Shannon entered the room with a tray of coffee and sandwiches. She spoke to Claire. "Won't you and Eden stay and have a bite with us?"

"I-I couldn't," she said. "But thanks, Shannon."

Eden left her chair and crossed the room to Jack's side. She placed a light kiss on his cheek. "Thanks for bringing me. I'll call you."

Colin gave Claire a hug. "Take as much time from work as you need to handle your affairs. There's nothing at the bank that can't wait. I'll be in touch."

When they had gone, Shannon joined Matt and ran her arm through his. "Glad you're back. You look tanned and rested."

"It was a wonderful two weeks. But it's good to be home, despite the sad business across the street."

Colin gave a somber nod. "It's a shame. They were a fine couple."

Matt took a seat by Jack at the island, and handed him a mug filled with hot coffee. "As a wise man once told me, you can't inherit or buy class."

Jack gave Matt a faint grin. "I don't let Claire Davenport get to me. She's a snob of the first order, and

Eden isn't much better. Taylor's a good kid, but her sisters think their blue blood makes them superior to us mere mortals."

"Blue blood?" Matt asked.

"Yeah. Judge Bittermann is their aunt, and they also have a renowned heart surgeon in the family tree."

"Then you're not serious about Eden?" Matt asked.

"Far from it. She called yesterday and invited herself over. Her two boys were at their dad's in Oklahoma City. When the weather turned bad, she invited herself to spend the night. It's not like I don't have room for house guests. I could put the Cowboys up for the weekend."

Matt chuckled. "I guess you could at that. Who's Win?"

"Winston James Charles Seymour." Jack grinned. "He's Claire's significant other. Minor English royalty of some kind."

When the crime scene cleared for the day, Matt's officers and detectives trooped into the kitchen, followed by Sheriff Joe Wilson. Word must have spread about the food.

Shannon had been right. All the drive-through places and restaurants never opened, or closed early due to the weather conditions. His hungry crew dove into the impromptu spread like a pride of hungry lions.

She and Joe Wilson stepped up behind Matt. Shannon put an arm around Jack's neck. "Since Sara took Matt off the market, you are now the state's most eligible bachelor."

Jack wrinkled his brow. "Don't spread that around. I have enough problems without advertising."

Joe Wilson scowled at her. "What does that make me, chopped liver?"

She slapped his shoulder. "No, Wilson, you're number two because you're spoken for."

Joe grinned down at her. "You have a silver tongue, Shannon Connelly, but you have severely bruised my ego."

"You'll survive." She winked at him then lured Jack into helping her bring in more food from the kitchen.

Joe took the stool Jack vacated. "I didn't expect to see

23

you here. When did you and Sara get home?"

"Late last night."

Joe shifted his big frame and inclined his head toward the street. "I did a walk-through of the crime scene before your people closed up shop. Can't make up my mind whether it was random or personal."

"Or a madman on the loose," Matt added. His mind played with the possibilities. The knife wounds seemed to make it personal.

"Find any witnesses so far?" Joe asked.

"None. Davis had officers question the neighbors. No one saw or heard anything. The storm kept everybody inside, close to the fire. The gunman must have used a silencer." Matt gave a nod in Shannon's direction. "She thought she saw something around seven this morning, but wasn't sure. That squares with Lisa's time-of-death window."

Matt pushed off the barstool and gave his friend a pat on the shoulder. Nothing more could be accomplished today, and he needed to get home. "I think I'll head out. If I hurry, I can get to the house in time to have dinner with my bride."

Joe shook Matt's hand. "Smart move."

Matt made the rounds, saying goodbye, and stopped at Miles Davis' side. "I'll see you and Turner in the morning so we can compare notes."

Matt walked to the window and peered into the darkened street. Snow and sleet had begun to fall again. He retrieved his coat from the entry closet where Shannon had stored it, and left the warmth of the Connelly home.

He walked gingerly to his SUV. A broken bone or concussion would be inconvenient. Inside the car he gripped the cold steering wheel and started the engine, and then speed-dialed Sara's number. "Hey, I'm on my way."

"Hey, yourself. I hoped you'd call soon. I didn't want to bother you on the job."

"I'll stop by the house and pick up some clothes. We can spend the night at your place so we don't have to bring the kids out in this weather. Soon, we're going to have to discuss which domicile we're going to call home. Is Beatrice making something special for dinner? I'm starved."

"I don't know what it is, but it smells wonderful. Hurry home. I missed you."

"Me too. More by the minute."

He made a U-turn in front of the Davenport home, now dark and foreboding, and compartmentalized the day's events. The case held secrets he would have to peel back, layer by layer. But the case could wait until tomorrow. It wasn't going anywhere tonight.

CHAPTER 4

Sara Bradford's Home
Twin Falls, Texas

When the police siren on Matt's phone sounded at five a.m., his hand shot out and shut it off. He might need to rethink that alarm tone.

Through the open drapes, a soft glow of moonlight shimmered like liquid silver across Sara's face. She stirred then turned to face him. "No need to be quiet. I'm awake," she said with a sleepy yawn and snuggled close to him. "Do you have to rush off to the station?"

He stroked her hair, and then kissed the tip of her nose. Slipping his arm under her head, he drew her nearer. "Yes. Big murder case from yesterday. I have a meeting with Davis and Turner this morning."

Wide awake, she raised up on one elbow. "Anyone I know?"

"Do you know Art and Kathy Davenport?"

"Not personally, but they're members of our church. I do know their daughters, Claire and Eden, from the country club. Eden's twin boys took swimming lessons last summer with Poppy and Danny. What happened?"

"Art and Kathy were murdered sometime Sunday morning. Shot. Shannon Connelly found Kathy's body. That's about all I know right now."

"How awful for Shannon, and even worse for the family. I'll have to contact them and see if there's anything I can do." Sara sneezed and reached for a tissue from the nightstand. "I hope I'm not coming down with the flu."

"Did you get the shot?"

"No. Too busy. Besides, that's no guarantee. Guessing the right strain is a shot in the dark for the CDC. No pun intended."

"If you start to run a fever, go to the doctor."

"Aye, aye, Chief," she laughed. "I would salute, but

it's impossible to do properly from a prone position."

"Don't be impertinent, woman. I'm just doing my job as a doting husband." He would have to watch becoming paranoid about Sara's health. Losing Mary had made him overly-sensitive. He didn't want to smother Sara with his phobia. She was a strong, intelligent woman and could take care of her own well-being, something he would have to keep reminding himself.

"I appreciate your concern, but I don't want you to worry about me." She ran her hand over the stubble on his face. "We didn't get a chance to talk about our living arrangements last night."

Hair had fallen across her face, and he brushed it back off her brow. "Sorry, I wanted to spend time with the kids before they went to bed, then the evening got away from me. Danny is becoming quite the chess-player." He chuckled. "I thought I'd go easy on him and let him win, build his confidence. But he was too smart for me. When I made a dumb move, he looked over at me and knew exactly what I was doing. Give him ten years and he'll be a chess master. I had to struggle to beat him.

He rested his chin on her head and stroked her arm. "I will always make time for you, Sara Louise."

She sneezed again, grabbed another tissue, and held it to her nose. "That's one of the things I love about you, but you have more important things to take care of. We'll just wing it until things settle down."

He tossed the cover back. "I'm good with that. Think I could find something to eat downstairs, or should I grab a bite on the way to the station? It's no problem. I usually don't have time to eat in the morning. I'm well known at Starbucks and The Sunny Side Up Café."

"I'll take care of breakfast while you shower," she said, and slipped into her robe. "Beatrice made fresh tortillas last night. I'll whip up a few egg, sausage, and potato burritos in no time and join you."

Twin Falls Police Station
Twin Falls, Texas

Murder was major news in most cities, and especially in places like Twin Falls, because of its rarity. And bad news traveled fast. Only one news van had made it to the crime scene yesterday. Roads were still a mess, but the city's trucks had sanded most of the thoroughfares. No snow or sleet in today's forecast, and nothing to keep the news hounds away. The Dallas and Ft. Worth news crews would be out in force.

Matt called his boss, City Manager Doug Anderson, and the District Attorney, Gabriel Morrison, last night after he left the crime scene, to give them a heads-up. Hopefully they would keep the press off his back while he did his job.

Matt pulled into the parking lot leading to the back entrance to his office. A cold wind whipped around the building's corner, hitting him in the face before he reached the door, and he missed seeing Abe Harris, the crime-beat reporter for *The Twin Falls Herald*, waiting for him.

Busted.

"Hey, Matt. Help a hard-working man out. Give me the lowdown on the Davenport murders."

"You'll have to talk to the DA, Abe. You know that. All news releases will come through his office."

"Come on, Matt, give me something I can use. I'll make it worth your while." The guy was relentless.

Matt laughed. "What, you're going to bribe an officer of the law? I thought you and Mayor Hall were bosom buddies and he gave you inside information."

"Not any more. He's given me too many bum leads. The paper had to write a retraction because of him, and my boss was not happy."

Guilt washed over Matt, but not a lot. Last year, the mayor planted a snitch in the police department, and when Matt discovered the identity of the informer, he had planted that bum information where Hall's mole could find it.

The mayor was always looking to get his name in the news, and he'd been a major pain in Matt's backside since his election last year. His Honor had been quiet since the fiasco with the retraction. A quiet Terrance

Hall made Matt very uncomfortable.

"Sorry, Abe, the answer is still no. See Gabe. He'll give you the news as it develops."

The reporter mumbled under his breath and shuffled back to his car.

Matt entered his office, dropped off his briefcase, and made his way upstairs to the second-floor detective bureau.

A white-haired senior volunteer met him in the doorway. Martha kept the lunch room and conference rooms spotless. She leaned in and whispered, "I made some fresh cinnamon rolls and put them in the conference room, chief. I'm putting two in your office. Otherwise, Chris will hog them all."

"I heard that, Martha," Chris Hunter said. "I thought we were going steady."

She ignored him and went on her way.

All four detectives were at their desks. Chris Hunter, Davis' partner until the recent switch, saluted him with a breakfast sandwich in hand. "Good morning, chief."

The division's unchallenged clown, Chris looked like a dark-haired Pillsbury Doughboy, always upbeat. His unruly mop of dark curls was regularly in need of a trim.

Chris was as different from his debonair ex-partner as chic from grunge. He was five-feet-eleven, and about forty pounds overweight, due to his penchant for fast-food. He sat sideways at his desk, feet propped in the open bottom drawer.

His latest partner, Cole Allen, held the title of the youngest detective in the unit. He gave Matt a wave of acknowledgement, and then returned his attention to the computer monitor.

Matt pulled up a chair next to Chris. "You guys got anything going this morning?"

"We're winding up an assault/robbery case. A biker dude with full-sleeve tats called in a report that his girlfriend beat him up and stole most of his electronics," Chris said. "We went to the woman's apartment, and she had his stuff. Didn't even bother to deny the charges. Seemed kind of proud of her skills. He was over six feet, she was barely five-two." Hunter grinned. "If I were him, I'd drop the charges rather than let anyone know that little girl could take me. We just deposited her in a cell. Cole is finishing up the paperwork."

"Good. You guys can join Davis and Turner for a meeting in fifteen minutes."

At nine o'clock, Matt stepped into the conference room. The area was standard police- department-dull: white paint, a large oval table with eight faux leather chairs, a six-foot white erase board on the wall. TV, VCR, and an overhead projector stuck in a corner.

The detectives were already assembled and waiting.

Matt helped himself to a cup of coffee from the pot at the counter and, as Martha had predicted, the rolls were gone. "Okay, who wants to go first?"

"Ladies first," Davis said. "So, Chris, I guess that means you're up."

Chris and Cole laughed. Lucy Turner scowled.

Lucy came to the detective bureau a little over a year ago with a huge chip on her shoulder. Matt hadn't been sure she would make it. She was an intuitive investigator, but didn't play well with the rest of the team. Davis' tutelage had smoothed off a lot of her rough edges, but not all of them.

"Just kidding, Turner." Davis' lip turned up in a grin. "Tell us what you've got."

She flipped a sheet on her notebook. "Not a lot, just some Internet research on the Davenport siblings. It's amazing what you can find out on the Net. I'll start with Claire. We already know she's a VP at Colin's bank. Never married. Probably doesn't make enough money to support her lifestyle. Maybe has an inheritance. Lives upscale in a home near her parents, owns a late-model Bentley. Has a live-in boyfriend with no visible means of support I could find, but drives a new Jaguar. No children. Country club membership. Maybe financed by her folks or the boyfriend."

"Does the boyfriend have money?" Davis asked.

"Possibly. He has a title of some kind, so there may be money there. He played professional tennis some years back."

"See if you can get a warrant to look at the financial records of all the players," Davis said.

Turner jotted an entry in her notebook and continued, "Eden Russell is an interesting case. A perpetual student. She's thirty and still in college, going for her second master's. My guess would be school was financed by her parents. She's divorced from Dr. Stephen Russell, of Oklahoma City. They're in a bitter custody battle over their twin boys. Articles didn't go into detail. She probably gets hefty child support, but owns a so-so condo on the better side of town. Drives a new car, but appears to have little cash flow." Turner wiggled her eyebrows. "Maybe that's why she has Jack McKinnon in her crosshairs.

"Taylor Davenport is enrolled at Hockaday Girls' School in Dallas, very upscale, very pricey. Excels at tennis and swimming. That's all I could find on her."

Turner pulled a handful of photos from a manila folder. "I have some shots from Google Images, mostly society page stuff."

"Make copies for me, Lucy when you get a chance," Matt said.

"Good work," Davis said. "That's it?"

She nodded.

Davis reached into his jacket pocket and placed his notebook on the table but didn't open it. "Guess it's my turn, since Chris and Cole just joined the party. Neighborhood interviews last night were a bust. They were all inside, huddled close to the hearth. No one saw anything. No one heard anything. No one knows anything.

"As soon as possible, we need to get family members to walk through the house and see if anything is missing, ask about the empty briefcase. See if they know what their father might have carried in it. May not be important, but it's puzzling.

"Davenport owned an architectural firm, The Drawing Board. We'll check with his manager and inquire if Davenport would have carried anything confidential home. I can't imagine what that might be, but we'll ask. I'm also checking VICAP for similar cases in the past year."

Matt stood and pushed his chair back under the table. "Looks like we're on the right track. You guys know the drill. Chris, you and Cole work with Lucy to get the phone and credit card records of Art and Kathy, and Claire and Eden, for the last thirty days. Reconstruct their movement over the last twenty-four hours as near as possible. Where they went, who they talked with in person or on the phone, etcetera." He looked around the table at his detectives. "Any questions, suggestions, anything we missed?"

"Lucy and I are going back to the residence today," Davis said. "The victims had a home office. We'll check that, see what shakes out."

"I'm interviewing Kathy's sister, Judge Bittermann, today." Matt tossed his empty cup in the trash can. "If that's it, let's get to it. Same time, same place tomorrow. We'll see where we stand."

Matt had a list of the Davenport siblings. He would start with Judge Judith Bittermann. The judge and he went back a long way. He wanted to offer his condolences and see if she had thought about a possible motive. She was intelligent and organized, but also grieving.

The judge was a local legend. After ten years on the county bench, she was appointed as a state judge for the Fourteenth District Court in Dallas, where she remained until President Ronald Reagan, in his last year in office, appointed her to the United States District Court for the Northern District of Texas. She retired last year.

Back in his office, he picked up the phone and dialed her home number and asked her to lunch.

He hung up the phone, and a shadow blocked the light from the corridor outside his office. Sheriff Joe Wilson stood in the doorway, with an envelope in his big hand. "I'll let you buy my lunch if you twist my arm."

"Can't, I just asked Judge Bittermann to lunch. You're welcome to join us if you wish," Matt said, "or I'll spring for coffee in the lunch room."

"I'll take a rain check on the lunch." He waved the

envelope. "I brought you a hard copy of Lisa's autopsy report. She is also emailing you a copy."

Matt joined Joe in the hallway, and they made their way to the lunch room. He filled foam cups from the coffee bar. "You running errands for Lisa these days?" he asked with a grin.

Joe snorted a laugh and handed Matt the report. "Whatever the woman wants."

"Any surprises?" Matt asked as he unfolded the document.

"Haven't read it, but, if there was anything unusual, Lisa would have mentioned it. She gave Davis a copy when he picked up the bullets she removed."

Matt gave the file a quick read while Joe sipped his coffee. "Both died from the head gunshot wounds. Kathy Davenport's knife wounds were postmortem and look to have been inflicted by a serrated hunting knife."

His friend nodded and crushed the empty cup in his hand. "Yeah, Lisa sent photos to McCulloch, to see if he could determine the make and model."

"When are you going to marry that woman?" Matt asked.

"In June. She wanted to wait until school was out. Paul spends every other summer with his dad, and this is his summer, which works out well for us. He can attend the wedding, and then go have fun with his father rather than stay with his grandmother while we're on our honeymoon."

"You need a best man, I'm available," Matt said.

"I wouldn't consider anyone else."

The Big Catch Restaurant
Outside Twin Falls, Texas

Matt had persuaded the judge to meet him for lunch at her favorite eatery. The Big Catch was one of the best-kept secrets in Twin Falls. The restaurant sat on the shores of Lake Palmer, with a spectacular view of the water and tall pine trees, not to mention the best seafood in the state. He picked a table by the window and glanced out across the lake's smooth surface. He shivered, remembering a jump off a bridge into its cold depths last year to rescue a drowning woman. The almost-victim had been Sara.

The judge opted to have her chauffer/assistant drive her, rather than let Matt pick her up. She had to meet with the family after lunch to make funeral arrangements.

He stood as the hostess led the judge to the table, and he held out her chair. "Sorry to bother you while you're grieving your sister's loss, Judge, but, as you know, the first forty-eight hours after a crime are crucial."

She took her seat and shrugged out of her coat, letting it rest on the chair back. "I know, and I needed to get out of the house and away from all the telephone calls. Besides, I want to find whoever did this as much or more than you do."

A waiter took their drink orders. The restaurant served wassail during the winter months, a hot apple cider, with orange juice and spices. They both opted for a mug.

"I hate to hit you with routine questions, but they have to be asked. Do you have any idea who might have wanted your sister and her husband dead?"

"If I had any idea, I would have called you already. It seems senseless to me, Matt. As far as I know, they didn't have an enemy in this world. Kathy was the baby of our family. She could have been a great actress if she had seriously pursued it. She wasn't a great beauty, although she was certainly attractive. Her theater group performed the play *Separate Tables* Saturday night at the Cultural Center Theater on the square."

The judge's gaze drifted out the window. "She gave a great performance. I'm going to miss her terribly."

"Any possible conflict in the theater group?"

Their server brought the wassail and took the food orders. Grilled salmon for her, Cajun fried catfish for him.

When the waiter left, Judith answered. "I doubt it. The cast is mostly stock company actors, and even if they held a grudge against Kathy, there would have been no reason to harm Art."

"Was she happily married?"

"I think so. They weren't openly affectionate, but they teased each other in a friendly, flirty way, and seemed to genuinely like each other. Art was her greatest fan."

"How about the children? Any problems there?"

"As the oldest, Claire had a close relationship with Kathy. As did Taylor. Kathy doted on them, but she and Eden had their differences. Not an unusual occurrence between a mother and daughter. Who can explain why some mothers and daughters are best friends, and others barely speak?"

"Were they speaking?"

Judith waited a beat before answering. "Yes. I don't think there was any unusual tension in the relationship until recently. Kathy tried very hard to never let it get out of hand. She always gave in to Eden to keep the peace. She loved her grandsons and wanted to keep the relationship on good terms for their sake. Eden can be difficult to deal with."

"So, there was a recent quarrel between them?"

Judith gave a slight nod. "Kathy wasn't happy about Eden divorcing her husband. She thought Eden should have tried harder to make a go of it for the boys' sake. And Art agreeing to testify for Stephen in the custody battle drove a wedge between Eden and her father, with Kathy caught in the middle."

"Do you know why she divorced her husband?'

The judge gave a slight shrug. "I don't think there was a specific reason. It seemed to me Eden just didn't like living in Oklahoma."

Their food arrived, and the judge looked down at her grilled salmon, then across at Matt's platter piled high with golden, crispy catfish, its spicy fragrance filled the air around them. "I'm trying to watch my cholesterol, and you're not helping."

"Sorry, I'll share. There's enough here for two people." He took a bite, trying not to enjoy it too much, and then returned to their previous conversation. "Seems a trivial reason to end a marriage."

"Yeah, well, Eden is a woman of strong opinions.

Things are either black or white. No grays allowed. She has a real hate on for her ex."

Judith forked a small piece of fish from his platter and grinned. "One little piece won't hurt me."

"Any other problems between Eden and her mother?"

Judith looked down at her plate. "Not that I know of."

She continued. "We are all grieving the loss of Kathy and Art, but the one hurt most by their deaths is Taylor. She idolized her parents, and she was never particularly fond of her sisters, particularly, Eden. Her young life has been turned on its head."

On the drive back to Twin Falls, Matt switched on the radio to a local country music station. They were playing George Straight's "I Cross My Heart", one of Matt's favorites, and his thoughts drifted to Sara and the lovely image of her making breakfast this morning.

The music swelled and filled the inside of his SUV as he turned onto the freeway. A sudden thought struck him. Judith Bittermann hadn't told him everything she knew about her sister's family.

The good judge was holding something back.

CHAPTER 5

Grayson Manor
Twin Falls, Texas

Jack McKinnon stared at the lavish tray Perkins had just delivered to the library. Tea cakes, Devonshire cream, finger sandwiches, strong black tea, and French roast coffee included.

The butler insisted on acting the servant since Jack became master of Grayson Manor.

It would have been simpler had Jack not grown up in this house as the gardener's son. He'd been on personal terms with the household servants his entire life. Perky, as Jack had always called the butler, wasn't handling the transition well.

Jack's father and Perkins had been best of friends, playing chess in the kitchen in the evenings, and Perkins no longer knew how to relate to his friend, Sean McKinnon. One just didn't play chess with the master's father, or so Perkins believed.

Jack took a sip of tea and drew his lips back across his teeth. Wearing the mantle of the Grayson heir was not as easy as it might appear.

"I thought I saw Perkins headed this way with tea," his father said, hastening to the fireplace and spreading his hands to its warmth. "I'm hungry."

Despite his new position, Sean McKinnon still felt he had to oversee the garden and give advice to the new groundskeeper. He took a seat next to Jack, poured a cup of tea, and grabbed a sandwich. "I hate drinking tea from these fancy china cups. It goes cold too soon. Think we could get him to bring us a proper mug when it's just the two of us?"

Jack laughed. "You can try."

Jack took a seat in front of the fireplace and rested a booted foot on the stone hearth. An oil painting of his wife, Victoria Grayson, hung above the fireplace. A local artist had painted it, using Jack's favorite snapshot as a model.

His wife of only two months was pregnant with their child when she was killed. Vic, both of her parents, her brother, and their cook had been murdered in the manor a little less than a year ago. Jack had been arrested for the murders before Matt Foley found the real killer.

His father's gaze followed his, and his voice became husky when he spoke. "Aye, it's a bonny portrait, Jacky. Victoria was a lovely, sweet lass." He gulped down his last sip of tea, poured another, and sat silently, watching the embers drift up the chimney. After a while, he exhaled a deep breath and headed back to the garden.

Jack smiled as his father hurried from the room. Perkins wasn't the only one having difficulty with the transition.

The muted buzz from the cordless phone at Jack's elbow brought him back into the moment.

Caller ID reflected *Eden Russell*. He groaned inwardly and pushed the talk button. "Hello, Eden."

"Hi, Jack. Glad I caught you." Children's voices in the background filtered through the phone. "I was wondering if the boys and I could drop by Wednesday. They want to play billiards. They love it out there."

"Hey, Eden, I'd love to, but I have a board meeting at Grayson Limited starting tomorrow. Since the roads are bad, I'm staying in town." All true now, though if the roads cleared, and they probably will, he would come home. She didn't need to know that.

The line was silent for a beat or two. "Are you avoiding me, Jack?"

"Why would I avoid you?" Answer a question with a question when the answer is yes.

Even if she had been an angel, no way did he want Claire Davenport for a relative. And Eden was no angel.

"It just seems when I want to see you, you're always busy. Have I made you mad? I thought after Saturday night..."

Saturday night had been a mistake. "No, of course I'm not angry. I just have a lot of obligations as chairman of the Grayson board." Again, all true. She hadn't made him mad, but had turned him off with her obvious favoritism between her twin boys. The boys weren't identical. Brandon looked like his dad, Brian like her side of the family. Brandon couldn't do anything right. On their last visit, she had ragged on the boy until Jack wanted to throw her out of his home. Verbal abuse of a child was inexcusable, and often just as damaging as the physical kind.

She rang off, with her tidy-whities in a twist.

He was busy. So much so, he decided to interview several secretarial applicants to handle the correspondence coming in. Calls from charities wanting money, social invitations, and his personal bank account information came in so fast he couldn't handle the deluge.

His thoughts returned to Eden—how unlike Vic she was. Eden's persistence might force him to tell her flat-out he wasn't interested.

Like most men in such entanglements, he'd always been a coward. He hoped she would get the message and just drift away. He wanted to avoid a confrontation if possible, but he could be direct if he had to.

Sara Bradford's Home
Twin Falls, Texas

After Matt left for work, Sara took her coffee into the library. She curled up in a leather chair in front of the fireplace, enjoying the quiet that gave her time to think. The children had another snow day, and were sleeping in.

She loved this room, with its rich paneling, mahogany book shelves, and heavy, masculine furniture. This had been Josh Bradford's domain before he died. She'd never changed anything after his death. The décor suited the rest of the house.

Her home held good and bad memories. More bad than good. She could put it on the market in a heartbeat and not look back. With its three stories, seven bedrooms, and manicured grounds it was too big for a family of four.

Josh had wanted a showplace to entertain friends and people from his law firm. She had offered no resistance, but the place cost a fortune to keep up.

Now was not the time to make a firm decision. She had calls to make.

Less than a minute later, she dialed Shannon Connelly's work number.

"Shannon, it's Sara. Matt told me about Sunday. I'm just checking to see how you're doing."

"I've been better, but the shock is wearing off. I really liked Kathy and Art. Since the roads are passable, I opened the club up today, but only a few members have shown up. I'm glad you and Matt are back. I missed my daily mental therapy sessions."

"Those therapy sessions go both ways, my friend. So, you're good?"

"Well, I'm now the proud owner of a white female bulldog named Sugar. Claire has a cat and didn't want her, and Eden already has two dogs. Taylor wanted to keep Sugar, but she's living with Claire now, so, no go. I couldn't stand the thought of sending Sugar to a shelter." She laughed. "The new addition to the family is costing me money. We'd had to install a doggie-door and buy an electronic fence to keep her on our property. She keeps trying to go back home."

"Poor little thing. That's so sad."

"I know," Shannon sighed into the phone. "The crime scene tape is still up. I saw two of Matt's detectives go inside earlier. Claire told Colin she's going to put the house on the market as soon as it's released to them. Can't say I blame her."

The tone of her voice brightened. "On the positive side, Sugar and Colin have become best friends." She chuckled. "I'm getting jealous of an ugly dog with gas problems."

"Funny, but you don't have anything to worry about. Want to have lunch later in the week?" Sara asked.

"Sure, I'd love it. Give me a call when you're free."

After she rang off with Shannon, she called Eden to offer condolences, but got no answer.

The Davenport Home
Twin Falls, Texas

With a search warrant for the Davenports' financial records in his jacket pocket, Davis and his partner eased into the driveway and stopped behind a gas-guzzling black Bentley sedan. The warrant might not have been necessary, but he didn't want any evidence they might find compromised when the killer was brought to trial.

Claire Davenport waited in her car and stepped out to meet them.

"You want to come in while we look through your parents' office?" Davis asked. "Sometime today, we'll need you to see if anything inside the home is missing."

She shook her head. "I have to get back to the bank. I'll pick up Eden later and bring her back with me. She'd be more help in that department than I would."

Davis handed the banker the warrant. As Claire turned to leave, he called out to her. "Do you have a copy of the will?"

"No," she said. "There might be one inside. If not, I'll get you a copy from Dad's attorney."

Inside, the residence was as cold as the temperature outside. Davis cranked up the heat before he and Turner made their way to the second floor.

For a home office, the room was large. Against the back wall, a group of colorful Italian prints hung above a small brown leather sofa. Bookcases and a credenza sat behind the oversized hardwood desk. Nearby were two built-in four-drawer file cabinets. Davis tried the handles. Locked

The desktop computer was missing. Dale McCulloch had loaded it and a laptop into the mobile crime lab Sunday. SOP, standard operational procedure.

He and Turner would go through the paper files. With luck, they would find a copy of the will, and with more luck, a motive for the murders.

It took him only a minute to find the key to the files, stuck in the back of the middle desk drawer in an envelope. Why lock files and keep the key where anyone could find it?

"Turner, you take the files; I'll take the desk."

She gave him a narrowed-eyed glance. "Figures you get the sit-down job."

He chuckled. "One of the perks of being the lead."

"How well I remember."

"Don't be bitter, Turner. You can pull up a chair."

"Who's bitter? I like being your flunky." She softened the words with a slight grin that meant she was only half-kidding.

After almost three hours, Turner stood and stretched her back. "At least the files aren't stuffed, just copies of credit card and bank statements. Also, some investment portfolio documents, and family birth certificates, trusts, etcetera. I'm thinking we should box this up and take it back to the bureau for closer inspection. You find anything?"

"Yeah, the will."

"Anything important?" she asked.

"No smoking gun. Just what we might expect. The bulk of the estate is split among the three girls, with a trust fund for each of the grandsons. Some items are left to the sisters and brother. Looks like family heirlooms."

Voices sounded below, then footsteps moved upstairs and down the hall to the office.

"We're here. Anyplace you want us to start?" Claire asked.

Davis came around from behind the desk. "You guys know the place better than we do. But you might want to concentrate on things of value, items that would be the most obvious to be taken. You guys have any idea what your dad might have carried in his attaché case? It was empty, and the papers burned in the fireplace."

Claire shrugged and looked at her sister. "I've no idea. How about you, Eden?"

She shook her head. "I haven't a clue."

The two sisters turned back down the hallway towards the master bedroom.

"I'll check the jewelry," Eden said.

Davis went to the car and brought up cardboard boxes for the files, then he and Turner packed the cartons. "You make a property list of what we're taking?"

She glared at him. "I'm not a rookie, Davis. This isn't my first crime scene."

He held up both hands. "Just asking. Don't go defensive on me."

They took the boxes to the car and then went in search of the Davenport siblings. He found them in the kitchen. "Anything missing?"

Eden perched on a stool at the island bar. "Only one item, as far as I could tell, a diamond pendent that belonged to my great-grandmother. Was Mom wearing her wedding rings?"

"Just the band, no engagement ring," Turner said.

"Then the engagement ring is gone. She always wore it. It was a rare four-carat pink diamond," Eden said.

Davis flipped through the will, and stopped when he found what he was looking for. "The necklace was left to Amy Bauer. Your mother willed the wedding rings to Taylor."

A sad smiled tilted the corners of Claire's mouth. "Aunt Amy loved that necklace."

"Can you suggest any reason for just those two items being taken? Seems odd the killer would leave behind the other expensive pieces." Davis said.

Claire nodded. "Those were the two most valuable, but it does seem a thief would have taken everything."

He and Turner exchanged a glance. How did the killer know the articles taken were the most valuable, unless someone told them? The fact that only two pieces were missing also indicated the killer wasn't a professional jewel thief.

Davis handed Claire the property list. "This is a receipt for the records and papers we've taken. Thanks for your help."

He pulled away from the mansion with one

realization. Half a day and two cups of Starbucks Grande Pikes Place and they were no closer to identifying the Davenports' killer than when they started.

CHAPTER 6

Twin Falls Police Station
Twin Falls, Texas

Matt Foley strode into the detective bureau conference room and plunked down two dozen assorted donuts. The four detectives came in behind him.

Chris Hunter grabbed a paper plate and took one cake and two chocolate with sprinkles. "I love you, Matt."

"Just don't hug me, Chris."

"Okay, your loss."

Matt grinned. "I'll try to live with it. You folks ready to get started?"

After everyone sat, Davis pointed a finger at Chris Hunter. "Let the B-Team go first."

Chris glanced at Matt. "Just in case you didn't know, the B stands for best. Okay, enough frivolity. The cell phone stats showed something interesting. Art Davenport made four calls to Dr. Stephen Russell in Oklahoma over the past two weeks. Just to refresh your memory, that's his ex-son-in-law, Eden Russell's husband. The calls lasted more than five minutes each."

"Good work, Chris, Cole," Matt said. "Which pair wants to make the scenic drive to Oklahoma City to talk to Dr. Russell, find out what those calls were about?"

Lucy Turner's brow wrinkled. "I'd rather work the investigation from here."

Lucy's abusive ex lived in Oklahoma, and she didn't want him to know where she and her sons were living. He was under a restraining order, but the daily news proved just how much that piece of paper was worth.

"You got it. Chris, that means you and Cole get to make the trip."

Chris gave Matt a two-finger salute. "No problem, as long as the weather stays clear. Otherwise, as Cole's wise mentor, I'll let him drive."

Cole shook his head. "You're so full of it, Chris. You just like passing down all the dirty jobs to the new kid."

Chris barked a laugh. "That, too."

"Not to interrupt Comedy Central, but, Davis, what do you and Turner have?" Matt asked.

"Mostly, a lot of questions," Davis said. "According to Claire and Eden Russell, there were only two items missing from the Davenport residence, an heirloom pendent and their mom's engagement ring. Apparently because those items were the most valuable. Makes you wonder how the killer came by that information. Neither of the sisters had any idea what was in Art's briefcase, nor why he might have burned the contents."

Turner flipped her notebook open. "Nothing unusual about their financial records, except that they were doing very well. And the will was straightforward." She looked over at Davis. "I've brought the murder book up to date."

She turned to Chris. "I need copies of the phone records."

He passed her a handful of papers. "Here you go, milady."

"Lucy and I have an appointment to interview Eden Russell at her condo this afternoon." Davis removed a sheaf of papers, and squared the corners. He tapped the pile with his index finger. "These are reports from VICAP and the Texas violent crimes data base for similar cases over the past two years. Not as many as I feared there would be, but enough to keep us busy. I'll split them with Chris so we can narrow it down quickly."

He divided the stack in half and Chris grabbed the closest pile.

"I spoke to Judge Bittermann yesterday," Matt said. "Nothing much there, except Eden and her mother were not on the best of terms, for whatever that's worth.

"I'm going to catch a flight to Houston and visit Dr. Alden Davenport, Art's younger brother, see if he can shed any light on who might have wanted his brother dead."

Matt pushed back his chair and stood. "If that's all, I'll see you folks tomorrow morning."

Home of Eden Russell
Twin Falls, Texas

Davis pressed the white button mounted on the jamb and rang the doorbell at Eden Russell's condo. The ring didn't sound inside. Perhaps out of order. He waited a minute and, when she didn't answer, he knocked.

"You think she left?" Turner asked. "She did know we were coming, right?"

"She knew." Davis raised his hand to knock again just as the door opened.

"Sorry," Eden said, breathless. "We're remodeling the upstairs bedrooms, and I barely heard the knock. The bell is broken, but it's on our to-be-repaired list."

Davis wondered who *we* and *our* were, but didn't ask. "Our condolences for your loss, Mrs. Russell. We have a few questions we need to ask you. May we come in?"

"Sure. Sorry. I'm just a little frazzled, with my parents' death and the remodeling. Would you like something to drink? The kitchen is in good shape."

"Nothing for me, but, before we get started, may I use your restroom?" Turner asked.

"Of course." She pointed down a corridor, past the stairs. "It's just down the hallway on the right."

"Nothing for me, either, thanks," Davis said. No sign of a grieving daughter here. She seemed almost chipper.

The large living room smelled of varnish and turpentine. Leather sofa, love seat, and oversized chair were good quality, but covered with a light film of sawdust. A desktop computer sat on a corner desk, the screensaver a camouflage Hummer.

Eden ushered him in and wiped dust from the sofa so they could sit. "Have a seat, and please excuse the mess."

Davis checked out the magazines on the table. Mostly military field gear and weapons. Hopefully not reading material for her kids.

Turner rejoined them and sat beside him.

A tall, muscular man wearing jeans and a white T-shirt with a tool belt cinched at his waist came down the stairs. Two young boys followed him. He wore a full, well-trimmed beard on his olive-toned face. His dark eyes narrowed as he looked from Davis to Turner, then back to Davis. He stepped forward and stretched out his hand. "I'm Jim Bauer, Eden's cousin, as well as her attorney."

Davis shook his hand. "She doesn't need a lawyer. We just want to ask some general questions about her parents."

He smiled, but it didn't reach his eyes. "I'm also her carpenter." He sat on a bar stool, his eyes focused on Eden. The boys took seats on each side of him.

Although the boys were twins, they looked nothing alike, except in size. One was fair, the other dark. They sat in silence, occasionally glancing at him and Turner with intelligent eyes.

"Where can we reach you, Mr. Bauer?" Turner asked.

Bauer grabbed a card holder off the bar, removed one, and handed it to Lucy. "That's my office address. It also lists my cell number."

"And your home address?" Turner asked.

He rattled off a street address, and Turner logged it in her notebook.

"When was the last time you spoke to either of your parents?" Davis asked Eden.

She spread her hands and shrugged. "It's been more than a month." Subtle, cool anger flashed quickly in her blue eyes before it disappeared just as fast. "I wasn't really close to them."

"Why not?" Davis asked.

"Eden, I advise you not to answer that," Bauer said.

"It's okay, Jim," Eden said, "my differences with my parents are common knowledge within the family. If I don't tell them, someone else will.

"There were many things that came between us. They tried to interfere in how I live my life, tried to choose my friends, and sided with my ex-husband in our custody battle, just to name a few."

That could explain her indifference to their deaths. Even so, it seemed a little cold-blooded to Davis. "To your knowledge, did they have any enemies, anyone who might want them dead?"

"I've given it some thought." She paused to look at Bauer, then back at Davis. "You see...my ex-husband has Mafia connections. He knew my parents were wealthy; perhaps he hoped to get his hands on the boys' inheritance."

Bauer nodded.

"Do you have any proof of that?" Davis asked.

She shook her head. "No, but it's well-known in Oklahoma City."

"Can you tell us about your schedule the days before and after the murders?"

"Don't answer that, Eden," Bauer said. "She'll provide you with a written response once I've had a chance to look it over."

"I don't have anything to hide, Jim," she said.

"Nevertheless, I want to look over your schedule and make sure it's correct."

She shrugged and stared down at the floor. Davis wondered if she was angry with her cousin for interrupting her a second time.

"Can you tell us where you were last weekend, Mr. Bauer?" Davis asked.

"Yes, I was at the Indian casino in Durant, Oklahoma with a buddy, Earl Locke. We spent three days there then drove home Monday around noon."

"Do you have his phone number?"

Bauer checked his cell phone and read off the number.

"How are the accommodations at the casino?" Davis feigned ignorance, although he'd been to the casino many times.

"Comparable to mid-size hotels in Vegas," Bauer replied, "doesn't have the bling of Vegas but the win/lose margins are about the same. Do you want a copy of my hotel receipt? It's in my briefcase upstairs."

"Yeah, we'd like to have it, if you don't mind," Davis said. "We just need to confirm the alibis of those close to the family."

It took only a minute for Bauer to return with the paper. He handed it to Turner.

"Thanks." Davis stood and Turner followed. "If you think of anything that might help, give me a call." He handed Eden his card.

Davis didn't bother to offer his condolences again. Apparently, she didn't need them.

<<>>

Turner steered the black sedan away from the condo. "Did that seem a little strange to you?"

"Very," Davis said. "Did you notice the motion detector and floodlights rigged above the door? That would blind anyone trying to enter undetected. Could just be a paranoid prepper or survivalist precaution, but, coupled with the weapon magazines, I think we need to take a closer look at Mr. Bauer. Anything interesting in the bathroom?"

"Birth control pills, aspirin, over-the-counter cold remedies, and migraine headache pills. No drugs or prescription meds," she said.

Turner made the turn around the old county courthouse on the square. "Do you buy her story about her ex-husband's Mafia connections?"

"It sounded like a bitter ex-wife attempting to discredit her former spouse. But I'll ask Chris and Cole to check it out while they're in Oklahoma. Can't see that a guy in the Mafia would need to steal money from his kids. Let's also get copies of the paperwork on the divorce and ongoing custody battle. See what that's all about."

"I didn't like the fact she made the charge against her husband in front of his kids," Turner said, "and perhaps it's just my suspicious nature, but I think we need to ask the neighbors about the relationship between Eden and Bauer. It looked a little too cozy for cousins."

The Foley Residence
Twin Falls, Texas

Sara picked up the children at school and drove back to Matt's place. Thank Heaven he had given her the Jeep this morning. Roads had frozen over since last night and the Jeep held the road without skidding.

The housekeeper's blue Focus sat in the driveway. Sara pushed the garage door opener and pulled inside as the door lifted clear. At least they wouldn't have to navigate their way up the snow-and-ice-covered front steps.

Rowdy jumped out of the car and headed inside, the children behind him with their backpacks. "You guys get your homework done by the fire before dinner," Sara said.

Stella met them at the kitchen entrance. "I wasn't expecting you and the children this evening. I only made dinner for Matt."

"That's my fault. I should have called. Could you make pancakes and sausage for Poppy and Danny? That will be easy, and they love breakfast food for dinner. Beatrice made chicken soup for me, seems like I'm coming down with something." Sara placed the soup in the fridge.

Stella nodded and disappeared into the kitchen. She didn't look happy, but by now she should realize Matt would no longer be eating dinner alone.

Sara's brow felt flushed with heat and her head pounded with a dull ache. She headed to the bedroom and changed into PJs and robe then went back downstairs. A loud voice made her head towards the kitchen.

Stella stood at the island, her back to Sara, pouring apple juice into two glasses with quick, angry movements. A white-faced Danny stood at her side. "You are NOT to come into this kitchen and help yourself. If you need something, you ask me and I'll get it." She slapped the breakfast food onto the island surface beside the juice. "Eat in here. I don't want food all over the hardwood floors."

Heat ran up Sara's face that wasn't from her fever. She didn't want Danny to see, so she took two deep breaths, calmed her voice, and strode into the kitchen. She jerked the food from the counter. "I think it'll be okay to let them eat on the coffee table by the fire tonight. They're really very neat with food."

Stella's eyes widened, her mouth set in a grim line, but she didn't say anything.

Plates in hand, Sara carried the food into the living room and deposited it on the low table. She tousled Danny's blond curls. "Here you go, Champ. I'll bring your drinks right back."

Sara brought their drinks and returned to the kitchen. Matt's home had an open floor plan, with the great room, kitchen, and dining room all visible from any area. A game room opened off to the left. Sara didn't want to confront the housekeeper in front of the kids. "Stella, may I see you for a moment in here?" She held the door open.

Stella didn't answer, but she followed Sara and shut the door behind her.

Sara took a deep breath and counted to ten. "I understand that you are not accustomed to dealing with children here, but this is Poppy and Danny's home now. They are not to be restricted from *any* area. And you are never to speak to them in the tone of voice you just used with Danny. If you have a problem with them, tell me. I'll handle it. Are we clear on that?"

The housekeeper's face burned red, but she nodded and returned to the kitchen.

That went well, Sara thought. She was off to a great start with her husband's housekeeper. Stella was afraid the children were going to make her job more difficult. In truth, they would. There would be more laundry, more dishes, and more beds to be made. They should probably offer to increase Stella's salary, since the size of the household had more than doubled.

She'd speak to Matt. But she wouldn't have handled the situation any differently. No one was going to be rude to her son and daughter. Not when she could prevent it.

CHAPTER 7

Office of Dr. Stephen Russell
Oklahoma City, Oklahoma

Roads had been cleared of snow, and Chris and Cole made good time on the 195-mile trip to Oklahoma City. Chris had arranged to meet the doctor after office hours, before he made his evening hospital rounds.

The office was in a high-rise building next to the hospital. Cole found an empty spot in underground parking near the elevator. A bitter wind enveloped them as they hurried to the elevator and punched the up button on the panel next to the door.

The chill worked under Chris's collar and his nose and ears were starting to go numb. He hated the cold. He stretched achy muscles while they waited for the steel doors to open and rescue them from the elements.

Once inside, Chris pressed the fourth-floor button. "I'm getting too old for this weather, makes me want to retire to Florida to live out the rest of my days in a balmy climate."

Cole shot him a grin. "You're too young to retire."

"It's not the years, my man, it's the miles."

The doctor's office door stood open, no receptionist in sight. Still wearing his green scrubs, Dr. Russell waved them inside. Stephen Russell looked to be in his late thirties, and bore a strong resemblance to the marshal on the TV show, *Justified.* He shook hands and motioned them to two chairs in front of his desk. "You fellows have had a long drive on not-so-good roads, so I assume the trip is important. I have about an hour and a half before I have to make rounds. I'm at your disposal."

Cole shrugged out of his overcoat and took out his notebook.

"Thank you, that should be more than enough time to cover the questions we have," Chris said. "Primarily, we want to cover conversations you had the past two weeks with Art Davenport. His telephone phone records show he recently made four calls to you. Can you tell us what the calls were about?"

The doctor hesitated and a shadow fell across his face. "I was sorry to hear about Art and Kathy. They were always kind to me. And, yes, I can tell you what Art and I discussed."

He came from behind his desk and sat on its corner. "My ex-wife and I have been in a vicious custody battle over our sons, both during and after the divorce. I'm asking for rotating summers with the twins, a week at either Thanksgiving or Christmas, and every other weekend throughout the year. Art had agreed to testify on my behalf. He felt the boys needed more time with me. Of course, Eden is fighting my request with everything in her arsenal. Art's death will most likely force a postponement of the hearing."

"Do you think the hearing had anything to do with your in-laws' death?" Chris asked. "Your ex-wife has a solid alibi for the morning of the murders."

He folded his arms and nodded. "I don't say this lightly, Detectives, but Eden is a cold-blooded witch who is capable of anything. Before we separated, the children's pediatrician called Child Protective Services on us. My son Brandon had three broken bones in three years. The doctor felt that was excessive. I didn't want to believe my wife would harm the boy, but since our divorce ...I've learned what she's capable of. When I question the boys about their treatment at home, they are evasive and frightened. That's why I'm determined to spend more time with them."

He fingered a paperweight on his desk, his brow wrinkled in thought. "If Eden has an alibi, then it was probably her loony cousin who's responsible."

Chris's mind ran back over the crime scene pictures. It didn't look like an assassination. Most assassins get in and get out. They don't go through the victim's personal belongings. "Who's her loony cousin?"

"His name is James Bauer. He's an attorney, mostly an ambulance chaser, or so I heard from Eden's parents. They didn't like him and the influence he had over Eden.

"He doesn't need to work too hard. His dad left him well-off. Not a millionaire, but comfortable. The guy has an arsenal, of everything from hand guns and assault rifles to explosives."

"Why would he want to kill Eden's parents?" Cole asked.

Russell ran a hand over his mouth and shook his head. "Probably no reason at all. You'll have to forgive me. I'm just venting my frustration. But I can't help but believe my in-laws' deaths are just too convenient for Eden. I liked Art and Kathy, and the boys are going to miss their grandparents. Their deaths put me back to square one in the custody battle."

Cole turned a page in his notebook. "Where were you last Sunday morning?"

"I'm a suspect? I had no reason to kill them. Quite the contrary." He looked away, and then shrugged. "I was at home with my fiancée until 10:00 a.m., and then I made my hospital rounds. I had a patient who was critically ill."

He rose from the corner of the desk and returned to his chair. "I understand that you have to look at everyone as a suspect, but I would never have harmed those two people. They were unbelievably kind to me, considering I was no longer married to their daughter. I hope you find out who did this. For my children's sake, I hope their mother wasn't involved."

Chris stood, and his partner followed suit. He handed the doctor his business card. "Thank you for your time, Dr. Russell. If you think of anything that might help with our investigation, let us know." He slipped into his overcoat and gloves. "We'll let you get to your rounds, and we'll be in touch if we have any further questions."

Chris shivered as they left and stepped back out into the cold. Not an unusual reaction for anyone in Oklahoma in January.

"What do you think?" Cole asked.

Icy wind seeped through Chris' coat, and he turned up the collar, pulling it tight around his neck. "I think it's too early to know what I think."

"Where to now?" Cole asked.

"The nearest police station," Chris said.

GPS led them to the closest police department. Chris flipped open his badge case and asked to speak to a detective. After a few minutes, a man of obvious Indian heritage crossed the lobby and introduced himself. "What can I do for you?"

Chris explained why they were in the city and asked if they had any records on Dr. Stephen Russell.

The detective led them back to his cubicle and did a quick search of the state database. "Nothing on our end unfavorable to him."

"His ex-wife suggested he might have Mafia connections. You know anything about that?" Chris asked.

The detective shook his head and tried to smother a smile. "You're kidding, right?"

"Nope, I'm as serious as cancer," Chris said.

The detective sobered. "I think the wife has an overactive imagination. That's one problem we don't have in our fair city. Yet."

The Texas Heart Institute
Baylor St. Luke's Medical Center
Houston, Texas

The Southwest flight passed so quickly, Matt felt he'd barely buckled up before the wheels touched down at Houston's Hobby Airport.

Matt stepped into the brisk morning. Not as bad as Twin Falls, but cold enough. He hailed a taxi outside the terminal and crawled into its warmth. Midmorning traffic clogged city arteries as the cab maneuvered to the medical center and stopped at the entrance. The usual twenty-minute drive had taken twice that long.

The Cooley Center was one of the premier heart-transplant centers in the country. It was here, in May of 1968, that Dr. Denton Cooley and his associates made news around the world by taking the still-beating heart of a fifteen-year-old girl and placing it into a forty-seven-year-old man...the first successful heart transplant in the United States. The patient survived for 204 days after the transplant.

Matt shared the elevator with an older woman and a man, who looked to be her son. Both wore expressions of concern, whether for themselves or a loved one, he had no way of knowing. One of the reasons he avoided hospitals whenever possible. The gloomy aura was as contagious as the flu.

He stepped into a wide hallway and a receptionist directed him to Dr. Davenport's office. The doctor had agreed to see Matt with the stipulation that he might have to leave in a hurry. He had a patient prepped for surgery. When the harvested heart arrived, he would have to start the operation immediately.

Harvested seemed an odd name for the removal of a human heart. Retrieved sounded more compassionate.

He found the doctor's office easily and the secretary waved him towards the open doorway. Matt knocked on the jamb, and Dr. Davenport looked up. "Good morning, Chief. Have a seat." He came from behind the desk and sat in the chair beside Matt. The doctor probably had a great bedside manner.

Expensive modern Swedish furniture filled the large space. Framed pictures of Davenport with various celebrities and politicians covered one wall, including a photograph with former Surgeon General, C. Everett Koop, that held center stage.

Dressed in green scrubs, Alden Davenport bore a remarkable resemblance to his older brother, with fewer wrinkles and less gray hair, slim and of medium height, with the same dark hair and facial features. His warm brown eyes held a deep sadness. "I'm not sure what I can tell you that will help you find whoever killed Kathy and Art, but I'll do whatever I can."

"You have no idea who might have held a grudge against your brother and his wife?"

"I'm clueless, Chief. I don't know anyone who didn't like them. I assumed it had to be a robbery attempt gone wrong. Was I mistaken?"

"It's too early to tell. We're just covering all the bases to get as much background on the victims as possible. How was their relationship with their children?"

"Good, I think. Claire and Taylor were model children. Eden gave Kathy a lot of problems in her grade school years."

"What kind of problems."

He paused for a moment, and an expression passed over his face Matt couldn't identify. "Raging temper tantrums that lasted as long as six hours." Davenport hesitated a long five-count, and then took a deep breath. "Kathy asked me about it at the time. I'm a heart surgeon, not an analyst, and I suggested she take Eden to a psychologist. The doctor assured Kathy that Eden would grow out of it, which she apparently did. But it was very touch and go for a while. When the rages lasted for hours, Kathy could only bring Eden out of it by sticking her under the shower. Perhaps not what a pediatrician would recommend, but it worked. Would you like some coffee? I'm going to grab a cup while I can."

Matt nodded, and the doctor asked the receptionist to bring in two cups.

She returned shortly with coffee and sugar and creamer packets.

"What can you tell me about your brother's work? Would he bring home any sensitive documents in his briefcase?" Matt asked.

"I don't think Art handled anything sensitive. He had blueprints, but those remained at his office. I can't believe anyone other than Art would have use for them. There would be no reason for him to take them home. Why do you ask?"

Matt shrugged. "His briefcase was empty, and it appears papers were burned in the fireplace."

The doctor rubbed a finger across his bottom lip. "That's strange. I guess you know he planned to testify for his former son-in-law in the custody trial coming up. Could be there was correspondence between them in his attaché. It was general knowledge, and I can't see why anyone would want to destroy that."

"It could be your brother was simply cleaning it out, and it has no bearing on the case at all," Matt said, but he still wondered, why burn the contents? Why not just toss the papers in a trash bin?

"How about his finances or business contacts? Any disgruntled employees or business associates that you know of?" Matt asked.

The surgeon shook his head. "Not to my knowledge. Art was an easygoing guy, and smart enough to avoid those kinds of conflicts."

The secretary stuck her head in the door. "The heart's here, Dr. Davenport."

The doctor downed the last drop of his coffee, then rose. "I've got to run, but I'll be at the funeral tomorrow afternoon if you have any more questions."

<<>>

Matt caught a taxi in front of the hospital, and the driver fought the rush-hour freeway traffic back to Hobby. Unsure how long the interview would last, Matt had purchased an open-ended return ticket, and was forced to wait on standby. While he waited, he again had the feeling a family member was holding something back. Was the family circling the wagons to protect one of their own? And, if so, who and why?

He forced the case to the back of his mind and called Sara. "Hi, sweetheart. I'm waiting on standby in Houston."

She coughed twice before responding. "Sorry you've been delayed. Looks like my fears have come to pass. I have the flu. I took the Tamiflu shot today. Maddie and Don picked up the children to get them off to school tomorrow."

Maddie was Sara's legally-blind aunt who had lived with Sara since the death of her parents when she started her senior year of college.

"That's good. I could have gotten the kids to school, but this will save you having to take care of their baths and tuck them in. Stay in bed. I'll hurry home as soon as I can catch a flight. I may bribe someone to give up their seat if I don't get on the next plane."

The Foley Residence
Twin Falls, Texas

It was after eight p.m. when Matt stepped through the garage entrance to a very quiet house. Even Rowdy greeted him without the usual enthusiasm.

Matt hung his coat in the closet just as his cell phone sounded a text message. It was from Shannon Connelly.

Need a sitter for Sara tomorrow? I'm free for the next four days. She sounded terrible when I called today.

Good. One problem solved. He texted Shannon, *Yes, thanks.* That done, he mounted the stairs to check on Sara.

The lamp on the nightstand cast a soft glow across the room. No fire in the hearth. Funny, in winter months, Stella usually started a fire before she left. He felt his wife's brow. Her skin was hot to his touch. From the medicine cabinet downstairs, he emptied two aspirins from the bottle into his palm, then grabbed a bottle of water, and hurried back to the bedroom.

He shook her gently. "Hey, babe, I have some pills for your fever. Can you sit up and take them for me?"

She nodded, swallowed the pills and a couple of sips of water between coughs then slid back under the covers. "So sorry about this, Matt. Our first week back, you have a big murder case to solve, and now you have to take care of me."

A coughing spasm racked her body. When she caught her breath, she ran trembling fingers through her mussed hair. "I must look a fright."

He brushed her hair away from her face and kissed her fevered brow. "You couldn't look bad if you tried, Sara Louise. Besides, flu happens. We'll deal with it. Your job is just to take it easy until this mess works its way out of your system."

Before going to bed, he brought a glass of white grape juice up and cajoled Sara into drinking most of it. After lighting the logs in the fireplace, he slid into bed. Sara's skin was still hot, and chills made her shiver. He wrapped his arms around her and drew her close.

Illogical as it seemed, he flashed to the bad days with Mary's illness. He pushed it back. Those days were behind him. Sara just had the flu.

CHAPTER 8

Twin Falls Police Station
Twin Falls, Texas

Matt merged onto the eastbound lane on Highway 75, glad he'd rescheduled the detectives' meeting for an hour later. Before leaving home, he'd waited until Shannon arrived and settled in to take care of Sara, and then headed to the station.

The meeting went quickly, with each team outlining their interviews from yesterday. The finger of guilt seemed to point to Eden Russell, but she had a solid alibi for the night before and morning of the murders. She'd spent the night at Grayson Manor with Jack McKinnon. Double checking that alibi with McKinnon was at the top of his priority list.

"Okay, we're all set for today. Davis and Turner, you're interviewing Claire Davenport." They both nodded. "And Chris, you and Cole are going to check into James Bauer's background. I will be interviewing his mother, Amy Bauer, this morning."

Matt stopped in the doorway and glanced back. "Before we head out into the cold, dark world, breakfast is on me at The Sunny Side Up, if anyone is interested."

Chris Hunter stood and rubbed his hands together with glee. "If you're buying, I'm eating."

Home of Amy Bauer
Twin Falls, Texas

The Bauer home sat on the outskirts of Twin Falls, a large, rustic, two-story log structure, with a cattle guard rather than a gated entrance. No animals in sight, but a classic red barn stood about twenty yards from the big house.

The woman who answered the door looked very much like Judith Bittermann, but younger and slimmer. She wore no makeup, her eyes red and swollen. Her gray hair was pulled into a neat ponytail, and she wore jeans, boots, and a red flannel shirt on her slim, almost frail, body.

"Good morning, Chief Foley. I'm not going to have much time. The funeral is at three, and I'm meeting Judith at her place at one."

"It was kind of you to agree to see me," Matt said. "This won't take long."

She led him into the large living room, filled with heavy, unfinished western furniture, and pointed him to a seat. The acidic smell of tomato sauce hung in the air. Through the kitchen doorway, rows of canning jars contained what appeared to be tomatoes.

"Forgive my appearance. I'm into organic foods, and I've been canning all morning. Staying busy helps keep my mind off..."

"My condolences for your loss, Mrs. Bauer; I know this is hard for you," Matt said. "Do you have any idea who might have killed your sister and brother-in-law?"

"None at all." Amy Bauer shook her head and looked directly into his eyes. "It wasn't robbery?"

"It doesn't appear to be. Only an heirloom diamond pendant and Mrs. Davenport's engagement ring are missing."

"Really? The pendant belonged to our mother." She gave a wistful smile. "Mom left it to Kathy when she died. I always loved that piece. But Mom knew Judith and I seldom wore jewelry."

"When was the last time you spoke to your sister?"

"We had lunch about a week ago. Kathy was concerned that Eden hadn't brought the twins by to see them in a while." She chewed her bottom lip. "You see, Eden and her mother had issues between them, and it wasn't all Eden's fault. She spends most holidays here with me and Jim. That's my son. Well, he isn't really my son, although I certainly love him like he was my own flesh and blood. His mother died when he was born, and I married his father when Jim was a year old."

"I understand your son is a hunter," Matt said.

"Yes, he's quite the outdoorsman," she said, "and a

great handyman. He can fix anything. He keeps his guns in a storage room in the barn. I have no idea how many weapons that boy has out there. I just don't want them in the house. My two daughters have small children who visit often."

"Would it be possible for me to take a look at your son's gun collection?"

"I don't have a problem with your looking at them, but I don't have a key. Jim keeps it on his key chain."

"Fine, I'll check with him. He lives here with you?"

A slight hesitation, a glance to the left, then back at him. "Yes."

Matt left the Bauer residence and drove slowly back to the station, using the alone time to step back and look at the evidence his team had gathered. One thing stood out. He'd left Amy Bauer, having a definite picture of her son, and he didn't like what he saw.

Lone Star Bails and Process Servers
Twin Falls, Texas

The funeral forced Davis to reschedule the interview with Claire Davenport. He and Turner fell back on plan B, checking out Jim Bauer's alibi, and Eden Russell's neighbors. Since she would be away from her condo, they were free to talk to the other residents, undetected.

Chris and Cole were running a background check on Bauer. They also planned to ask questions of his peers in and around the courthouse. Gossip might offer some insight into Bauer's character.

Earl Locke's bail bond office sat conveniently a half-block from the city jail. He'd agreed to see them at the office at eleven. Davis and his partner parked in the courthouse parking lot and walked the short distance to Locke's place of business.

A buzzer sounded when Davis opened the door. A pretty blonde dressed in jeans and a red sweater looked up. "Good morning. May I help you?"

The office wasn't fancy or aesthetically pleasing, but it didn't need to be. Bail bond customers weren't usually the country club set. Tan sheetrock walls were clean, and four framed black-and-white pictures of local scenes were mounted above the reception desk. A fake rubber plant sat next to the picture window that looked out at the courthouse.

"We're here to see Mr. Locke. I'm Detective Davis." He waved a hand in Lucy's direction. "And this is Detective Turner. Mr. Locke is expecting us."

Ponytail bouncing, the receptionist came from behind the counter and led them down a short hall to a door on the right. She knocked and stuck her head into the office. "Earl, your eleven o'clock appointment is here."

"Thanks, Bree. Show them in."

She stepped aside and motioned them into the small room.

Locke stood and shook hands. He was of medium height and muscular, with the short neck of a bodybuilder. He wore khakis, a light-blue turtleneck, and a navy blazer. A photo of an attractive brunette and two little girls sat on a credenza behind his desk. He motioned them to two chairs and returned to his desk. "How may I help you folks?"

"We understand that you spent last weekend with Jim Bauer at a casino in Oklahoma. Can you tell us when you left on your trip, and when you returned?"

Locke leaned back in his chair and fingered a ceramic coaster on his desk. "We drove out early Friday morning, then drove back to Twin Falls late Monday morning. We got home around noon."

"Did you win?" Davis asked.

Locke chuckled. "Does anyone? It was just an extended guys' night out; a harmless way to let off steam."

"You picked a really bad weekend for your outing," Turner said.

"Yeah, but the bad weather didn't hit until after we arrived at the casino. I guess braving the elements is a guy thing."

Turner nodded her head. "I guess it is. So, you and Bauer were together all weekend?"

"That's right."

"Do you have a copy of your hotel bill?"

"Sure, it's right here." He pulled out the desk's center drawer and retrieved a piece of paper. "I'll have Bree make you a copy. Any reason the police are so interested in the trip?"

"We're just verifying the whereabouts of people close to the Davenport family," Davis said. "You read about their murders?"

"Yes, sad business."

Davis moved on. "What can you tell us about Jim Bauer? What kind of guy is he?"

"Jim's okay. He knows everything there is to know about guns and surviving off the land. He's a crack shot with a hand gun or a rifle. On the downside, he's somewhat racist." Locke quickly added, probably because Davis was black. "Which I don't agree with, but he's not confrontational. Keeps it to himself."

"How long have you known Mr. Bauer?" Davis asked.

"About eight years. He's an attorney, and he referred a couple of clients my way. That led to drinks after work. We both like to hunt, and a friendship developed."

A woman in the doorway caught their attention; the woman in the photograph on Locke's desk. "Oh, sorry to interrupt, Honey. I was in town and thought we could have lunch together."

"Sure thing, as soon as I'm finished here. Ask Bree to come back. I need her to make a copy for me."

She left and Bree appeared in the doorway. "I tried to stop her from coming back, Earl."

"No problem, Bree. She's my wife. She can come back whenever she wants." He handed her the hotel bill. "Make a copy of this for the detectives, please."

Bree didn't look happy, but took the bill and went back up front. She returned moments later and handed a copy to Turner.

"Anything else we need to know about Bauer, Mr. Locke?" Davis asked.

He shook his head. "Can't think of anything."

"Thank you for your time." Davis rose and handed Locke his card. "If you think of anything that might be helpful, give me a call."

They passed Mrs. Locke in the lobby. She was

sending frosty glares at Bree.

On the way back to the car, Turner glanced at him and grinned.

"What?"

"I'm thinking Locke's having an affair with the secretary."

"How do you figure that?"

"Did you notice Bree seemed a little possessive?"

"No."

"That, Davis, is why women make good detectives. Where are we going for lunch?"

"Your choice, as long as it isn't fast food or deep fried."

<<>>

Over lunch, Turner said, "So Bauer is a racist-slash-survivalist. Think it has any connection to the case?"

"No, and the two are not mutually inclusive. Most survivalists aren't racists. They're just men who don't like the direction this country is headed and want to protect their families—whatever comes down the pike; and, yeah, clinging to their guns and Bibles."

"A little paranoid, if you ask me," Turner said.

"Look around you, Turner, at what's happening in the world, and tell me they're wrong. I wonder how the anti-gun crowd would feel about guns if they met an ISIS terrorist coming towards them with an ax or a machete."

"You have a hidey-hole, Davis?"

"No, but I have a cabin in the backwoods of East Texas, a year's supply of MREs, and an AK-15."

"You're kidding."

"For now, but maybe not for long."

"How did you like being a Marine, Davis?"

"You never stop being a Marine. I was in for eight years. Did two tours in Iran and one in Afghanistan."

"Why did you leave?"

"It's complicated. The Marines are the best fighting unit anywhere. But there are some internal problems they need to work out."

"Like what?"

"Hazing. Maybe it happens in all service branches, but I can only speak for the Marines."

"I thought hazing was outlawed."

"It has been on paper. But, believe me, it still exists. Recruits don't dare complain or it gets worse. Just before I finished boot, twelve corporals took me out and told me I had to fight them all, one at a time. By the time I got to the eleventh man, I was so tired I could barely lift my arms. The last two guys took it easy on me, but I was still sore for a week."

"Do you think it was a racist thing?"

Davis shook his head. "No, two of the corporals were black, and two white guys in my unit went through the same thing. In my opinion, it's just a bunch of sadistic punks taking advantage of their rank. Recruits enlist to fight the enemy. They shouldn't have to fear their own noncoms."

He finished the meal and pushed back his chair. "But that was then and this is now. And we have a killer to catch. Different battle, different rules of engagement."

Turner sent him a cheeky grin. "Well, I'm glad those bullies didn't mess up your pretty face."

He emitted a deep laugh. "Yeah, that would have been a real shame."

It only took an hour to cover Eden Russell's neighborhood. The only significant information he and Turner gathered was that Bauer had moved his clothes and other belongings into the condo three weeks ago. Most of the residents thought they were married or living together.

Christensen Memorial Park
Twin Falls, Texas

Matt met up with Davis and Turner at the funeral home to attend the Davenport services. The clan opted for a small, intimate group of family members.

Art and Kathy Davenport were laid to rest on a hill overlooking the cemetery, no trees or shelter to block the brisk, cold wind.

Matt got his first look at James Bauer, who stuck

close to Eden's side. The two were basically ignored by the rest of the family, except for Jim's mother, Amy. Strange that the two were being shunned. Did the family share his suspicions that Bauer and Eden were somehow involved in the murders, or were they simply embarrassed by the close relationship of two cousins?

After the interment, Matt shook hands with Dr. Davenport, and then hugged Judith Bittermann, who stood beside her nieces, Claire and Taylor. This was also Matt's first meeting with the youngest Davenport. Unlike her older sisters, twelve-year-old Taylor apparently resembled her father, with dark hair and hazel eyes. She had the lanky figure of a pre-teen, with the bone structure of a future beauty. Her face revealed more anger than grief. Who could blame her? She'd lost both parents in one awful day.

Claire wore a somber countenance befitting the occasion, her posture ramrod straight. A scowl wrinkled her patrician brow when Matt stopped to offer his condolences. "I expect you to find out who killed my parents, Chief. For this to happen to..." She gulped a breath, "is unconscionable. I expect a quick resolution and justice for my family."

Before Matt could respond, Judge Bittermann threaded her arm through Claire's. "I know you're hurting, Claire, we all are. These things don't solve themselves overnight. It takes time. Matt has the best team of investigators in the state. If this case can be solved, Matt will do it."

"Thank you, Judge," Matt said, then looked directly into the young woman's eyes. "Be assured, we're putting all our efforts into finding the people responsible."

He pulled on his leather gloves and turned to leave when Taylor hurried over to him. She looked young, sad, and lost. "Chief, are you really going to find out who killed my mom and dad?"

"You heard what I told your sister. I meant every word of it." He placed his hands on her shoulders. "Do you know anything that might help?"

She chewed at her lower lip, and then glanced back at Claire and Judge Bittermann. With a slow shake of her head, she turned and rejoined her family.

After the funereal crowd dispersed, Matt strolled over to the Grayson mausoleum, a great white edifice built to house the earthly remains of the Grayson family, the victims of a mass murder last year. Matt hadn't been here since the monument's construction. The building was impressive, as was the man whose family lay inside.

He opened the door and entered. In the center of the crypt stood a six-foot marble angel statue, its wings draped forward, its head bowed. The angel's hands held an eternal flame censer.

A bronze plaque, engraved *Ethan Grayson,* drew Matt's attention. He walked over and read the inscription under the plaque, a line from Mark Anthony's speech at Julius Caesar's burial. *"Here was a man, when comes such another?"*

Matt swallowed the lump that formed in his throat, remembering the gentle man who had been his friend.

The outside door opened, and Jack McKinnon stepped inside. He startled, then chuckled. "You scared me out of my wits, Matt. Of the many times I've been here, I've never run into another soul."

"Sorry, I was here for the Davenport funeral and thought I'd pay my respects."

Jack nodded. "Me too, although I come here frequently to visit Victoria."

Matt understood. He had visited his own wife's grave often after her death. "I've been meaning to call on you, to ask a few questions about the morning of the murders. Is there any way Eden could have left your home before six a.m. without your knowledge?"

"Is she a suspect?" He shook his head. "Guess you can't answer that. I'd like to help, Matt, but Eden was there all night."

"How can you be sure?"

"Because her car was still in the garage, no snow or ice on it."

"Could someone have picked her up?"

Jack punched his hands into his overcoat pockets, and kept his eyes on his boots. "No, Matt. She spent the night in my bed."

"I thought you said there was nothing serious between you two."

Jack flashed an angry glance at Matt. It quickly receded, replaced by embarrassment. "There isn't. And I've cut her loose. Look, it was her idea and...that's no excuse and I know it. I'm not proud of myself for letting it happen. I've been kicking myself ever since. Vic would be disappointed. She deserved better from me."

"You don't have to explain, Jack. It's your life. But I would caution you, don't let your loss and your grief lead you places you don't want to go."

CHAPTER 9

Thursday, The Foley Residence
Twin Falls, Texas

When Matt steered his Escalade into the driveway, Shannon Connelly's Lexus sat in the circular drive.

He entered through the garage and walked into the living room.

Sara sat on the sofa in her robe and pajamas, thick brown hair tousled around her face, hazel eyes glaring at Shannon.

Her gaze found him as he hung his coat in the hall closet. She grabbed a handful of tissues from a box on the coffee table and stumbled across the floor, into his arms. "Matt, I'm so glad you're home. Sham...Sam...Shannon's being mean. She won't let me go outside, and I'm hot."

"Well, good for Shannon. You should be in bed, not outside."

Shannon released a breath and plunked down on the sofa. "I've practically had to sit on her for the past hour to keep her inside."

"See, she's...mean," Sara said.

He raised an eyebrow. "What's going on, Shannon?"

She grinned and shook her head. "I made tequila sunrise cocktails in a plastic container and set it in the fridge to chill. Sara came down thirsty, thought it was orange juice, and..."

He expelled a long breath of irritation. "She's drunk?"

Shannon lost her smile and winced. "I'm afraid so, and it's my fault. I'm sorry."

He shook his head and lifted Sara into his arms. "Come on, my tipsy one. I'll take you up to bed."

Sara put both arms around his neck and rested her head on his shoulder. "I love you, Matt. The orange juice tasted ba-a-ad."

"Yeah, she only drank two glasses." Shannon tried

unsuccessfully to hide a grin.

"We'll talk about it later," Matt said, heading for the stairs. "I'm not sure what effect this will have on her flu."

Sara nuzzled her head against his neck. "I love you, Matt. Mmmm, you smell nice."

"I love you, too, babe."

"Everybody doesn't love me."

"Tell me who doesn't love you, and I'll shoot'em."

"Stella doesn't love me." Sara pushed a curtain of hair away from her face and wagged a shaky finger in front of her face. "She was mean to Danny, and I made her stop."

"Well, I may have to rethink shooting Stella. She's been around for a while. Do you want me to talk to her?"

"Nope, I fixed it."

He suddenly realized he hadn't seen Stella. "You fixed it, huh? I don't have any dead bodies in the house, do I?"

She giggled, "Noooo, silly."

Upstairs, he sat her on the bed and helped her off with her robe. "How do you feel?"

She still had her arms around his neck. "I love you, Matt and...ohhhhh...I'm going to be sick..."

He grabbed a nearby wastebasket and held it while she regurgitated the offending orange juice and everything else she had eaten that day. When she finished, she lay back against the pillows and moaned. He grabbed a clean set of pajamas and handed them to her. "Get into these and I'll get a cool washcloth for your face."

When he returned, she stood, waving like a leaf in the wind.

"Need some help?"

"I don't think show," she lisped.

"I beg to differ. You're buttoned up wrong." He sat her on the bed and re-buttoned her top. When he'd finished, she slumped back against the pillows. He tucked the covers under her chin and positioned the cloth on her brow, then stayed with her until she fell asleep.

Confident she was resting peacefully, he picked up

the offensive wastebasket and headed for the dumpster.

<<>>

What now? Shannon paced as she waited for Matt to come back inside. She was in for a well-deserved tongue lashing. However unintentional, she had made her friend's illness worse.

There was no liquor in the Foley household. And she knew why. After the death of his parents, he'd been raised by an abusive, alcoholic uncle.

Well before she'd finished beating herself up, the door opened, and she met his gaze across the room. "Do you want me to leave?"

Matt motioned her toward the sofa, then sat beside her, his arms crossed, brow furrowed. "Not unless you had planned to leave when I got home." A long silence fell between them before he spoke again. "You know how I feel about liquor in my home. And it's even more important now with the children around. They would have made the same mistake Sara did. You know I have no problem with folks who drink responsibly, but that doesn't mean I want it where I live. I know you love Sara, and would never deliberately harm her..."

"I'm sorry, Matt, very sorry. I just didn't think; one of my big character flaws."

"No need to keep apologizing. I accepted the first one. All I ask is that, in the future, you respect the house rules."

She stood, and silence fell again. "How could I forget? Guess I'll go home to Colin. He's usually around to keep me straight. By the way, I dumped the *orange juice*. I'll be back tomorrow, if you still want me."

He walked her to the door and opened it, a slight twitch at the corner of his mouth. "Absolutely. Tomorrow you get to pay for your sins. She'll probably have a terrific hangover, plus she still has the flu. She'll be a very bad patient." He planted a kiss on her brow. "Drive safely."

She gazed into his serious brown eyes. "How did you get to be so wise?"

He gave a sheepish grin. "I've always surrounded myself with wise people."

Friday, Twin Falls Police Station
Twin Falls, Texas

The meeting in the detective bureau lasted only fifteen minutes. Nothing new to report, except that Bauer and Eden Russell had solid alibis. Matt wasn't satisfied with that answer, but it was what it was.

He returned to his office and found a note from Doug Anderson, asking that he call when he got a chance. He grabbed the phone and speed-dialed the city manager's number. "What's up, Doug?"

"You have an opening in IAD?"

"Yes. One of my men in Internal Affairs is leaving in April."

"Our mayor wants to install his brother-in-law, Luther Donnell, in that vacancy."

Even though his boss couldn't see him, Matt shook his head. "It's not happening, Doug. Hall tried once before to get that guy into the department. Human Resources checked him out. At the time he applied, we didn't know he was related to Hall. The man has been a problem in every place he's worked. The last thing Internal Affairs needs is an insecure cop with a grudge against other law enforcement officers. Have HR send you a copy of their report."

"Think about it, Matt. It would go a long way towards easing tension between the mayor's office and the police department."

"I don't want to play politics with this station or my people. If I'm forced to hire the man, I'll also have to hire someone to keep an eye on him. That's hardly cost-effective."

Matt heard a deep sigh on the other end of the line. A sigh of frustration. "Just think about it, Matt. That's all I ask."

He would think about it, but he wouldn't change his mind. Soldiers and cops had the hardest jobs on the planet. They didn't need bureaucrats second-guessing their actions. He couldn't do anything about the military, but he could protect the guys who worked for him.

Internal Affairs was needed because, like it or not, there were bad cops. He wanted people who were interested in finding the truth, not railroading an officer to satisfy public opinion, or whitewashing a dirty cop. Guys who put their lives on the line everyday deserved nothing less.

His boss certainly knew how to ruin the start of a good day.

Claire Davenport's Home
Twin Falls, Texas

Davis made an appointment to interview Claire Davenport at one that afternoon. She lived three streets over from her parents, in a house of similar design and floor space. It was a chic address on the upscale side of town, and Ms. Davenport had probably chosen it for that reason.

When he and Turner pulled into the circular drive, snow and ice had been removed from the entrance. He and Turner made their way to the front door and rang the bell. Claire answered, wearing green wool pants with flared legs, a white long-sleeved sweater, and no makeup. Her eyes were red and swollen, her grief seemingly genuine. The contrast between her and Eden's reaction to their parents' deaths was obvious.

She didn't look happy to see them, but she moved aside for them to enter, and they stepped into the foyer. "We're in the den. I only have about an hour before I have to take my sister to swim practice. She's on the school swim team."

They moved through double doors into a room with high ceilings and mahogany paneling, topped by elegant crown molding. A sofa and chairs formed a seating arrangement in front of the fireplace, where a fire blazed away.

The décor wasn't what he'd expected from Claire. He figured her for something out of *Architectural Digest,* a showplace to impress her friends. Instead, it was comfortable French Country, something you could put your feet up on.

An attractive man stepped forward to meet them. He was tall and slender with collar-length brown hair, who looked to be ten years older than Claire. He was well tanned despite the season, and didn't appear to be the type to frequented tanning booths.

"I'm Winston Seymour, but everyone calls me 'Win'," he said, and offered his hand. He spoke with a cultured upper-class English accent. "And the lovely young lady in the chair is Taylor, Claire's sibling."

The girl nodded, and then glared at Win. Davis introduced himself and Turner. "We won't take up much of your time, just a few questions for our records."

Win took on the role of host, and pointed them to a mustard-colored sofa with a triangle-patterned skirt and matching throw pillows. "Would you join us for coffee? We were about to have some."

"Yes, thank you," Davis said.

Win turned to Taylor, "Would you like hot cocoa?"

Taylor sat detached, her eyes downcast, playing with the sleeve of her sweater. When he spoke, she looked up and shook her head.

The Englishman headed toward the kitchen and stopped before an elaborate coffee maker.

Davis followed him. "I've never seen a machine like this one."

Win smiled. "It's new. I'm a fresh-coffee snob, and when I found this coffeemaker that roasts and grinds the beans, then brews the finished product, I was sold." He placed the beans inside, measured the water, and went to the china cabinet and pulled down four heavy mugs.

"You must have just gotten back from vacation, with that tan of yours," Davis said.

"I just returned from Melbourne. I was at the Australian Open the week leading up to Art and Kathy's deaths. I played professional tennis until about ten years ago, when the younger competitors became too much for me."

Claire made her way into the kitchen. "He's too modest. He came in second in the men's singles at Wimbledon ten years ago." She sent him a glowing smile and squeezed his hand.

He slipped his arm around her shoulders. "Now, I just coach."

The machine finished its cycle- filling the room with the aroma of the dark roasted beans.

Claire selected a silver tray,poured coffee into the mugs, and they returned to the living room.

Taylor was nowhere in sight.

Davis glanced at Claire. "How is Taylor doing?"

"Not well." Claire shook her head. "I'm not sure how to help her. Perhaps it will just take time, like the rest of us."

Win settled on the sofa next to Claire. "Perhaps we should take her away for a while, if you can get away from the bank."

She shook her head. "We're into year-end reconciliations. I can't leave now."

Win turned his attention to Davis. "How may we help you?"

Davis directed his question to Claire. "When you spoke to your mother Saturday evening, did she seem upset about anything?"

"No more than usual." Claire perched on the edge of the sofa, both hands wrapped around the coffee cup. "My parents have been upset about Eden's custody battle. My father was going to testify on behalf of Stephen. They didn't like the boys spending so much time with Jim Bauer, and felt the twins needed more time with their father. Eden was dead-set against it. Mom and Dad hated the division it was causing between them and Eden. After Dad agreed to testify for Stephen, she stopped bringing the boys to visit, and it broke their hearts."

"When was the hearing scheduled?" Turner asked.

"In two weeks."

Taylor came back into the room with a huge yellow tabby in her arms, and knelt in front of the fireplace. She stroked the cat and didn't look at anyone, but Davis suspected she was listening to every word.

Turner jotted a note on her pad. "Will the hearing move forward without your parents?"

"Of course, but I'm not sure how it will effect Stephen's request for more time with the twins. Eden's lawyer is a shark."

Taylor opened her mouth as if to speak, then closed it and turned her attention back to the cat.

"Do you think Eden is a good mother?" Davis asked.

She swallowed and glanced at Win. "If you tell Eden I said this, I'll deny it. Eden loves those boys, but that's not the same as being a good parent. I have no children, but to me she seems possessive and overprotective. And her choice of companions is certainly questionable—a two-bit lawyer and an accused murderer."

Taylor looked up. "I like Jack. He's nice."

Claire cast a cold glance at her sister and rolled her eyes.

"Just for the record, the murder charges against Jack McKinnon were dropped after the killer was found," Davis said.

"Whatever." She gave a dismissive wave. "The fact remains the men she is hanging with are a bad influence. Stephen Russell is a well-respected doctor and the boys' father. They should see more of him than just two weeks every summer and every other Christmas. Eden never should have divorced Stephen."

"Anything else you can tell us about your parents' affairs that might help us? Problems with anyone outside of Eden? Business problems?"

"No, nothing. That's why their murder is so bizarre," she said.

"How about you, Win? Any ideas?" Davis asked.

"I have to agree with Claire. There doesn't seem to be any personal reasons for their deaths. They were generous, kind people."

"When did you return from Australia?" Davis asked.

"Unfortunately, my client didn't make it through the quarter-finals in Melbourne, so there was no need for me to stay. I arrived home Saturday afternoon, and was here with Claire until she received the phone call about her parents."

Davis thanked the couple for their time, and he and Turner left.

He looked up before getting into the driver's side. The sad face of Taylor Davenport watched them from the second floor window.

"Any thoughts?" Turner asked.

"As far as our case is concerned, no," Davis said. "I was prepared not to like Win, but he seemed like an alright guy. No airs, and he appeared to be genuinely fond of Claire. Did you get the impression the girl had something on her mind?"

Turner placed her head against the seat back and sighed deeply. "Yeah, I did. I'd like to talk to her alone. I think I'll drop by her school next week and buy her lunch, see what she has on her mind." She looked over at him. "Want to call it a day? We both have to work tonight."

"Sounds good to me," he laughed. "We can start early tomorrow to make up for it."

The drive back to the station didn't take long, but Davis was running on empty, and Turner looked to be in the same shape. They hadn't had a day off since the Davenports' murders.

Today's visit with Claire Davenport yielded nothing they didn't already know. However, it did support the theory of Eden as a prime suspect in the murders. And, there was no such thing as a wasted interview.

<<>>

Taylor Davenport stood at the window and watched the two detectives leave. She should tell them what she suspected, but she had no proof. Her first thought after Claire told her that Mom and Dad were dead, was that Eden was somehow responsible. Taylor didn't want to believe her sister could do such a horrible thing, but she had always known something wasn't right with Eden.

She pressed her face against the window pane. *Please, God, let this be a terrible nightmare and let me wake up. I don't want to live with Claire, and I would*

80

never, never, never live with Eden. Not even if I have to become homeless.

Claire's tabby, Liszt, rubbed against her leg. Taylor issued a soft sigh and lifted the cat into her arms. Claire was such a poser, naming a cat after a famous pianist.

Taylor snuggled the cat to her breast, stroking his soft fur, and then nuzzled his head with her nose. "I like you, Listy, but I miss Sugar. Claire wouldn't let me bring Sugar, because she thought you two couldn't get along."

Claire was hinting that Taylor should consider living at school. The academy provided residence for those who wanted it. Claire worked, and she didn't want to drive into Dallas every day. Win had been driving her to school, but he wouldn't always be there.

Taylor didn't want to live at school. It would be too lonely. She'd lost Mom and Dad. She couldn't bear to lose Sugar and her home as well.

She dropped Liszt and flung herself onto the bed. Grief overwhelmed her, and great gulping sobs shuddered through her body. *Oh, Jesus, what is going to become of me?*

The tears finally subsided, leaving behind a bad case of hiccups.

Maybe, just maybe, she could live with Aunt Judith. She liked Sugar, and she liked Taylor. And her assistant, Elijah, could drive her to school. But how to ask, without making Claire mad? Dare she tell Aunt Judith of her suspicions of Eden? Best not to. Everyone thought of Taylor as just a kid.

No one would believe her. Not even Claire.

CHAPTER 10

Élan Club
Las Colinas, Texas

Lucy Turner and Ben Stein pulled up in front of the club, just ahead of Miles Davis. Her partner had gotten Lucy a night job at the club last year. She'd been falling deep into debt and the money she earned at Élan was top-notch. And, since she only worked on Friday and Saturday nights, she could spend more time with her boys. Ben Stein, another TFPD officer, also worked at the club.

Ben gave her a wave and hurried through the entrance.

Davis stepped up beside her. "Hey, nice dress, Turner. Is that one of Sierra's creations?"

Élan was an elegant establishment that catered to the upper-crust of Dallas society, sports stars, politicians, and required security personnel to dress like their clientele. Davis' significant other, Sierra Jackson, was a buyer for Nordstrom's and she gave Lucy a call whenever something in her size went on sale. Lucy couldn't have afforded Élan's dress code without Sierra's help.

Sierra had suggested the gray silk dress she wore tonight. Its neutral color brought out the red in her hair and green in her hazel eyes.

"Yes, your lady has great taste, Davis."

They entered the club together, and Davis stopped just inside the door. "You got a minute before you check in?"

"Sure. What's up?"

He ran a hand down his face, in an embarrassed gesture that was totally unlike him. "First, this is none of my business, but are you seeing Stein outside of the job?"

She agreed it was none of his business, but Davis had

been good to her. He wouldn't pry into her personal life without a reason. She nodded. "Yes. We're both single, so there shouldn't be a problem."

Her marriage to Hank Turner had been a disaster from the beginning, and she had barely escaped with her life. Ben Stein was one of the nicest men she'd ever known. He was attentive to her and seemed to love her boys, taking them to Ranger and Cowboy games without her. The boys loved the male attention they'd never gotten from their father. She didn't want to give that up. She wouldn't give him up, period.

"There are rules at the club. They have a policy of no dating between co-workers or club clients. So keep it low key, and tell Ben to do the same."

"Thanks for the heads-up. Any problems with our dating at the station?"

"There's no written policy, but it's frowned upon. Of course, it goes on all the time, so just be discreet. Got it?"

"Got it."

The evening passed without serious problems, only one middle-aged matron who drank too much. That was Lucy's job: keeping the female patrons from embarrassing themselves and ensuring they left the club safely.

As she re-entered the lobby after putting the customer in a cab, Ben Stein and the club manager, Giles Beneoit, escorted James Bauer out the double doors. He pushed past her, apparently without recognition.

She stopped inside the lobby and waited for Ben, wanting to find out why Bauer had been evicted.

"You're not welcome at Élan any longer," Beneoit said in his heavy French accent. "Your affiliation with the club is revoked. We will refund the balance of your membership fee within the next ten days. Give me your valet ticket."

Bauer's face flushed a dark red, and he slapped the ticket into the club manager's hand. "I'll sue you, Beneoit, and close this place down by the end of the week."

Beneoit signaled the valet attendant and handed him Bauer's ticket. "Get this gentleman's car." He turned to Stein. "Make sure he leaves the property."

Ben stood beside the seething lawyer until he got into his car, and then watched him peel out of the lot.

"What happened?" Lucy asked when Ben came back in.

"Bauer was spouting his fascist philosophy to a redneck oilman who wanted to deck him. I stepped in just in time to keep it from getting ugly. You know that guy?"

She nodded. "He's involved in the Davenport murder case Davis and I are working. This squares with everything we've heard about him."

Ben squeezed her arm, and twin creases formed between his eyebrows. "Watch your step, Luc. I don't want you to get hurt. That guy is a couple of rounds short of a full clip."

The Foley Residence
Twin Falls, Texas

The living room was empty when Matt got home. Rowdy bounded down the stairs, wagging his nub of a tail in greeting, leading Matt to conclude Shannon was with Sara.

He climbed the carpeted staircase and stepped into the master bedroom. Sara was propped up against the pillows, and Shannon sat in a wingback chair beside the bed.

"How's our patient doing?"

Sara flashed him a bright smile and spoke through a stuffy nose. "Early this morning, I didn't think much of my chances for survival but, around three this afternoon, I decided I was going to live. I think the shot is doing its thing."

"Actually," Shannon said, "Beatrice sent over more of her miraculous chicken soup. After one bowl, Sara started to get color back into her cheeks."

"I'm happy to hear that," Matt said, and sat on the bedside. He leaned over and kissed Sara's brow.

There was cautious humor in Sara's eyes. "I hope I don't give this plague to you."

"I don't think there's any danger, but it's worth the risk."

Shannon rose from the chair with a grin. "I'm going to leave you two honeymooners alone, and get home to my husband and my new baby. By the way, Matt, Stella left your dinner in the oven. Not sure what it is."

"No matter; I'm not picky."

"Thanks for staying with me, Shannon," Sara said, "and give my love to Colin and Sugar."

As Shannon left, Matt's cell phone vibrated. He retrieved the phone from his pocket. "Yeah, Miles, what's up?"

"Thought you might like to know that McCulloch identified the gun in the Davenport murders. It's a Beretta .92."

"Good, that gives us something to put on our radar. Anything else?"

"We'll check ATF to see how many are registered in Texas. That's an older model, and there could be a gazillion of them out there. I had one while I was in the Marines."

"It'll be worth checking out. Let's see if any of our suspects have one registered. I'd also like to get a look at the arsenal Bauer has in his mother's barn. See if you can get him to open it up. We don't have enough cause to get a warrant."

"Yeah, but if he has a Beretta .92 and it's the murder weapon, he'll get rid of it before he lets us inside."

"We still need to know what kind of firepower he has if we have to bring him in."

"That, too," said Davis.

Matt ended the call. Sara watched him with troubled eyes. "Problems?"

He should have taken the call in another room. She didn't need to worry while she was trying to recuperate. "Just routine follow-up on the murder weapon and trying to prepare for any contingencies." He grinned down at her. "How about I warm up some more of that chicken soup for you?

The Foley Residence
Twin Falls, Texas

Matt took his coffee into the living room and switched on the local FOX news channel. Outside, the day was gray and cold, but no snow in the forecast. The soft padding of footsteps on the stairs told him Sara was up. Fresh from a shower, she strolled into the kitchen, brought back a glass of orange juice, and joined him in the oversized chair.

He slipped his arm around her, inhaling her fresh, soapy fragrance. "I was going to let you sleep in before I made breakfast."

"The juice is fine. The flu seems to have zapped my appetite." She placed her legs across his lap, pulled a throw from the chair back, and tucked it around her body. "I thought I'd bring Poppy and Danny home today. I think I'm up to taking care of them now. What do you think?"

"Let me pick them up tomorrow morning and take them to church with me, then bring them home after services. An extra day of rest will help you regain your strength."

A "Breaking News" alert flashed on the television screen, and Matt turned up the volume. A video showed an aerial view of a white colonial mansion set on acres of land, almost invisible in patches of snow. A voice-over told the story.

". . . double murder last night in Norman, Oklahoma. An elderly couple, Barton and Emme Russell, were shot in their home on the couple's fortieth anniversary. Barton Russell was a prominent attorney in Norman and active in local politics. Investigators are still at the scene. There are currently no suspects in the brutal murders. We'll continue coverage as the story develops."

Sara's hazel eyes searched his face. "You think this has something to do with the Davenports?"

He rubbed the back of his neck as he considered his answer. "Possibly. It has the same MO. I'll give the Norman sheriff's office a call. It's worth checking into."

DOWNFALL

He finished his coffee and set the cup on the end table. "I'm hungry. Can I interest you in breakfast?"

She shifted her legs to the floor and shook her head. "Still not hungry, but I'll keep you company. You can describe Stella's duties so I'll know what the guidelines are."

As they stepped into the kitchen, Rowdy bounded through the doggie door with a dead bird in his mouth, which he proudly placed at Sara's feet.

"Oh, no, you don't, Buddy. Outside with your trophy," Matt said.

Rowdy dropped his head, picked up the bird, and slunk back through his personal entrance.

Matt glanced over at Sara. "I forgot to tell you he brings in gifts from time to time."

While he whipped up a batch of pecan waffles and bacon, he explained Stella's responsibilities. "She has mostly been a housekeeper, but made dinner for me on week nights, with weekends off. If you need more than that, we can expand her duties and compensation, or replace her if she's unwilling. What about Pete and Beatrice?"

"They want to retire, go back to South Texas to be near their family. And with Maddie and Don getting married this summer, Maddie will live in Don's home, so it will work out well."

Matt turned from removing a waffle from the iron. "Maddie and Don are getting married? When did you find this out?"

"Last Sunday night, when we spent the night at my house. Sorry, I guess the flu gave me a lapse of memory."

"No problem. That's wonderful news." He set the food and two plates on the table. "Try to eat if you can. It'll help you kick that flu bug faster."

Before he could sit down to the meal, his cell phone chimed the James Brown classic, "I Feel Good". He'd left the phone in the living room. The ring tone told him the call was from Miles Davis. He hurried to answer it. "Hey, Miles, what's on your mind?"

"You see the Russell murders in Norman, Oklahoma,

a little while ago?" Miles asked.

"I did. Thought I'd call the sheriff up there to see if he'll let us take a look at the crime scene."

Miles chuckled. "Great minds think alike. When do you want to go?"

"Today, if the sheriff is agreeable. Let me give him a call and I'll get right back to you."

"Did you know they were Dr. Stephen Russell's parents and Eden Russell's in-laws?"

"The thought occurred to me, since it happened in Oklahoma, and the last name is Russell."

He disconnected with Davis and made the call to the sheriff in Norman, then called Davis back and told him they were set to meet the sheriff this afternoon.

Back in the kitchen, he scarfed down the waffles and downed a cup of coffee. After giving his mouth a swipe with his napkin, he leaned over and kissed Sara's brow. "Sorry, babe, I'm going to have to make a fast trip to the Okie crime scene. Will you be okay here alone?"

Sara stood and circled her arms around his waist. "Of course; don't worry about me. I'll miss you, but if this is connected to Eden's parents' murder, the sooner you find the killer, the safer we'll all be."

CHAPTER 11

Max Westheimer Airport
Norman, Oklahoma

Matt connected with Miles Davis at Love Field, where Matt had chartered a small jet to the Max Westheimer Airport operated by the University Of Oklahoma. Westheimer was a general aviation reliever airport, capable of handling aircraft up through and including executive class jets. Flying into the small facility would allow him to get a look at the crime scene while it was still fresh, without the usual airport hassles.

Davis had stopped by the station and put the murder book in his briefcase. The flight to Norman gave Matt time to refresh his memory. Nothing new had been added since the detective team's last meeting.

The plane landed at Westheimer on the grounds of the university, one of the most beautiful campuses in the country.

Sheriff Walter Gates said he would have a deputy pick them up at the airport. True to his word, a uniformed deputy waited inside the small terminal. Matt and Davis introduced themselves, and the deputy ushered them to the waiting county SUV.

The short drive from the airport into Norman took about four minutes. One of the streets they turned onto was James Garner Avenue, a Norman native. Matt had always been a fan of the famous Okie movie star.

The deputy remained silent on the thirty-minute drive from the city to the crime scene. Matt didn't know if the man was naturally reticent, or if he just resented having out-of-state cops involved in a local murder.

Sheriff Gates waited inside his county vehicle. He opened the door and stepped out as they pulled into the driveway. Walter Gates was black, six-foot-three, with a linebacker's build, and a neck the size of most men's thighs, likely an OU alumni. The university routinely fielded one of the most formidable football teams in the Big 12, and was the University of Texas' number one rival.

Gates had pulled a leather jacket over his uniform, and his face wore the seasoned expression of a man who'd seen a lifetime of violence. He approached them with an easy, athletic grace.

Matt made the introductions, and the sheriff reached out with a firm handshake.

"Chief Foley, I appreciate your getting here so fast. I sure hope you have some information that will help us find the people or person responsible. The Russells were good folks."

Gates strode towards the front entrance of the residence, and Matt moved into step beside him. "No promises, but this is similar to a case we're investigating in Texas."

They crossed the yellow tape and paused for a moment under the portico. Through the open double doors, two chalk outlines were drawn half in, half out of the entrance, shot in the back as they'd returned from a party—at least, that's what the news broadcast had said. The outlines seemed to bear out that scenario.

"The bodies have been removed, but I have photos for you inside." The sheriff led them to the back entrance, and provided booties and gloves. "I don't have to tell you not to disturb anything. Just look around as much as you want. I'll be up front when you're ready to talk."

"Sheriff, before you leave, did the killer enter the home?" Matt asked.

Gates nodded. "Looked as though he was looking for something in the bedroom."

Matt and Davis wandered down a long hallway with tumbled marble floors wide enough for a dump truck to drive through. The walls featured dark wood paneling, lined with paintings that looked to be original and expensive. Indirect lighting showed off the art to the best advantage. The decor was tasteful, and had been coordinated by someone with an eye for details and textures.

Davis commented as they moved into the equally-inspired living area, "These folks certainly knew how to live well."

Matt nodded but didn't answer.

They passed a broad marble staircase that led to the second floor, but Matt wanted a closer look at the photos the sheriff had left on a foyer table before checking upstairs.

The pictures showed the bodies lying face-down in the doorway, partially on the smooth marble entrance. The couple was Caucasian. He couldn't see their faces, but knew from the newscast they were in their early sixties.

The weapon of choice appeared to be a rifle. That didn't mesh with the handgun used in the Davenport murders, but there were no rules that said a killer had to always use the same firearm.

Both victims were expensively dressed. Mrs. Russell wore a long black skirt with a beaded top, her hair stylishly coiffed for the anniversary celebration. Her husband wore a black tuxedo, gold Rolex on his left wrist.

Provided the killer hadn't picked up the brass before leaving the scene, Gates would have them in his evidence kit. Otherwise, they would have to wait for the autopsies to try to determine the weapon and caliber.

Photographers and videographers on the ground floor were finishing their job, busily packing up their gear. Matt knew he and Davis needed to make this a fast inspection. Gates would want to close down the crime scene soon.

"Let's check out the master bedroom, and then we'll go find the sheriff," Matt said.

Upstairs, the scene in the Russells' bedroom mirrored that in the Davenports' home. The room had been tossed, a jewelry box dumped on the bed, diamond rings, pendants, and brooches glittering in the bright overhead lights. Robbery was not the motive, unless the killer looked for something in particular, as seemed to be the case in the Davenport killings. The CSU people upstairs were also closing up shop, so he and Davis went in search of Sheriff Gates.

He stood talking to a cop about twenty feet inside the crime scene tape, and crossed to meet them as they descended to the lower level.

"There's a pancake house down the road a few miles," Gates said. "Let's get some coffee. We can compare notes over the best java in the county."

<<>>

A pretty young woman in a beige uniform with a blue-and-beige-checkered apron led them to a booth in the back of the crowded restaurant, and promptly returned with three cups and an aluminum carafe. The coffee was good, fresh, and strong.

Sheriff Gates took a long sip and cast a brown-eyed gaze at Matt. "What do you think? Same perp?"

"Quite possibly. There are a number of similarities. The murder victims were members of prominent families, they lived in remote areas, and most important of all, they were connected by marriage to Stephen and Eden Russell."

Gate's eyebrows shot up. "Is that a fact?"

Matt nodded. "I assume you spoke to Dr. Russell before the news people flashed it on the air."

"Yeah, talked to him on the phone; he's driving over after his rounds tonight. He seemed pretty shook up. He'd planned to be at his parents' party, but had an emergency at the last minute."

"I don't suppose you've had time to confirm that?" Davis said.

Gate shook his head. "Too busy working the crime scene. We'll take care of it over the next few days."

"How long had they been dead when your crew arrived?" Matt asked.

"We lucked out there. They had a live-in maid who arrived home as the apparent killer drove away. She saw the bodies and called immediately. So we have near to the exact time of death, midnight, give or take twenty minutes while he searched the house. Unfortunately, she didn't get a good description of the vehicle, so setting up a roadblock would have been futile. Too many people around here carry rifles in their cars and trucks."

"You pretty sure it was a rifle?" Davis asked.

"Looks that way, but we didn't find any casings. Won't know for sure until the coroner removes the bullets."

"Did the maid identify the bodies?" Matt asked.

Gates waved the waitress over for a new carafe. "Yes, but there was no need. I knew Barton and Emme personally. They held an open house every December for first responders." He stirred the coffee with a spoon and looked up. "You people have a suspect?"

"We have a strong person of interest, but no proof," Matt said. "I'll send you photos of Dr. Russell's ex-wife and her cousin, James Bauer. You can see if anyone saw them around the time of the murders."

"That'll be a start. I'm going to ask Dr. Russell to take a polygraph. Even if the man has an alibi," Gates said, "he could have hired someone to kill his parents. I don't like to believe that, because I also know the doc, but I intend to cover all the bases."

Matt swallowed the last of his coffee, then set the cup back in the saucer. "Good idea. We'll send you copies of the forensics on our end, and would appreciate you sharing whatever your people come up with."

Highway 75 Service Road
Twin Falls, Texas

The flight back to Love Field was faster by twenty minutes. Matt found his Escalade in the parking garage. It was as cold inside as a refrigerator, but it wouldn't take long to heat up once he hit the highway.

Temperatures had risen to forty-five degrees on Saturday, and the sun had melted the snow sludge. But, as night fell and the thermometer dipped below freezing, the highway became an ice rink. Road conditions made the trip to Twin Falls longer than normal. Anxious to get home, he hissed an impatient breath as he eased to a stop at the red light just before going under the Highway 75 bridge. He glanced left as a pickup truck careened off the freeway.

Unable to intervene, Matt watched as the truck hit the ice and ploughed into a car stopped at the intersection. Sounds of crunching metal filled the silent night as the truck crushed the car like an accordion against the eighteen-wheeler in front.

Matt snatched his cell phone and described the situation to the 911 dispatcher in short, precise sentences, replaced his phone, and rushed across the icy street to the scene.

The guy in the pickup was already out of the cab. He was pale, but otherwise appeared unscathed. "I couldn't stop...the ice made me slide. I couldn't stop..."

Matt didn't have time to reassure the man. Quick strides brought him to the car in the middle.

The trucker jumped down to the street with a fire extinguisher in his hand. "Can I help?"

"Just keep that extinguisher handy in case we need it," Matt said, and leaned through the window of the compact car.

A young woman of about thirty was pinned against the steering wheel. The airbag had inflated, but must have burst with the force of the impact. The vehicle was so mangled it would take the fire department and the Jaws of Life to remove her. She must have sustained massive internal injuries.

Matt reached inside the driver's side shattered window. He felt her thready pulse. The hand was cold and thin, almost skeletal, the skin milky white. She turned her head and focused an intense blue gaze on his face. Her wire-rimmed glasses were askew, and he gently straightened them. "How are you doing? Are you in any pain?"

"No," she said in a weak, almost-whisper. "It probably should hurt, but it doesn't. That's not good, right?" Her gaze never wavered, and she must have seen the answer in his eyes. "It's okay. I know...I'm going to die."

Matt swallowed the huge lump in his throat and evaded answering. "I've called for an ambulance. It should be here soon." That wasn't exactly true. The same streets that caused her accident would delay the arrival of help.

A wisp of a smile touched her lips. "Don't look so sad. It's okay...you see, I'm saved. I know where I'm going."

"What's your name?" Matt asked.

"Julie, Julie Landers," she said, her voice a soft whisper. "My husband's name is John. His number is in my cell phone. Someone will let him know? He's a good man, a good husband." She inhaled a shallow breath. "I'm not afraid ...well, maybe a little. The unknown is always scary, but I think I know what to expect." Her eyes were luminous in the dim light. "I didn't really want to go so soon. I have two little girls. I hate to leave them now...they're so young. What's your name?"

He folded his jacket and placed it between her head and the remnants of the airbag draped across the steering wheel. "I'm Matt, Julie. And I'm going to stay here with you as long as you need me."

"My two girls, Amy and Pamela, Amy is the oldest. She's eight and she'll probably grow up to be president. She's so smart and articulate. My youngest is Pamela. She's five and she paints, sings, and dances. She's very talented. Everybody tells me so."

"What type of work do you do?" he asked, trying to distract her from the inevitable.

"I'm a teacher. Middle school English. Are you a Christian, Matt?"

"Yes." He squatted down on his haunches beside the car and placed one hand against her face. The lashes and brows were white-blonde, like her hair. The nose was a little too long, the lips thin. It wasn't a pretty face, but it was a good face, etched with character and kindness. "I think you're the bravest person I've ever known."

The corners of her mouth tilted upward in a faint, shy smile. "Not really...I just hide my fear really well. Will you pray for me, Matt? "

Holding her hand, Matt whispered the most fervent prayer of his life. He asked for God's mercy to save her life if possible, but he didn't ask God to give her dying grace. She already had that. Instead, he asked for God to keep the pain at bay, for Him to hold her close and lead her to the other side. He also asked for peace and comfort for her husband and children.

She gave him that beautiful smile again. "Thank you, Matt. You'll stay with me?"

"Wild horses couldn't drag me away."

"You married?"

He nodded.

"Kids?"

"Yes, two. A boy and a girl."

For a moment, her gaze focused somewhere behind him. She smiled then closed her eyes. And just like that, Julie Landers was gone.

Matt remained there for a long time, holding her hand until a firefighter walked up behind him. He hadn't even noticed when the emergency team arrived.

"I'll take over now, Chief."

Matt stood, released her hand, and placed it against her cheek. He filled his lungs with cold air, drawing it past the heavy weight in his chest.

The pickup driver looked at him with wide, frightened eyes. When Matt nodded, he burst into tears. "I couldn't stop...I tried . . ."

A sheriff's deputy walked over. "You want to notify the family, Matt?"

He shook his head. "No, I'm going to let you guys handle this one."

As he walked back to his car, a fireman called to him, "Chief, don't forget your jacket."

"Keep it until you free her. I'll pick it up later." Matt turned to the man. "Take good care of this one." His voice became husky, and he cleared his throat. "She's special."

The Foley Residence
Twin Falls, Texas

It was almost one o'clock when Matt called to say he was on his way home. Sara sat before the fireplace, and watched sparks float up the chimney like bright fireflies while she waited for him. She'd made the apple cider he liked, in case he wanted something hot before he went to bed.

He'd sounded down when he called. Being the wife of a cop meant she would have to understand that Matt would see things in his day-to-day job that most people could only imagine. Quiet moods were to be expected. After all, he'd just left a violent murder scene.

The purr of the high performance engine easing into the garage told her Matt was home. She stood as the kitchen door opened and he crossed the room to meet her. Without a word, he gathered her into his arms and held her close for a long time. "It's great to be home," he said, his breath warm in her ear.

"You hungry?" she asked.

"Not really. Davis and I grabbed a bite before we left Oklahoma. I'll keep you company if you want to eat."

"I ate earlier. Bad trip?"

"The worst." He put his arm around her waist, and they went upstairs to the inviting warmth of a blazing fire in the hearth.

Sensing it wasn't something he wanted to talk about, she didn't ask any questions. He would tell her when he was ready.

Twin Falls Police Station
Twin Falls, Texas

Matt was surprised to find Doug Anderson waiting for him in his office. His boss was a tall man, lanky, with auburn hair and honest brown eyes; a handsome man for his age of fifty-something years. Sunlight bounced off the melting snowbank outside, filling the room with blinding brilliance. Doug stood gazing out the window behind Matt's desk. He didn't turn when Matt entered.

"Hey, Doug, what brings you down from your tower?"

There was a long pause before Doug spoke. "I've made an executive decision," he said, still facing the window. "I didn't want to tell you over the phone."

"I guess it can't be good if you don't want to look at me. Spit it out, Doug."

The city manager swiveled around, his mouth formed a grim, straight line. "I want you to put Luther Donnell in the Internal Affairs slot when it opens up in April.

That's my decision. I expect you to implement it at the appropriate time." He turned back to the window.

Matt sat on the corner of his desk and let what the man said sink in for a minute. He had a responsibility to the people who worked for him. If he couldn't protect them from political appointments, he couldn't protect them at all. "It's inconceivable to me that you would want to put Donnell in such an important position. You've never interfered with the way I run the police department, so I have to assume you have a good reason for doing so now. But I can't do what you're asking."

"Can't or won't?" Doug asked.

"Whichever, it amounts to the same thing. I have three months until the IAD position opens up. The Davenport case should be wrapped up before that. You'll have my resignation on your desk before then."

Doug turned and strode to the door. "Don't threaten me, Matt. I don't want to lose you, but I won't be bluffed."

"You should know me better than that. I don't bluff."

A surge of deep disappointment seemed to wash over Doug's face as he reached for the door knob. "You're a cop. What else would you do?"

"I can always send out my resume, or take up the offers I've received to run for public office. Then again, I may decide to retire and just take care of my wife and kids."

He stood and walked around the desk to his chair. "Irrational people across this country have painted targets on the backs of the very people charged to protect them. I won't be a party to anything that puts them in more danger. That includes installing an incompetent individual in the IAD spot. When I leave, I'd like to recommend Miles Davis as my replacement. He'll make a fine Chief of Police."

"It's your choice." Doug opened the door and closed it silently behind him.

This move was totally out of character for Doug Anderson. Unlikely as it seemed, Matt couldn't help but wonder if the mayor had something incriminating on Doug and forced his hand.

Matt was still in shock when Chris Hunter knocked on the door jamb and stuck his head in. "Was that your boss I just saw in the hallway? He doesn't come around often." When Matt didn't respond, Chris said, "You got a minute to go over what Cole and I learned at the court house about Bauer?"

Feelings could wait. Matt had plenty of time to make a final decision about his future. But he needed time to compose himself. "I have a few things to take care of first. Give me an hour, and I'll meet you in the conference room."

The phone on his desk rang. Sheriff Gates was on the line from Norman. Matt put his personal issues aside as the sheriff brought him up to date on what was happening on his end.

<<>>

The smell of fresh brewed coffee greeted Matt when he entered the Detective Bureau conference room. He reluctantly avoided the refreshment counter. He'd had his caffeine quota for the morning.

Chris and Cole waited for him to be seated.

"We asked a lot of people in and around the courthouse about Bauer," Chris said. "Bottom line, most folks are afraid of him." He chuckled. "Women say he considers himself a ladies' man, and goes into a James Bond persona around them. He stops just short of sexual harassment."

Chris flipped his notebook open. "For the record, he has a concealed carry permit and, according to the deputies and courthouse staff, he's always packing."

"Anyone ever file a complaint?" Matt asked.

Chris shook his head. "Not that we could determine. Maybe out of respect for his father. Old man Bauer was admired by almost everyone. I got the feeling they were afraid to push Junior's buttons.

"Bauer was at the courthouse while we were there. Don't know if he suspected our purpose, but he didn't look happy to see us there."

CHAPTER 12

Indian Casino
Durant, Oklahoma

After checking in with Matt, Davis headed the new unmarked Dodge Charger east toward Oklahoma. He had liked the old Ford Crown Victoria, the most popular police car ever made, but Ford decided to stop offering it to police departments. Davis had been on a committee to find a replacement, and the group finally settled on the Charger. The reason was simple. Like the Crown Vic, the Charger was the only rear-wheel drive, V8, full-size vehicle available.

Davis and Turner needed to question the casino staff about Bauer's presence there.

Davis offered to take Chris Hunter with him because of Turner's aversion to returning to her home state, but she declined. "I'll go. I can't let that jerk ex-husband of mine interfere with my job. He's had too much power over my life as it is."

He admired her courage, but noticed she kept reaching for the cigarettes in her purse, then putting them back. There were rules against smoking in police vehicles, not that Turner always followed the rules.

The casino sat just across the Texas/Oklahoma border, a little over an hour's drive, barring traffic problems. It was a massive complex, with gaming of all kinds, and hotel facilities.

The parking lot was almost full when they pulled into the closest spot available. He shouldn't be surprised. Gambling could be as addictive as drugs. Davis led the way through a thousand slot machines to the reception desk.

He introduced himself and Turner to the pretty blonde girl behind the desk. He showed his credentials, and asked to speak to the manager.

Five minutes later, a man stepped through a door

behind the counter. His wide shoulders, long dark hair tied back in a ponytail, and high cheekbones reflected his Native American ancestry. He wore a charcoal gray suit, a black shirt, and a black-and-white-striped tie. Piercing dark eyes gave Davis a questioning look. He introduced himself as Waya Mann. "How may I help you?"

Davis again showed his credentials and explained they needed to speak to all hotel personnel who had direct contact with James Bauer, dealers, waiters, or whoever, from Saturday evening until his departure Monday.

The casino manager nodded. "Of course; I'll make sure you have the cooperation of the hotel and casino staff."

"We have a copy of Bauer's bill," Davis said, and handed it to Mann.

"Our records will be more detailed." Mann signaled to the clerk behind the desk. With nimble fingers, she clicked the keys on her terminal keyboard. After a few minutes, she printed off a copy of the hotel's account archives of Bauer's stay. She handed it to Mann. He scanned it quickly. "I see Mr. Bauer is a frequent guest here." He then passed the bill to Davis.

Having seen Bauer's copy, Davis gave it a light once-over. The symbols meant nothing to him. Bauer had ordered room service at twelve o'clock Saturday and breakfast at nine Sunday. "We'd like to speak to the room service waiter who delivered the meals Saturday night and Sunday morning; also the maid who took care of his room."

"It will take a few minutes to make them available. Would you like to wait in my office?"

Davis inclined his head towards the restestaurant. "Thanks, but we'll grab some coffee until you're ready for us. You have surveillance cameras in the casino." It was a statement, not a question.

"Yes, in all the gaming areas, and certain parts of the hotel."

"Parking lot?" Davis asked.

"Yes, all outside areas."

"Good. Then we'll also need to look at the gaming and parking lot surveillance tapes from the time he arrived until his departure."

"It'll take a few minutes," Mann said, "but I'll have security set it up."

It took more than the few minutes Mann alluded to for him to arrange the meetings. The waiter didn't come on duty until one. He and Turner decided to grab lunch in the casino's massive buffet dining area in the interim.

Shortly after one o'clock, they were led to a small conference room, where the Hispanic waiter sat stiffly in a chair, wrinkles of anxiety etching creases around his mouth. His name tag was imprinted *Antonio Perez*. "Am I in trouble?"

"This isn't about you. We just want to ask some questions about meals you delivered a week ago, late Saturday night and breakfast Sunday morning to room 209," Davis said, and placed photos of Bauer on the table. "You remember him?"

The waiter's shoulders relaxed and he studied the shots. "Yes, I see him before, many times."

"What time did you deliver the food?"

"Between eleven-thirty and twelve that night."

Davis pulled up a chair, straddled it, and faced the timid man. "Did you see Mr. Bauer when you made the delivery?"

"Yes, he was there, but a lady answered the door. The man was on the phone. I placed the food on the table, asked the lady to sign the ticket. She gave me a big tip and I left."

"Do you know the woman's name? Was she staying with Mr. Bauer?"

"I don't know her name; she is a regular at the casino. She dates many men."

"Does that mean she's a prostitute?" Davis asked.

The waiter's gaze dropped to the floor then back to Davis. "I don't know if she gets paid."

"But you did see the man in the room?" Turner asked.

Perez nodded.

Davis continued. "Did you pick up the tray later that

night? Were both meals eaten?"

"Yes, I gather the trays left outside the rooms before I leave. If the food had not been finished, I would have noticed. That would say they didn't like the food. The hotel is very concerned that food service customers have no complaints."

"You delivered breakfast Sunday at what time?" Davis asked.

"At eight o'clock. The woman was still there. She say he had gone to get cigarettes," the waiter said.

Davis placed his arms on the chair back and leaned forward. "So this time the man wasn't in the room? You never saw him?"

The waiter shook his head. "Yes, only the woman."

Next they questioned the maid. She had nothing to add to what the waiter said. She had not seen Bauer Sunday during the day or Monday when he checked out.

A knock on the conference room door sounded, and Mann said security was ready to roll the surveillance tapes.

The tech room was down a long hallway, large, quiet, and cold, probably in deference to the equipment. Men sat in suit coats and ties, watching banks of monitors; spotters trying to catch cheaters. Cameras covered every square inch of the large gaming room, but the main focus seemed to be on the card tables.

The security guard led them to a small room with more video equipment and banks of stored tapes. A man sat at a console, ready to follow their directions. He had already loaded the date parameters Davis asked for.

"We're looking for this man," Davis flashed a photo of Bauer. "Roll the tapes slowly; we'll see if we can spot him."

The tech pointed them to two chairs in front of a twenty-inch monitor, and started the tape feed. It was real time and slow-going, the pictures in grainy black and white.

Bauer showed up at the blackjack table at six-thirty Saturday night. A young woman with dark hair watched over his shoulder for a while then drifted off to the slot machines.

"Let's speed it up a little," Davis said.

With a nod, the tech made a few clicks of the mouse, and the film speed increased significantly. Judging from the chips Bauer started with and what he ended with, he didn't do too badly. He left the table at ten-fifteen, walked over and said something to the dark-haired woman, handed her some bills, then headed to the bar and out of sight. The girl stayed at the slots for another thirty minutes, and then exited towards the bar.

"Stop right there," Davis said. "Can you print off a picture of the girl?"

"Yes, no problem," the tech said. He made a print, and then resumed running the tape.

The parking lot video reflected the time of Bauer's arrival and when he and Locke left. They came in the same car, and the vehicle hadn't moved during their stay.

Davis tapped the tech's shoulder. "That's good. Thanks for your help."

Before leaving the casino, he located Mann again and showed him the print. "Do you know this woman?"

Mann nodded. "Yes, I've seen her around. She's one we watch. She never approaches men, they come to her. We never see any money change hands, except to give her money to gamble with. They usually buy her dinner. Sometimes she goes to their room, sometimes not. I can't keep her out since she does gamble...we just try to keep the pros out."

"I'd like to show this photo to Antonio, if I may, to confirm she was the woman in Bauer's room Saturday and Sunday."

"Sure," Mann said. He had the receptionist page Antonio.

After the waiter confirmed the woman as Bauer's guest, Davis pulled a card from his inside pocket and handed it to Mann. "If she comes in again, give her this. I'd like to make an appointment to ask her a few questions."

Mann slipped the card into his jacket and nodded.

Davis and Turner left the building and he got behind the wheel of the unmarked car. The parking lot was still full as they pulled away. "So what do you think?"

"I think Bauer is guilty as sin, but nothing back there proves it," Turner said. "His car was stationary the entire time, but he could have brought another car and left it close by. He wasn't filmed leaving the building at any time, but, again, he could have left through a side exit where there are no cameras. And since he is a frequent guest he would know where those are. He had plenty of time to leave after midnight, drive back to Twin Falls, commit the murders, and return to the casino, even with the bad weather. The woman in his room may have lied Sunday when she said Bauer left to get cigarettes. So what's next?"

"We try to run down all the calls Bauer made before and after the murders. We can split the job up with Chris and Cole. Also, we need to see if he rented a car during that time."

Turner groaned. "That's a tall order. He could have made a hundred calls, and there are about that many car rentals. Too bad we don't have enough evidence to get a court order for his credit card receipts."

Davis glanced over at her and shook his head. "I didn't say it was going to be easy."

Italian Restaurant
Plano, Texas

Matt asked Sara to meet him for dinner at his favorite Italian restaurant. He needed to fill her in on his conversation with Doug. After they were seated, Matt told her everything...what his boss wanted and why he'd refused.

Sara moved closer to him in the circular booth, her lovely eyes filled with empathy. She placed her hand over his. "I'm so sorry. I know how much your work means to you. And everybody knows you're one of the best at what you do. But you made the right decision to stand up for your principles. I'll be happy, whatever you decide."

Before he could respond, a slender man in black jeans and a black long-sleeved t-shirt slid into the booth beside him. The man was handsome in a rugged kind of way, about forty-five, with close-cropped dark hair sprinkled liberally with gray, and a nose that had been broken at least twice. "Who's the beautiful lady you're holding hands with, Foley?"

"Hi, Chaim. This is my wife, Sara. Sara, may I introduce Chaim Harel. This guy used to beat the stuffing out of me on a regular basis."

He took her hand and held it a little longer than necessary. "A beautiful name for a lovely woman. But what your husband said is not true. He's just looking for sympathy. By the way, Foley, why haven't I seen you at the studio? You don't use it, you lose it."

Sara shot him a questioning glance.

"I've been too busy to let you push me around," Matt said then added to Sara. "Chaim teaches Krav Maga classes. In fact, he taught the techniques to the Israeli military before he came to the States to take it easy."

"What does Krav Maga mean?" she asked.

The martial arts expert glanced across the table at Sara. "It's Hebrew, and means contact combat. You should take my classes. You look athletic, and a lot of women are enrolled. Not to be melodramatic, but it could save your life."

He turned his attention back to Matt. "One of your detectives takes classes three days a week, Lucy Turner." He chuckled and shook his head. "That woman has a lot of pent-up rage. I'd hate to be the guy she's holding a grudge against when she finally lets loose."

Sara gave him a sideways glance. "I don't know...I've never tried martial arts."

"Krav Maga uses your body's natural instincts and reflexes in a fight or flight situation, and transforms them into effective self-defense," Chaim said. "It eliminates the need to memorize techniques."

Matt nodded and mulled over Chaim's suggestion. "That's not a bad idea. Since you're no longer working, you have some extra time. I'm sure the master, here, can arrange to give you private lessons, which would speed up your learning curve. I'd join you whenever possible."

"Private lessons will be no problem," the instructor said and handed her his business card. "Just let me know when and how often."

"You don't have to decide right now," Matt told her. "Give it some thought and let him know if you're interested."

When their dinner arrived, Chaim left them to their meal. "Don't forget about the policemen's ball Monday night," Matt reminded Sara.

"It's formal, right?"

"Oh, yes. The wives love having an excuse to dress up, and the guys wear a tux. It's a very glamorous affair. Gives me a chance to mingle with the beat cops, which I don't often get an opportunity to do." He smiled. "It's a lot more fun than political and society gatherings. My guys know how to have fun. Unfortunately, some of the political types show up, but they don't stay long. That's when the party starts." He chuckled, "You haven't lived until you see a bunch of burly cop's dance 'the wobble'."

As they finished, Matt's former father-in-law, Blain Stanton, strode over to their table. "I thought I saw you when you came in." He bent forward and kissed Sara's cheek. "You're looking lovely as always."

"Thanks, Blain. It's good to see you." Blain's daughter, Mary, had been Matt's first wife and Sara's best friend, before she succumbed to cancer three years ago.

Matt shook his father-in-law's hand with genuine warmth. Blain Stanton was the richest and most influential political figure in the state, and he still treated Matt like a son. The man had won Matt's respect long ago, a rare, honest politician.

"Mind if I join you?" Blain asked.

"I'd be disappointed if you didn't," Matt said.

Blain slid into the booth beside Matt. "What's this I hear that you may be leaving your job in Twin Falls? I thought you were a cop first, last, and always."

Matt just managed to keep his mouth from dropping open. "It never ceases to amaze me how you know everything that goes on in this state as it happens."

Blain waved a waiter over and ordered Scotch on the

rocks. "Not everything. But I make it my business to keep tabs on people I care about. So, why are you leaving?"

Matt filled him in on his conversation with his boss.

Blain stirred the ice with his forefinger. "I know Doug Anderson. This seems way out of character for him."

Matt nodded and grinned. "That's what I thought. I figure Terrance Hall has some naked pictures of Doug and is blackmailing him."

Blain echoed a deep laugh. "I doubt that, but Hall might have enough on him to force Doug to hire the brother-in-law. I've heard of this fellow, Hall. Some people have been pushing to run him for state senator. But we already have too many of his kind in office."

"My thoughts exactly," Matt said.

Blain downed his drink and said goodbye before departing through the front entrance, where his driver waited.

Sara laughed when they were alone. "This where you come to catch up with old friends?"

"I didn't plan it that way, but looks like that's what happened. I need you to do me a favor."

She gave him a sensual smile. "I'm always at your disposal."

The smile distracted him momentarily, but he regrouped quickly. "Check with the funeral homes in Twin Falls, and find out when services will be held for Julie Landers. Send flowers, something extravagant."

"A friend of yours?" Sara asked.

"Yes, and that's how I want you to sign the card. No name, just *a friend*." He squeezed her hand. "I'll tell you about it sometime."

His phone dinged an incoming text message. He held up a finger to Sara while he scanned the script. He felt the blood leave his face. "Emergency. We have to go."

CHAPTER 13

Twin Falls Police Station
Twin Falls, Texas

Davis and his partner made it back to Twin Falls around four that afternoon. He dropped Turner at the station's back entrance. "I'll park and see you inside."

As she started through the door, movement in the building's shadow caught Davis' attention. It happened so fast, he wasn't sure he saw it at all. But his cop's instinct made his gaze flash back on the spot where the movement occurred. In one fluid motion, Davis slammed on the brakes, jammed the car into park, and jumped out of the vehicle. "Turner, watch out!"

Too late.

From the snowbank nestled against the building, the shadow morphed into a man who stalked into view. He wrapped a huge arm around Turner's throat and pressed a 9mm Glock to her neck.

"Take it easy, cowboy," the man said.

Turner stared at Davis, her eyes wide with panic, her voice strained. "Davis, let me introduce you to my ex-husband, Hank Turner."

P-229 Sig at his side, Davis stepped in front of Lucy and sized up the man behind her. He was as big as a bear, at least six-foot-six and solid as a steel battering ram, shoulders broad, hips narrow, and thighs like tree trunks. His shaved head bore a swastika above his right ear.

Great. Just what the situation called for. A crazed skinhead on a mission.

Hank had timed his move perfectly. The parking lot was empty of squad cars. The second shift was on the streets, and the third wouldn't arrive until after six in the morning.

Davis aimed his gun at the man, a futile gesture. He couldn't shoot. If he did, Hank would kill Lucy. "Okay, man, stay cool. Put the gun down and let's talk this out. That way, nobody gets hurt."

Hank barked a laugh that raised the hair on Davis' arms. The ex's eyes were bright and jerky. The man was high on something, crack, heroin, cocaine, Davis couldn't tell. Whatever it was, it upped the crisis level to critical mass. He of all people couldn't reason with a drug-crazed racist.

"I'll tell you how cool I am. You shoot me, my reflexes will pull the trigger, and Lucy is dead. I'm going to shoot you where you stand."

"If you hurt him, Hank, I'll kill you," Lucy said through gritted teeth. "You'll be afraid to sleep at night, because I'll be waiting to slit your throat."

He shoved the gun barrel into her neck and she yelped in pain. "This your new boyfriend, Luc?"

"He's my partner, and this isn't his fight. This is between you and me."

A yellow Hummer screeched into the lot and stopped two feet from where Davis stood. In his peripheral vision, he saw the car door flash open and another skinhead emerge, wearing a red hunter's jacket and armed with a Heckler and Koch MP5. These guys were better armed than the cops on the street.

The guy with the sub-machine gun yelled, "Drop the weapon and kick it away!"

Davis wasn't going to give up his weapon. They'd probably shoot him anyway if he did.

He never got the opportunity to make that decision. He sensed a presence behind him, and suddenly realized there had been more than one person in the Humvee, just before a crippling pain hit the back of his head and darkness claimed him.

<<>>

Hank tightened his grip on Lucy's neck and heaved her into the Hummer's backseat, then slid in beside her.

Stupid.

Stupid.

Stupid.

She'd been preparing for this confrontation for five years, and when it came, she'd acted like a novice and failed to focus on her surroundings. Whether weariness from the trip or the fact she never expected Hank to come for her at the station was immaterial. She'd been taught to always be ready.

Always.

Instead, she'd walked into his trap like a pig to a luau. "Where are we going?"

"We're going to pick up my boys at your place, and then I have a special destination for all of us. We'll be one big happy family again."

"The boy's aren't at home," Lucy said. "They went on a teen retreat with the church this weekend. They're spending the night with friends."

He grabbed her face with one hand and squeezed hard enough to make her eyes tear. "You wouldn't lie to me, would you, Luc?"

Of course she would lie. She'd lie, steal, and cheat to protect her sons from their maniac father. By the grace of God, it happened to be the truth. And she knew when Davis was free, he would take steps to see Charlie and Mack were safe.

Hank let go of her face and shoved her back against the seat. "No matter. I can always come back for them."

<<>>

The cold was the first sensation Davis felt, then the pain in his head hit like a sledge hammer. His mouth, hands, and feet were duct-taped, and he had been stuffed into the trunk of a car. Despite the cold, sweat broke out on his brow as his muddled thoughts raced back to the scene in the parking lot. The skinheads had Lucy. And he was trussed up like a Thanksgiving turkey, giving them a big head start. They could be a hundred miles away in any direction.

Apparently, they didn't intend to kill her, at least not right away. Otherwise, they would have shot them both in the parking lot. Still, she was in immenent danger. Nobody in their right mind kidnapped a cop at a police station. Were these guys too dumb to know that security cameras would get it all on tape? Perhaps they were so hopped up they didn't care.

He tried to maneuver his body so his fingers could reach the inside trunk release. No easy feat. His chest faced the release button, and his hands were taped behind his back. Footsteps outside told him someone was nearby. Friend or foe? Whichever, he had to take his chances. He couldn't yell with his mouth secured, so he kicked the trunk hull with his feet.

Steps paused and a voice called, "Is someone in there?"

Davis kicked the hull again.

An urgent voice responded, "Just a minute, and I'll have you out of there."

The car door opened and Davis heard the lock pop. Heavy footfalls hurried to the back and the trunk lid lifted wide. After the darkness, the lights in the parking lot sent stabs of pain to the back of his eyes.

Ben Stein stood silhouetted against the lighted backdrop, a dumbfounded expression on his face. He ripped the adhesive from Davis' mouth none too gently. "What are you doing in there? I thought some of the guys were playing a practical joke on me."

"It's no joke, Ben. Cut me loose. Lucy's been kidnapped by her ex-husband."

Once freed, Davis jerked his cell phone from his pocket and sprinted for the police station's back entrance. He called dispatch to put out a BOLO on the yellow Hummer, then punched the speed dial number for Matt Foley, and sent him a text.

Lucy Turner abducted by her ex.

Stein stayed right in step by his side. "Davis, I'm in on this. Don't try to stop me. I know what that guy is capable of. We have to stop him before he kills her. I'll call a car to pick up her kids and take them and their grandmother to a safe-house under protective custody until we find Lucy. Sure as God made little green apples, he'll come after his sons. He's a possessive, narcissistic, egomaniac ... among other things."

Davis gave him a solemn nod. "Okay, you're my

partner on this until we find her."

<<>>

Matt flew through the Detective Bureau entrance and strode to where Davis and Officer Ben Stein stood in front of a large Texas map. Davis had a white bandage wrapped around his head.

"You hurt?" Matt asked.

Davis gave Stein a dark look. "No, but Mother Theresa, here, wouldn't leave me alone until I let one of the EMTs next door check me out. No concussion, like I told him; just a big bump."

Matt slapped the officer on the shoulder. "Good work, Stein. At least one of you is thinking straight. Anything yet on Lucy?"

"Nothing. The BOLO hasn't turned up anything, but it's early. The yellow Hummer would stick out like a sore thumb, but they could have switched cars. Stein's running the description to see if it might be stolen. By my calculations, the kidnappers have been gone a little over an hour."

"We're also checking out white supremacy groups, the Klan, and anything else we can think of," Davis said. "I don't believe these guys are in the Klan. They didn't look like white-sheet types. They had no problem showing their faces."

Matt perched on the edge of a desk and gazed at the map. "I'll give Joe Wilson a call. Those groups tend to locate in remote areas. He might have some leads for us. If not, he can contact other sheriffs and see if they have any intel on Hank Turner. A rank-and-file member wouldn't be allowed to pull a snatch like this, so Hank is probably the group's leader. Any information on who the other two guys are?"

Stein grinned. "We pulled the parking lot feeds, but the faces aren't clear. Davis has been checking out the skinhead mug shots, but he says they all look alike. We ran Hank Turner through the system, but the file is pretty skimpy, mostly misdemeanors. If he's turned radical, the Feds might have a jacket on him."

"Have you called them?" Matt asked. Many law enforcement chiefs shied away from bringing in the FBI or Homeland Security, but Matt never got into turf wars with the alphabet agencies. He'd always found them helpful.

Stein shook his head. "Not yet."

"I'll take care of that after I speak to Joe. I've worked with Alan Forbes, who's in charge of the Dallas Bureau. He's a good man. We may get lucky. If Turner has been placed on the FBI or Homeland Security watch list, they may know the location of his camp."

Highway I-20
Abilene, Texas

Hank slept from Dallas to Abilene, but not before he taped Lucy's hands together, thankfully not behind her back. At least he didn't blindfold her. That might be bad news. It could mean he intended to kill her and wasn't worried about concealing the whereabouts of his hideout.

It was late when they reached Abilene. The car bounced down a potholed street and stopped in front of a paint and body shop. The driver pressed a garage door opener and the man in the passenger seat jumped out, then backed out a late-model Land Rover. The driver pulled into the vacated spot and the group made the transfer to the white SUV.

Smart move, Lucy thought. Every cop in the state would be looking for the easy-to-spot Hummer. Whatever Hank was into, it must pay well, judging by the expensive vehicles at his disposal, although they were most likely stolen, repainted, and tagged with pinched license plates.

At a nearby fast-food joint, the guy in the front passenger seat jumped out and returned a short while later with a bag of burgers, greasy fries, and a tray of drinks. Beer for them, a Coke for her.

Despite a loss of appetite, she forced down the burger. She would need all her strength for whatever Hank had planned. Past experience had taught her that, whatever he had in mind, it wouldn't be good for her.

Hank had removed the restraints to let her eat, but as soon as she finished the last bite, he slipped plastic handcuffs back on her wrists. He pulled her close and nuzzled her neck, whispering in her ear. "You look good, Luc. Real good. I'd like to spend some time getting reacquainted, but my new wife is the jealous type." He nodded towards the front seat. "Her brother is my driver. She'd probably cut your throat when my back was turned, and I'm not ready for that. Yet."

Supremacist Compound
Near Big Bend National Park

They reached their destination at around five in the afternoon, or so Lucy guessed. With her hands tied, her watch had slipped under her wrist and she couldn't see the face.

Unable to sleep in the SUV, she watched through the Land Rover's tinted windows as they traveled through mostly desert country. She caught a glimpse of the Chisos Mountain's Casa Grande peak, and knew she was in Big Bend country, the largest protected area of Chihuahuan desert landscape and ecology in America. Mountains and canyons made a great place to hide.

She gave an involuntary shiver. Big Bend National Park was hostile country. It sat on more than a million acres that bordered one hundred and eighteen miles of the Rio Grande and covered two counties—an area larger than the state of Rhode Island. The climate could only be characterized as one of extremes. Too hot or too cold.

As a teenager, she'd hiked the many trails and through temple-like canyons carved in limestone by raging rivers of the past. She'd walked through deep gorges with nearly vertical walls and loved every minute of it. But it wasn't a place you wanted to be stranded, especially on foot and without supplies.

The chilled, cloudless afternoon revealed what looked like an old Cavalry fort. A high wooden fence covered acres of arid land. A catwalk with gun towers around the perimeter stood stark and menacing. Mass paranoia in full bloom.

The gate swung open, revealing hundreds of mobile homes of every size and condition, from new to old and rusted. She wondered where the financing came from for an operation of this size.

"So what do you think, Luc?" Hank asked.

She didn't answer. She was too busy figuring out how she was going to escape.

The first whiff of air inside the compound told Lucy where part of the money came from. The unmistakable stench of a meth lab filled the enclosed area. The second clue was a paint shop with six luxury cars parked outside.

A lab meant most of the folks here were likely meth users, with an unlimited supply. And the bad teeth and skin on the two in the Hummer she'd met confirmed her suspicions.

Not good news.

As the car moved farther into the compound, children played kickball among various species of cactus and a few desert marigolds that added color to the otherwise dreary landscape.

The kids stopped their game and watched as the car passed. Visitors were probably their biggest form of entertainment. Without electricity, there would be no television or games in this remote area. Generators would have to be used to power the meth operation.

The driver parked the car in front of a new double-wide with metal skirting and a wide deck. Hank grabbed her arm, dragged her across the seat, then shoved her up the steps through the front door.

The place was nice and clean, even though cheaply furnished. It was very clean. But that was one of Hank's fetishes. His second wife must be his new slave.

A thin, almost skeletal, woman sat at the dining room table, drinking from a ceramic mug labeled *Don't worry, be Hopi.* Long, stringy hair framed her sore-marked face, the tell-tale signs of a meth addict.

The glance she sent Lucy's way held unabashed hatred. "So this is the ex-wife."

"Yep," Hank said, and then to Lucy, "this is Abby."

"You want some coffee?" Abby asked.

"Pour two cups and we'll join you."

The woman stood and slammed her chair back in place. "I'll pour yours; she can get her own. I'm not going to wait on her."

Hank was enjoying his wife's discomfort. "Her hands are tied, stupid. Pour two cups and don't give me any lip."

Abby stomped away and returned with the coffee, which she banged on the table in front of Lucy.

Hank removed the cuffs and Lucy took grateful sips. The coffee was surprisingly good. When she'd finished, Hank lifted her out of the chair by her arm and pushed her down the hallway into one of the bedrooms, then closed the door behind him. He leaned back against the portal, holding her arms. "Just like old times, Luc." One arm slid around her waist, his other hand behind her head, jerking her closer. He placed a hard, cruel kiss on her lips.

Past memories flooded her mind, and she was filled with revulsion and uncontrollable anger. She brought her heel down on his instep with all her weight.

He cursed, drew back his hand, and slapped her across the room. It happened so fast, she had no time to brace for the impact. Her head bashed into the bed frame, sending fingers of hot pain through her temple. She forced her eyes open and fought off the nausea, warding off the blackness. She must remain conscious.

Abby screamed from the other side of the door. "Hank, what are you doing in there?"

He chuckled and called back. "Just making sure she won't get free." With a tight grip on her shirt, he lifted Lucy from the floor, pulled a pair of restraints from his pocket, secured her wrists and ankles, and then pushed her to a sitting position on the bed. "I don't want you going anywhere. I'll see you later. Now, I'm going to get my sons."

CHAPTER 14

Twin Falls Police Station
Twin Falls, Texas

Matt left Sara asleep at six that morning and headed back to the station. He, Davis, and Stein had stayed at police headquarters until after midnight. He felt guilty about leaving Sara alone so much. They'd been married less than a month and he'd come in late too many nights after she'd gone to bed. Not the way he'd wanted his marriage to begin. Thoughts of retirement were beginning to look good. But sleeping in today wasn't an option. With the Davenport case still open, and Lucy missing, it was a gathering storm of no small proportion, and he and one of his people was dead center in the eye.

Davis pulled into the parking lot just ahead of Matt. They exited their vehicles and met at the station's back entrance. Davis wore his usual showroom style, but his face was haggard.

"Anything new on the Davenport case?" Matt asked.

"Chris and Cole are backtracking Bauer's and Eden's cell phone calls and looking at car rental agencies. Grunt work, but other than that we're stalled."

They found Ben Stein already brewing coffee in the conference room, his eyes puffy, and looking like he'd spent a night as sleepless as Matt's own. He'd heard rumors that Stein and Lucy were an item. Stein's miserable countenance appeared to confirm it.

Sheriff Joe Wilson and FBI agent Alan Forbes showed up right behind Matt, followed by Detectives Chris Hunter and Cole Allen.

Matt sent the younger detective out for donuts and sandwiches. He didn't want any of the players to leave until they had a plan of action in place to find Lucy. He prayed to God they weren't already too late.

Everyone grabbed coffee and donuts, then Forbes took the lead as they chose a seat around the conference table. He opened a thin folder he'd brought with him, removed photocopies, and passed them around.

"We've had Hank Turner on our radar for a while, but not under surveillance. Until now, he hasn't broken any laws we're aware of. The sheet I passed out lists the locations of some known supremacist camps." Forbes walked over to the large map on the wall and picked up a pointer. "A couple in the piney woods of East Texas, a couple in the hill country, and one near Big Bend. All of them are stockpiling weapons. No surprise there. Except for a few local clashes with town folks, they've kept their noses pretty clean. I alerted field agents in those areas to check leads to Turner's whereabouts. My people can ask to look inside their property, and if they agree, all is good. At present, we don't have sufficient grounds for a search warrant unless or until we sight Turner or can tie them to him."

"Thanks, Alan. We appreciate the information. It's a place to start," Matt said.

Joe Wilson leaned back in his chair. His bulk made the springs squeak. "I've sent out a BOLO and copies of Turner's mugshot to the sheriffs in these counties. The skinheads have to go into town to buy supplies. With any luck, deputies or nearby townspeople may know where Turner is holed up."

Matt glanced sharply at Ben Stein. "You think he's coming back for his kids?"

"I'd lay money on it," Stein said.

"Then we need to prepare for that. Plant decoys in Lucy's home. Any of our officers small enough to pass for a twelve-year-old boy?"

"Maybe a couple of women, if he doesn't look too close," Stein said.

"We'll make sure he doesn't get that close." Matt pushed back his chair. "See what you can find, Ben. Put one of our guys inside with the impersonator, and a couple of unmarked cars in the neighborhood. Keep them there in rotating shifts until we find Lucy."

Matt folded the sheet the agent had given him and

placed it inside his jacket pocket. "Thanks, Joe, Allan, for your help." He glanced around the table at his people. "We all know what we need to do. Let's get to it."

Supremacist Compound
Near Big Bend National Park

Lucy awoke stiff and thirsty. With her hands and feet tied, movement had been restricted, and her mouth felt like it had been packed with sponges. She'd searched the room last night for something to cut the plastic ties until, exhausted, she'd fallen asleep. Bars on the one window made her wonder if they'd been installed just for her. For now, her kidneys were sending an urgent message.

Rolling to a sitting position, she struggled to her feet and hopped to the door. "Hey, Abby. I need to use the bathroom."

No answer.

She tried again. Knocked, and then yelled. "I know you're out there and I need to use the toilet, bad."

This time she heard hesitant footsteps. The door creaked opened. The poor woman looked worse than she had yesterday. Her hair was mussed and the clothes she wore hung on her thin frame as limp as if on a clothes hanger. The gray tint to her skin underscored her unhealthy condition, and her pupils were pinpoints, eyes glazed over. She was feeling no pain

Abby stepped back from the door. "Come on, I'll show you the way."

"I can't follow you. You need to untie me."

"No way. I can't do that."

"I can't walk with the ties on my ankles. You're not afraid of me, are you?"

Abby gave a sardonic laugh. "No, I'm afraid of him."

"Come on. I need to go, bad."

She gave a weary shake of her head, then stepped into the kitchen, brought back a knife, and cut the ties. "He's going to beat the crap out of me."

When she finished in the bathroom, Lucy came back into the dining room.

DOWNFALL

Abby sat at the table, coffee in front of her, head resting in her hands, tears rolling freely down her gaunt cheeks.

"May I have some of that?" Lucy said, indicating the coffee.

Abby didn't answer, just waved a hand towards the counter.

Lucy grabbed a cup, filled it, and then sat across from the frightened woman. She knew that, with little effort, she could overpower Abby and leave. Heck, a five-year-old could take her. But she felt only pity. Besides, getting out of the trailer wasn't the problem. Getting out of the compound was the major hurdle. "What changed your mind? You were so angry with me yesterday."

"Who says I changed my mind? I had one of my lucid moments last night and realized you were no threat to me. You used to be in the same situation I'm in, but you got lucky."

"Not exactly. I wasn't into drugs, and he wasn't into white supremacy. Where does Hank's money come from? I know about the meth lab and car thefts." Lucy waved her hand around the room. "But I doubt that's enough to pay for all this."

"He's also into human trafficking. He even sends those poor people to help me keep this place spotless."

"Why don't you leave him, Abby? It will never get any better; you have to know that."

Arms crossed on the table, she lowered her head, and sobs shook her thin shoulders.

Lucy came around the table and stroked the woman's hair until the tears were gone. With swollen eyes, her face red and puffy, Abby raised her gaze to Lucy. "Look at me. Just look at me. I'm an addict, and I'm so ugly I couldn't even make a living as a hooker." She gulped back another sob. "I don't have anyone, except my no-account brother who's worse off than I am; except he doesn't get knocked around by a bully twice his size on a regular basis."

Lucy placed her hand over Abby's rough one. How long had it been since anyone had shown her even a tiny bit of compassion? "Crack does some ugly things to the human body, but it's reversible once you get clean. Help me get out of here, and I'll get you into a detox program. That's the only chance you have."

Abby snorted and her mouth twisted downward. "And why would you do that?"

"Because I've been where you are."

"If I help you," she closed her eyes for a moment before continuing, "you'll have to take me with you. Otherwise, he'll kill me."

Lucy went back into the kitchen, brought out the coffee pot, and filled both their cups. "Deal. This is your playground, so how do we get out of here before Hank returns? Do you have a phone?"

"Are you kidding? You think Hank would give me a phone to call someone for help?"

"Dumb question. There wouldn't be any land lines here or towers for cell service."

"Hank has a sat-phone, but he keeps it with him."

Lucy downed the last sip of coffee. "Before we make a break for it, I need a shower."

"I have some clothes I think you can wear. I used to be about your size." She went to her room and returned with a pair of leopard print slacks and a low cut black sweater. She handed them to Lucy.

Eyeing the outfit, her distaste must have registered on her face.

"I know it's not your style, but it's all I've got. Take it or leave it." Abby reached to take the clothes back.

Too late, Lucy realized she'd offended her new partner. She hugged the outfit to her chest. "I'll keep it. I was just thinking I should be as inconspicuous as possible."

She showered and dressed quickly, slipping her jacket on over the sweater. The least of her worries was that the fashion police would catch her in this outfit.

She wasn't completely sure she could trust Abby, but her reluctant agreement to help seemed sincere. The woman didn't have to cut the restraints. She could have called for help to come escort Lucy to the bathroom. She could also have had someone re-apply the plastic cuffs and leg restraints, which seemed to be abundant in the

Turner household. But the most significant reason Lucy was inclined to trust Abby... Hank's new wife had that desperate look that abused women wore...a badge of courage.

Twin Falls Police Station
Twin Falls, Texas

There was a note to call Sheriff Gates on Matt's desk, when he arrived at the station that morning. He punched in the number and waited while a deputy made the connection. "Walt, this is Matt Foley returning your call."

"Thanks for getting back to me. We did some checking on Dr. Russell's financial situation, and he's strapped. He pays hefty child support, and his practice overhead is heavy. He recently took out a second mortgage on his home. Bottom line, his parents' death came at an opportune time. The inheritance will put him in the black for the rest of his life. He's an only child, so it all goes to him."

"I haven't met the doctor, Walt. What does your gut tell you?"

"Experience has taught me you can't build a case on hunches, and the facts certainly make him our number-one suspect."

"But?" Matt said.

"I don't think he did it. Nor does he appear to be the kind of guy who would know where to hire a hit-man."

"Has he taken the second polygraph?" Matt asked.

"Yeah," the sheriff said. "The same results as last time. Inconclusive. It's not unheard of. Some people are just impossible to get a good reading on. That's why they're not allowed as evidence in the court room. Any news on your kidnapped detective?"

"Nothing yet. We're hoping for a break soon."

"I wish you luck. I know Lucy Turner. We met at a couple of functions here. She's a good cop."

"That she is," Matt said. "Thanks for the update. I'll let you know if anything breaks here."

Supremacist Compound
Near Big Bend National Park

Heart in her throat, Abby made her way to the meth lab in search of her brother, Clint. She had a feeling this escape plan was going to go south and leave her at Hank's mercy, and he couldn't even spell the word.

If Clint suspected what she was up to, he wouldn't hesitate to hold her and Lucy until Hank returned, and then Hank would kill them both.

The room was unbearably hot, with four stoves covered with boiling pots of meth. She wondered if the drugs were making her schizophrenic. Sometimes she thought she heard voices, like now. Not actual voices, but thoughts that flooded her mind. *Run. Go back home where it's safe. You owe Lucy Turner nothing. She's just using you like everyone else.* And on and on they went until she wanted to scream. She'd lived with debilitating fear for so long, it was all she knew. A new life free of Hank and drugs was a dream she'd never dared to consider. But what Lucy told her was true. If she didn't leave Hank, eventually he would kill her.

Clint must have seen her when she came in. She held her breath and watched him cross to her. He marched across to where she stood, stopping her from coming any farther into the room. "What are you doing here? You need a hit?"

She screwed up her courage and quelled the tremor in her voice. "No, I've got plenty at home. I need a car." The request wasn't too unusual. She'd done it before; not often, but often enough that it shouldn't send up any red flags.

"What do you need a car for? You didn't leave that woman unattended, did you?"

"Yes, but she's tied and locked in her room."

"Abby, if she gets away, Hank will gut you and throw the remains to the cougars."

"I know that, don't I?" she said. "Where can I get a car? I need to get away from here. He has some nerve bringing his ex-wife into my home." She hoped her acting was better received by her brother than it had been with Hank.

"You might as well learn to like it. You ain't gonna change his mind, whatever his plans are for her."

"Look, I need some space. I'll get one of the guys to watch her."

"Just be sure you do. And be back before Hank returns. I don't want to have to explain your absence." Her brother reached into his pocket and slapped the keys into her hand, but held on to them. "These are for the white Land Rover outside. Take it."

He started to walk away then turned back. "How long you gonna be gone?"

"As long as it takes. I'm gonna take some things back to Walmart and do some shopping. Don't worry; I'll be back before Hank gets here. He'll be gone at least a day, maybe more."

She had to concentrate to keep her hand from trembling as she started the car. She pulled around to the mobile home and parked in front.

<<>>

Lucy met Abby at the door. "You did it! I'm proud of you."

"Yeah, well I almost peed my pants. If Hank catches me..."

"Don't worry about that. With my hands free, I can handle Hank, unless of course, he has a gun aimed at me."

Abby scoffed. "You? Handle Hank?"

"You'd be surprised what a woman can do with the right training. I've been preparing to face him for a long time. Do you have any guns?"

"No, Hank would never trust me with a weapon. So, if you're so good, how did you wind up here?"

"I got stupid and let him catch me off-guard. That's history. It won't happen again. Now we have to leave this viper's nest without getting killed."

"I'm supposed to get one of the men to watch you." There was cautious humor in her eyes.

"You'll get to use your superwoman skills on him."

She smiled for the first time since Lucy met her. "I'll try to find somebody smaller than you."

Abby was gone only twenty minutes when she returned with a skinhead. True to her word, he was only about five-six.

"Where is she?" the man asked.

"Locked in the bedroom. You want a beer first?"

"Sure," he said. "She shouldn't give me any trouble if she's hog-tied."

Abby led him into the kitchen. When the man passed through the door, Lucy stepped from behind the door in front of him and brought her elbow back into his sternum. He bent forward, and a strangled sound rushed from his throat as breath left his body. She twisted around to face him and pounded her fist into his nose.

Behind the man, Abby picked up a wooden cutting board and slammed it into his skull. "Impressive, but this works, too," she said as his legs folded, and he fell face-first into the wall, blood streaming from his nose. She grinned. "I didn't want you to get too winded. We may need all your talents and then some before we get through those gates."

Lucy relieved the man of his pistol and secured his hands and feet with plastic cuffs from a bowl on the counter. She taped his mouth, and then they dragged him into the bedroom and locked him in. Hank would be surprised when he found his pal instead of Lucy. Too bad.

She closed the door and gave Abby an urgent glance. "Let's get out of here. And if you're a praying woman, I suggest you start now."

Abby tossed her purse and backpack into the back and stood lookout while Lucy slipped into the back, crouched between the seats, and pulled a blanket over her so the sentry wouldn't get wise to their prison break.

The Land Rover started, and then crept to the compound entrance. The vehicle stopped and Lucy heard the creak of the hinges as the gate swung open. Noise from another car passed them, apparently entering the compound.

Abby screamed and pounded the steering wheel.
"What is it? What's happening?"
She screamed again and gunned the motor. The wheels spun before the car shot forward. "It's Hank. He's back!"

CHAPTER 15

Wednesdat, Private Road
Near Big Bend National Park

Lucy tossed the blanket aside and scrambled over the seat into the passenger side. Abby's hands trembled, her face bloodless from stark terror. The Land Rover spit gravel as she jammed the gas pedal hard against the floorboard.

"Stay calm. This road is stirring up so much dust behind us Hank can't see well enough to shoot." There were two problems with that hypothesis that Lucy didn't want her friend to know. They didn't need to see them. Their automatic weapons could spray the road ahead with bullets, disable the car, and kill the occupants. And once the chase hit the paved highway, they would lose the dust cover.

They were outnumbered, and their pursuers had all the firepower they would ever need. Lucy only had the one full clip in the gun she'd taken from the skinhead.

Almost incoherent with panic, Abby mumbled, "I knew this was a bad idea...I just knew it. Nothing ever works out for me. Do you see them, are they gaining on us?"

Needing to keep Abby from going over the edge, Lucy spoke in a cool, steady voice. "The dust is too heavy for me to see the car, or even if there's a car behind us, but I'm sure they're back there." She said *they* because she knew Hank would pick up some of his cronies before he continued the chase. He was in no hurry. The women had forty-five miles of desolate country before they reached anything resembling civilization, and the Land Rover was by no means a race car. The odds were in his favor, and the scumbag knew it.

"If he catches us . . ."

"Don't think about that now. We've got a head start; maybe we can outrun them. Did you see what he was driving?"

"A new Mercedes," Abby said. "His latest acquisition."

"Sports model?"

"Didn't look like it. It's a four-door. He could have souped it up. He doesn't tell me things like that."

"Let's hope not. Our best chance is to stay out of gun range.

"Where did you meet Hank, Abby?" Keeping her mind off what lay behind them might help relax her jangled nerves.

She licked her cracked lips and glanced in the rearview mirror. "I was waiting tables at a truck stop near Austin. He came in, wore a hat so the swastika wasn't visible. It must have been right after you put a restraining order on him. Gave me a line about how his mean ex-wife had lied about him and wouldn't let him see his kids. I bought it."

"Were you into drugs then?"

She shook her head. "That came later, when I realized what I'd gotten into. It helped ease the pain. The drugs added another problem to my existing one. I'm so hooked, I could never afford to feed my habit on my own."

How much of what Abby was going through now was due to the drugs working out of her system? That made an additional difficulty to worry about. "Slow down as much as you can without stopping," Lucy said. "I'm going to try to take over the driving. I'll hold the wheel and slip under you into the driver's seat while you move to the passenger side."

The move was dangerous, and it wasn't pretty. They swerved to the wrong side of the road more than once, but it worked. Secure in the driver's seat, with the seatbelt fastened, Lucy jammed the gas pedal and the car shot forward. "Did you bring drugs with you?"

Abby snorted as she removed pill bottles and paraphernalia from her purse, a glass pipe, and a bottle of capsules. The pipe was probably her preferred method because the high came faster, but not easy to do in a moving car. "If you know anything about drug addicts, you know I did."

"I'm a cop, Abby, and meth is an illegal substance."

She heaved a breath of resignation. "But this is an emergency, and I can't expect you to be any help if you're in withdrawal. When we get somewhere and find help, the drugs have to go. Period."

Abby swallowed two caps dry. "I'll deal with that when I have to."

The drug would take a half-hour to work, and she would have to keep popping pills to remain high.

The gravel road ended fifty feet ahead, and, with it, their cover.

Twin Falls Police Station
Twin Falls, Texas

Matt left the detective bureau and made his way back towards his office. Davis and Stein were glued to their phones, pacing and wearing holes in the tile, waiting for something to break on Lucy's whereabouts. He met Chris and Cole in the corridor as he was leaving.

"Hey, Chief," Chris said. "The desk sarge told me you were up here. We may have a break on the Davenport murder weapon."

Matt stopped. "I can use some good news about now. Follow me back to my office." He nodded toward the room he'd just left. "Stress in there is thick as fog."

He opened his office door and pointed the two men to chairs in front of his desk. "So, what's the good news?"

"Cole and I have been checking Bauer's phone records, and we hit something today. Bauer made frequent calls to a gun dealer, not a licensed store-front operation, sort of a private broker. You have a gun you want to trade or you're looking for a particular model, this guy brokers the deal and gets a commission."

Matt sat up straight in his chair. "You think he knows who has the murder weapon?"

"Not a sure thing, but it looks like it. I asked the dealer if Bauer had recently traded a Beretta .92. He said Bauer brings guns in all the time, all in A-1 condition. The Beretta was in a group of five other weapons he wanted to trade. Want to guess when Bauer brought the guns in?"

It was a rhetorical question and Matt didn't bother to answer.

"The Tuesday following the Davenport murders," Chris said.

"Tell me the man knows who has the weapon," Matt said.

Chris replied, "I wish. Apparently Bauer's guns are in great demand, and the dealer's record-keeping is manual and sloppy. He said he could run it down, but it might take a week or more. I told him I needed it yesterday, and all we want is the name of the person who has it. We'd take it from there. I also informed him if he told anyone we were asking questions, I'd arrest him for obstruction of justice."

"Good work, guys. This could be a big step in bringing Bauer down."

"Any news on Lucy?" Cole asked.

"Just some unofficial Hank Turner sightings, worth about as much as the paper they're written on."

Cole glanced out the window, and then brought his gaze back to Matt. "I want to participate in the search for Lucy, Chief. She was my partner for over a year. I owe her."

"You're helping by doing her job, Cole. We have an army of foot soldiers beating the bushes to find her. One more wouldn't help. I'll keep you in the loop as leads come in."

County Road
Near Big Bend National Park, Texas

The Land Rover bumped onto the smooth pavement and picked up speed, leaving the dust behind. "You okay?" Lucy asked.

"I'm good," Abby said.

Of course she was. She was high as a kite.

Five miles down the road, there was still no sign of Hank. Maybe they had outrun him. God help them if he knew a short cut and managed to get in front of them. The Mercedes was too close to the ground to risk an off-road trail. In the Land Rover, yes. But not in the

German luxury vehicle.

Lucy's anxiety level lowered, her breathing returning to normal. Until two sets of head beams jumped into the rearview mirror. Two cars, not just one, moving fast.

She stomped the gas pedal, but it was already smashed against the floorboard.

"What?" Abby asked.

"Hank is behind us. Can you shoot?"

"Are you kidding me? I've never even fired a gun, but it doesn't look hard." That was the meth talking. Addicts could feel invincible or paranoid when they were high. Abby was in the former stage.

Lucy couldn't shoot and drive at the same time. And, as an untrained marksman, Abby might shoot herself or Lucy. Too bad, because a well-placed bullet through the tires or radiator would stop their pursuers dead cold.

Playing the *if only* game in her head wouldn't change their predicament. It was what it was. And they were in a world of trouble. Abby could drive now, after her hit, but they didn't have time to switch places again.

Bullets from automatic weapons shattered the back window and pinged the auto's metal shell. The next one might get their tires. Or them.

"Abby, Are you hurt?"

Abby scrunched down in the seat, her voice unnaturally calm. "No...I'm good. Whoever is shooting must be a bad shot."

Lucy took the only option they had. "Make sure your seatbelt is fastened tight. We're taking an off-road detour."

If they stayed on the highway, eventually the cue balls chasing them would blast the tires and they'd be stationary targets.

She slowed and jerked the wheel right, leaving the paved road, and hit the soft shoulder, bounced into an arroyo, up the bank, and onto the desert floor. "The Mercedes can't follow us, but I'm not sure if the other car can."

The answer soon became clear when the second vehicle pulled around the Mercedes and became visible after it dipped into the arroyo. A Jeep Cherokee.

And Hank Turner was at the wheel.

On the positive side, they'd just reduced the hunters' force by half. Small comfort that.

No time to pat herself on the back. Two gunmen leaned out the Jeep's windows and bullets rained around them, but the shots were wild. The rough desert floor played havoc with their aim.

"The Land Rover's wheels are kicking up a dust storm behind us. Can you jump from the car if I slow down, and hide behind a bush?"

Panic widened Abby's gaze. "Are you crazy? They'll catch us on foot."

"They have automatic weapons, Abby. If they blow out our tires, we're done. Can you jump without killing yourself?"

"Sure, no problem." She emitted a chuckle, "I've never done anything like that. But I'm more afraid of Hank than I am of jumping. Maybe it'll kill me, and I won't have to deal with him."

In spite of the danger they were in, Lucy laughed. "That's right, think positive. Hand me your backpack from the back seat."

"Why?"

"Must you question everything? I'm going to put it on the gas pedal to keep the car moving after I jump. I'm hoping it will take them a while to realize we've bailed. We need all the time we can get. When I see some vegetation we can hide in, I'll slow, and you go for it. Stay hidden until they pass us."

"Yeah, right. No need to worry, the way those guys shoot," Abby mumbled under her breath.

Lucy spotted another ditch ahead on the right, with squat little bushes on one side. She whispered a short prayer for Abby. "This looks like the place. Get ready."

When the vehicle slowed, Abby thrust the door wide, threw her purse out, and bailed.

Lucy mentally shook her head in amazement. No way would the woman leave her drug cache behind. She shoved the driver's side open, dragged the backpack onto the driver's seat and dropped it onto the gas pedal, then leaped before the car accelerated.

Air left her lungs when she collided with the hard-packed dirt. She hit the ground with a roll, and the gun slipped from her waistband. She sucked oxygen into her chest and scrabbled around in the sand, patting the ground, looking for the gun. Nothing. She gave up. It was lost in the gathering darkness. She'd worry about the gun later. Right now, finding cover was priority one. No way to judge how far Hank was behind them. At the moment, what she needed most was the dust cloud to provide cover until she reached shelter. The alternative was something she didn't even want to consider.

Lucy glanced at her watch as Hank's Jeep whizzed by. He'd been almost three minutes behind them.

This was turning into a suicide mission. She didn't know the country, and she didn't have a compass or water. Not to mention she had a hard-core drug addict for a traveling companion. It was after six in the evening, and the sun had slid behind the western hills, and with it, temperatures would drop rapidly.

No use fretting about things she couldn't change. She brushed the dust from her clothes and turned towards the spot where Abby landed.

Twin Falls Police Station
Twin Falls, Texas

Miles Davis tried to ignore the ringing phone on his desk. He'd asked the station operator to field the calls unless it was an emergency. Finding Lucy had become an obsession, and any information on his partner would come to his cell phone, not the office line.

He blamed himself for letting her ex just walk in and take her without any resistance. Letting a partner come to harm was the worst mistake a law enforcement office could make. He pictured Lucy, crumpled and bloody, life leaving her eyes. It was his fault. It was his job to watch her back.

They'd started their partnership as antagonists. She'd had a gigantic hate-on for the world in general but, with time and patience, she had morphed from a bitter, whiny feminist into a caring and warm friend. She still had her sass, she would never lose that. He wondered if he would ever see her alive again. *Hold on, Turner. Help is coming. Just hold on. You're tough, you can do this.*

The phone kept ringing and he huffed a deep breath, snatched the phone from its cradle, and said gruffly, "Davis."

"I think you're going to want to take this one, Miles," the operator said. "It's a Mrs. Earl Locke. She says it's important."

Davis waited for the receptionist to disconnect. The name was familiar but, with his brain scrambled the last two days, it didn't register. "Hello, Mrs. Locke. How may I help you?"

"I don't know if you remember me, but we met at my husband's bail bond office."

The name clicked into place. "Of course; what can I do for you?"

"I'm not making any accusations, Detective Davis, but I have some information that might be useful to you. My husband told you the truth when he said he went with James Bauer to the Oklahoma casino the weekend the Davenports died. But he left out one important item. Earl took his secretary with him. And, knowing my husband as I do, I'm sure he didn't spend any time with Mr. Bauer."

Davis had set the Davenport case aside because of Lucy's abduction, but his antenna went up. "How did you find out?"

"I love my husband, Detective, but I've suspected for some time he was having an affair with Bree. When he told me he planned a trip with Jim, I hired a private detective to follow him. I received the PI's written report yesterday, complete with pictures."

"I'd like to have a copy of that report, if I may."

"Certainly. I'll drop off a copy later today after I pick up my girls at school."

"Thank you, Mrs. Locke. I appreciate your contacting me. I know it wasn't easy for you. This information just may help us catch a killer."

"As I said earlier, I'm not saying Jim Bauer is guilty of anything. But he isn't a very nice man. And he can't use

Earl as an alibi."

"Whatever you decide about your husband, I hope it works out the way you want it to."

"I intend to try to salvage my marriage, provided it can be mended. My girls need their father. If that's not possible, he's going to pay through the nose. And, if we can put our marriage back together, the next secretary he hires will be fifty, fat, and wear support hose."

Davis disconnected and pushed back his chair. With the lead on the murder weapon, and Bauer's failed alibi, the case was finally coming together. He'd wait for Mrs. Locke to drop off the file, then a visit with her husband and his secretary was in order. Sitting in the office wasn't going to find Lucy anyway.

CHAPTER 16

County Road
Near Big Bend National Park, Texas

In the evening twilight, Abby limped towards Lucy from a low depression hidden by barrel cactus and creosote bushes. Thin arms still held a death grip on the handbag hanging from her shoulder. Glad to see the frail woman wasn't seriously injured, Lucy met her halfway. "You okay?"

Abby glowered at her. "No, but I can walk. Barely."

"We need to get away from here quickly. As soon as they discover we're not in that car, they'll come back." Lucy pulled up a small bush and began sweeping the ground where they had landed.

Hands planted on her hips, Abby asked, "What are you doing?"

"Trying to erase our tracks. It always worked in old John Wayne westerns. Let's hope it will keep Hank off our trail." Lucy didn't have time to search for the gun. Hank could be back any minute. She hitched up her stylish leopard-print slacks and tramped north, parallel to what she hoped was the highway, with Abby behind her.

"My daddy use to watch old John Wayne movies all the time," Abby said.

Lucy smiled. "I think everyone's daddy liked the Duke. He stood tall in more ways than one. You have anything besides drugs in that purse? Like water perhaps?"

With an impish grin, Abby pulled out a bottle of water.

"Good girl." It wasn't much, but it was way better than nothing.

Lucy hurried the woman across the scrub-brush wasteland with hidden slumps and prickly pears, ready to twist an ankle or fill pant legs with sharp needles. A lonely coyote's yip echoed in the distance.

"Where are we going," Abby asked.

"Good question. Our best bet is to try to get back to the highway, keep out of sight, and follow it. Eventually, we should reach civilization and help." Staying near the road was risky, but it was their only course of action. Without water, food, or a compass, they could wander around the desert forever.

Her biggest problem now was finding the highway. She hadn't paid attention while being chased by a carload of drugged-out crazies. Following the tire tracks back the way they came would have been easy, if they could have done it without being seen. But Hank would be expecting them to go that route. The surrounding desert was flat for miles in all directions. She'd have to depend on her instincts and the darkness to prevent Hank finding them.

On landscape that resembled a moon walk, the temperature grew colder after the sun set. Despite the chill and lack of sufficient clothing, Lucy appreciated the quarter moon that dimly lit the bleak terrain, and trudged onward, the heels of her boots sinking into the sand from time to time, making her legs feel like weights were attached to her ankles. Lucy considered herself to be in good physical shape, so this must be torture for Abby. It only took one glance to see the woman wasn't in good health. If she didn't get off drugs soon, she likely would never see her fortieth birthday.

Abby had been pensive for the last hour. Putting one foot in front of the other looked to be a struggle for her during the peaks and valleys as the meth wore off. Finally, she asked, "Lucy, do you really think we're going to get out of this alive?"

"I always try to think positively. Negativity breeds failure."

"If we don't...do you believe there really is a Heaven and a Hell? I've thought about that a lot over the past couple of months."

Lucy put a few paces between them and studied Abby's face in the bleak light. "I absolutely do. I admit to having had doubts, especially while I was married to

Hank. I blamed God for my circumstances. That's probably normal for abused women. But the fact is my decision to marry Hank created my problems. Many women spend more time picking out their wedding dress than getting to know the man they're engaged to. There were signs of Hank's controlling nature that I chose to ignore."

Dim shadows hid Abby's gray pallor and facial imperfections. She looked like a skinny kid playing dress-up in her momma's clothes. "I used to go to Sunday school with my grandma. She was a sweet lady. After she passed away, I never went back to church."

"When we get out of here, you can start going to church again. It'll help you stay off the drugs."

They continued their trek across the parched earth, stopping only for short periods. Lucy reached for the water bottle and took one sip. They pushed on for another hour on the sunbaked dirt, dodging cholla and avoiding holes pressed into the sand by animals or the climate.

"Can we rest for a while?" Abby asked. "I'm tired."

"Yeah, let's take ten," Lucy said. Thirst was beginning to make her tongue feel like leather. Her stomach growled a reminder that she hadn't eaten all day.

They each took another sip of water. Even taking it slow, the bottle was only a quarter full.

Abby eased down next to her on the sand, and downed another capsule.

Lucy had spotted flashes of light ahead. It had to be car headlights. They were headed in the right direction. Hopefully, the flashing lights weren't Hank's men searching for them.

"You think there are snakes out here, Lucy? The men found a couple of rattlers in the compound." She shivered. "I hate snakes."

Lucy wanted to roll her eyes, but couldn't do so without Abby seeing. Didn't they have enough to worry about without bringing up her phobias? "There probably are snakes, but I don't think they travel at night." Lucy had no idea if what she just said was true. Her knowledge of reptiles was limited to 'some bites could kill you'. But maybe her words would relieve the woman's fears.

Abby wrapped her arms around her body and trembled. "You cold?"

Goose bumps pricked on Lucy's arms, and she rubbed them to restore circulation. "I wasn't until we stopped moving. Guess that's an incentive to keep going. You ready to give it another go?"

Abby nodded, and a scowl wrinkled her brow. She clutched her purse close to her chest, maybe for warmth, or protecting her drug stash. "Do I have a choice? It's either walk and drop dead in my tracks, or stop and freeze to death."

Lucy chuckled. "Anybody ever tell you you're a pessimist?"

"That's the story of my life. Never had anything to be optimistic about."

Their progress seemed slower than Lucy had expected, and she sighed a relieved breath when she saw a rise just ahead. A gully lay about fifty yards in front of them. If Lucy's calculations were correct, the road should not be far from the top of the rise. She figured they could use it for a lookout and, if no bad guys were in sight, they could move closer and catch a ride, preferably with someone who had a cell phone, although good luck with getting service this far from civilization.

Weary from their long trek, she gave Abby a hand up the steep incline as they trudged to the top.

Something moved in Lucy's peripheral vision just seconds before two sets of bright headlights almost blinded them. A profile took form and pushed night-vision goggles to the top of his head. The unmistakable outline of Hank Turner. "I thought you might head this way."

Abby screamed and dropped to her knees, sobbing.

Hank cursed and stepped in front of Abby, lifted her upright, and backhanded her with a blow Lucy feared might break Abby's jaw. She was in no shape to defend herself. When she fell, he drew his foot back to kick her in the stomach.

Lucy dived at his knees, knocking him sideways and off his feet. "Stop; you'll kill her!"

He stood and again lifted Abby from the dirt then shoved her into her brother's arms. "Take her home. I don't have time to deal with this now. She'll get what she deserves when I get back."

Lucy looked daggers at Hank, with hate so palpable she could taste it. "God has prepared the hottest places in Hell for people like you."

"I'm not worried. I don't believe in Hell."

"You will when you get there. And I hope it's soon."

He looked as if he might hit her, but changed his mind for some reason. "I'm going to finish what I started and get my boys. And you're coming with me." He jerked the car door open, pushed her behind the wheel, then walked around the vehicle and slid into the passenger seat. He jammed the keys in the ignition. "You're driving."

The car's warmth wrapped around her and, despite her dire situation, she was grateful. She prayed Abby was warm, and that her injuries weren't life threatening.

"What made you come back?" she asked.

"Something told me I couldn't leave you two alone together. You're too smart, and she's too dumb not to follow you."

Lone Star Bails and Process Servers
Twin Falls, Texas

Davis had filled Matt in on the phone call from Mrs. Locke. "You ready to roll?" Matt asked when Davis stepped into the office. Since Lucy was gone, Matt decided to accompany Davis on his visit to re-interview Earl Locke.

"Are we taking your wheels or mine?" Davis asked.

"Mine is closer," Matt said, opening the back door to his office.

The bail bond reception area was empty when they entered the office. A buzzer sounded, and a male voice called from the back. "Be with you in a second!"

An attractive, but worn-looking, man with blood shot

eyes and deep creases around his mouth strode towards them down the hallway. He stopped when he saw Davis. "I think I know what you want. Come on back."

Davis introduced Matt, and Locke waved them into his office.

Locke called out, "Dad, cover the front for me for a minute."

"Sure thing," said an older guy, who stepped from a second office and headed to the reception desk.

Locke waved them to seats and sat behind his desk. "How much do you know?"

"We have a copy of the report from the detective your wife hired. But it doesn't tell us what happened between you and Bauer that weekend," Davis said.

"Nothing happened between us. We arrived together, but I didn't see Jim again until just before we left on Monday."

Matt struggled to keep disgust from his tone. "So you have no idea if Bauer left the casino?"

Locke shook his head and looked away.

"How about your secretary; can we speak to her?" Davis asked.

"She doesn't work here anymore. I can give you her number, if you like. But she won't tell you anything different. She was with me the whole time."

"Do you have any idea how Bauer might have left the casino without using his car?" Davis asked.

"Not really," Locke answered. "Bree and I were gambling for a while, and I saw him with a woman there, but I doubt he would have asked her to take him anywhere."

"Do you know the woman's name?" Davis asked.

Locke shook his head. "I assumed she was just someone he picked up. He does that a lot."

At the end of the interview, Matt stood and waited for Davis to exit, then he turned back to Locke. "Just a word of advice, Mr. Locke. Concealing evidence in a murder investigation is a serious offense. You might remember that next time someone asks you to give them an alibi."

Highway I-20
Headed for Twin Falls, Texas

The winter sun rose above the tops of tall pines, sending a kaleidoscope of light flashing between the narrow tree limbs inside the Mercedes. Lucy had driven straight through to the south side of Dallas, with Hank holding the gun on her all the way. She rolled her neck to loosen her tense muscles, and blinked to moisten her dry eyes.

He had her pull into a McDonald's drive-thru and order breakfast sandwiches to go, threatening to shoot the clerk if Lucy tried to signal for help.

She wouldn't have tried anyway. Part of her police training was to protect the lives of civilians, and it was rooted in her psyche.

Not that she was afraid to die. She just wanted to ensure Hank didn't get away to harm her sons or Abby. She took a long gulp of the strong black coffee, welcoming the warmth as it slid down her throat. She had to grit her teeth and take his orders. Wait for the right moment. A time with just her and him. No one else around to get hurt.

Throughout the long drive, Hank tried his old sob story. He loved her, he'd never intended to hurt her or the boys, if she'd give him another chance he'd make it up to her, etcetera...etcetera...etcetera.

The same refrain abusers had been singing since the beginning of time.

She didn't reply. There was nothing to say. She'd go back to Hank when ISIS terrorists converted to Christianity.

Her life had gone disastrously off course over the past forty-eight hours. Leaving Hank had been the first step in the right direction of putting her life together. But now, five years after the fact, she was again in a battle to the death with her ex-husband.

She'd always known Hank wouldn't just go away— knew it was only a matter of time before he would come after her. It wasn't in his DNA to let go of anything he thought he owned. And he didn't like to lose.

Although her finances had been rocky, it had been an immense improvement over her wreck of a marriage. She and her boys had almost recovered from the physical and emotional abuse of their father. Now this.

Over the past year, she'd come to know Ben Stein, her second chance at a normal life. Ben was the man she should have married. He was everything Hank wasn't. And she'd come to realize, over the long drive back to Twin Falls, that she might never see him again.

Lucy Turner's Home
Twin Falls, Texas

Ben Stein took the graveyard watch inside Lucy's home. Experience had taught him that, if Hank came for Charlie and Mack, it would be late at night or in the early morning hours.

He spent the night pacing, worrying about Lucy, praying she was still alive. Lucy was the soul mate he'd searched for all his life. A confirmed bachelor, Ben told himself when he met the right woman, he would marry, and not until. He wanted a lifetime relationship. Then Lucy Turner walked into his life.

She'd had a hard shell when they first met, but he'd soon learned it was like a turtle's covering, to protect her from being hurt. And he was scared to death he would lose her.

Two unmarked cars were his backup. One sat in the driveway of the house across the street, in case they had to give chase. Another was parked on the street behind Lucy's house.

The hands on the bronze sunburst clock over the mantle inched toward seven o'clock. Charlie and Mack would normally be getting ready for school. Ben had grown fond of Lucy's boys. Their abusive dad would take them only over Ben's dead body.

A petite female police officer, about Charlie's size, dressed in jeans, sweat shirt, and a baseball cap, made a few passes in front of the living room picture window. Ben had talked her into pretending to be Lucy's oldest son. The officer knew the danger, but decided to take the gig anyway.

An extended yawn made him stride towards the kitchen. "You want a caffeine fix?"

She rubbed her eyes and echoed his yawn. "Sugar, no cream."

He went into the spotless kitchen and put on his second pot of the day. When the red light blinked on, he poured two cups, doctored hers, and took them into the living room. Before he could take his first sip, his phone vibrated. "Yeah?"

"Heads up, Stein," the officer across the street said. "A black Mercedes circled the block twice. Heavily-tinted windows, but it looks like a man and a woman. You guys set?"

"We're set. Do you think he saw the decoy?"

"He couldn't miss her."

"Let me know if he parks."

"Roger."

Stein drew his gun. "We've got company. He's seen you, so stay away from the window."

"You don't have to tell me twice." She threw the hat in the corner and tugged her weapon from her back holster.

The phone vibrated again. The officer didn't wait for an answer. "The car's pulling to the curb in front."

*****

Lucy spotted the two unmarked cars the first time she circled the block, and prayed Hank hadn't noticed. She eased out a slow breath. Although it looked like Charlie in the window, it had to be an imposter; probably a police woman. The authorities would never place her son in danger.

Hank had been snorting cocaine for the last hour, so his mind was fuzzy. His gaze darted from side to side, his breath coming in quick gasps. Nervous. Good, that gave her an edge.

"Circle one more time, and then park in front of the house. Once we've stopped, slide across the seat and get out on the passenger side behind me. Walk to the front door, and I'll take over from there."

Despite the cold, sweat trickled down her neck as she followed his instructions. She made the second trip around the block, parked, then stepped onto the sidewalk with him behind her, the gun pressed into her spine. The officer across the street wouldn't shoot as long as Hank held the gun on her.

She took two steps forward and faked a stumble. When he reached for her, she turned, hooked her elbow into his windpipe, and tore the pistol from his hand, bashing the gun butt into his nose with everything she had in her. The bone cracked, and blood gushed down his shirt.

Hank roared like an enraged grizzly.

Adrenaline spiked, and she sent a sharp, powerful kick to his right knee, bent it backward in a way nature never intended. He screamed and crashed to the ground.

"Lucy, stop," Ben Stein said behind her. "We've got him now."

Dazed, she looked back at Ben. She been so intent on taking Hank down, she'd lost focus. She nodded and started to step away, taking her eyes off Hank.

An unforgiveable mistake, when dealing with Hank Turner.

He grabbed her ankle, pulled her off her feet, and she hit the ground hard. In a flash, both big hands wrapped around her throat, cutting all breath from her body. "I'm going to kill you, if it's the last thing I do."

She thought as the morning sun became dark, and breath left her lungs, at least Hank would never hurt anyone ever again.

A shot shattered the neighborhood quiet. "Not today, you won't," Ben said.

Hands released the crushing grip on her neck and he rolled off her. Flashes of light burst before her eyes as she sucked air into her vacant lungs, straining to take a deep breath.

A red stream slithered down Hank's neck from the bullet hole in his temple, eyes open, staring into nothingness. He fell back onto the grass beside her.

Ben holstered his gun and lifted her to her feet. She shivered and looked into his gentle brown gaze. "He's dead."

Ben nodded and pulled her into his arms. "It's over, Luc. You're home-free."

Thanks to Ben, that was true in more ways than one.

As he held her, the street filled with squad cars and sirens. Cops came forward to pat them both on the back.

A dark figure backlit by sunlight moved towards her. "You alright, Turner?"

Ben released her, and she stepped close to Miles Davis and put her arms around his waist. "Yeah, I'm good. Thanks for the back-up."

"Better late than never," he said. "I'm glad you made it out." He gave her a lopsided grin. "I was worried about those skinheads."

Laughter bubbled in her throat. And it felt good.

She so wanted to see her sons, Charlie and Mack, to hold them close. Assure them that all was well.

But she still had a promise to keep.

CHAPTER 17

Supremacist Compound
Near Big Bend National Park

Lucy sat strapped in the back seat of the chopper flying low over Big Bend country, and tried to spot the compound. She knew it was there, somewhere, lost in sagebrush and sand that covered the landscape as far as the eye could see. The sight of the Chisos Mountains told her they were close to their destination.

Ben had wanted her to let the local sheriff and DEA handle the bust, but she'd refused. Abby was there, and Lucy had to know the woman was okay. She felt responsible for the physically- and emotionally-abused addict. And she'd made Abby a promise.

A DEA agent whose name, unbelievably, was Clark Kent, met her at the helipad. She thought he was joking until he flashed his credentials. His face turned a light shade of pink. "My mother had a weird sense of humor," he chuckled, "but I learned to fight early."

"I'll bet bullies made you live up to the name. Kinda like the Johnny Cash song, 'A Boy Named Sue'."

"Exactly," Kent said.

And she thought she'd had it bad in school living with The Beatles', "Lucy in the Sky with Diamonds". The song was long before her time, but mean kids seemed to hang onto such nonsense.

The chopper dropped altitude, and the sprawling racist camp came into view in the dimming evening light. Strobe lights flashed on dozens of county and government vehicles. The cavalry had arrived to clean out the nest of vipers.

Helicopter rotors whipped up a dust storm as they landed just outside the gate. Lucy ducked her head and followed Agent Kent inside the compound. Deputies and agents hauled people out of mobile homes, Abby's brother among them. Women screamed, kids cried, and

the men called the authorities everything but a child of
God.

Lucy gave Kent a wave and trotted to Hank's trailer,
an ambulance sitting in front with the motor running.
She'd told the sheriff to take medical help because of
Abby, and apparently he'd listened.

A deputy stood at the mobile home's entrance. Lucy
fished out her credentials, and he let her pass.

The inside was as spotless as ever. Lucy couldn't
believe it had been less than forty-eight hours since
she'd arrived here, a kidnap victim. And, without Abby's
help, she might well be dead.

She proceeded down the hallway to the master
bedroom, stopped at the partially open doorway, and
knocked on the lintel. The antiseptic odor reminded her
of emergency wards. The smells evoked bad memories.
She'd spent more than her share in ER while married to
Hank.

A medical tech was in the process of hooking an IV
into Abby's thin white arm.

The frail woman looked up from the gurney with wide
eyes, and her gaze locked on Lucy. She emitted a soft
whimper. "You came back for me. I didn't think you
would remember."

Lucy smiled. Her friend looked much better, not
healthy, but her color was better, and although her jaw
wore a big, black bruise, it apparently hadn't been
broken. "How could I forget my roadie? Besides, I made
a promise. These guys treating you well?"

"My jaw is so sore, I can barely open my mouth, but
they tell me it will go away in a week or so." She
grinned. "Maybe I can lose some weight. Right now I
would kill for a hamburger."

Lucy chuckled. "Yeah, you really need the weight
loss. The fact that you're hungry must mean you're
getting your appetite back. That's a good sign." Lucy
reached down and touched Abby's hand. "Just so you
know, Hank is dead."

"Yeah, they told me. Can't say I'm sorry."

"I don't think there'll be any tears shed over him. You
ready to head for rehab when the hospital releases you?"

"Not really, but I'll do it. Where?"

"I'll have you registered someplace close to Twin Falls...so I can check on you and keep you straight, make sure you do as you're told."

"Lucy, I don't know how I can thank you." Her lashes lowered and she had a lost little girl expression, and then she looked up, her eyes suddenly bright with tears. "No one has offered to help in a very long time. When Hank sent me back to the compound, I just knew he would come back and beat me to death. I couldn't believe it when the sheriff arrived with an ambulance. He told me you sent them."

"I did. I had no way of knowing how badly you were injured. We have to stick together; we're charter members of a not-too-exclusive sisterhood."

"Clint?" Abby asked.

Lucy nodded. "The authorities have your brother in custody."

Wrinkles formed on Abby's brow and the air in her lungs eased out in a low hiss. "He was never much of a brother, but I hate to see him go to prison."

Lucy stepped back from the gurney as the tech readied Abby for transport. "Nothing you could do to help him. It was his choice."

On the mobile home's deck, Lucy pulled a twenty from her pocket and handed it to the tech as he carried equipment to the van. "Buy her a hamburger with the works, and the largest shake you can find. She needs the calories."

"I'll see to it," he grinned and stepped into the ambulance.

Sliding her hands into her jacket pockets, Lucy walked across the compound to find the DEA agent she came with. The scene was still utter chaos. The racist camp was a bad thing, with drugs and human trafficking, but the shock and fear in the eyes of the women and children touched her heart. They were the other victims.

Agent Kent spotted her and they met halfway. "You finished here?"

She looked back over her shoulder as the EMTs

pulled away with Abby. "Yeah, I saw what I came to see. Can you give me a ride home? I'd rather not make the long drive back to Twin Falls."

"Lady, I'll take you anywhere you want to go. Thanks to you, this is the biggest bust we've made in a long time. The sheriff wants to pin a medal on you."

"Thanks, but I'll settle for a ride home. It's been a long time since I've seen my boys."

Twin Falls Police Station
Twin Falls, Texas

Matt threaded his way down the corridor to the detective bureau on the second floor. His four detectives waited for him around the conference room table at the appointed hour. Lucy was back, against his wishes. She'd asked for vacation time once the Davenport case was closed, but, until then, felt she needed to be back on the job

"Davis, let's put a twenty-four-hour surveillance team on Eden Russell's condo." Matt said. "If James Bauer leaves, have him followed. I don't want any more dead bodies until we find that gun."

"Will do," Davis said. "We didn't have enough evidence to get his credit card receipts, so we're doing the car rental agency search the hard way. So far, nothing."

"It won't be the first time. If Bauer is guilty, he had to have transportation other than the vehicle he drove to the casino. Sheriff Gates said folks in the Russells' neighborhood reported seeing an older model, dark pickup truck the night of the murder. Not sure of the color or make. That leaves a lot of trucks to look for."

Davis slumped in his chair. "We can take another look at the casino parking lot tapes, and zero in on that description. It probably covers seventy-five percent of the trucks there, but it's a place to start. May be faster than checking the rental agencies." He glanced over at Lucy. "You ready for another road trip?"

She leaned back in the chair and nodded. "I'm in for whatever it takes to get this guy."

"Anything more from the gun dealer, Chris?" Matt asked.

"The guy is getting put out with me calling him twice a day. Keeps saying he'll call me when he finds it," Chris chuckled. "I offered to help him go through his records. He refused. Probably afraid I'll find something illegal."

Matt's phone vibrated. It was Sara. He stood and stepped out into the hallway.

"I'm in the lobby. Want to buy a girl lunch?"

"Need you ask? I'll be right down."

He stuck his head back into the conference room. "Are we through here?"

"That's all I have," Davis said.

Chris nodded. "Me, too."

The Burger Shack
Twin Falls, Texas

Matt placed his hand on the small of Sara's back and guided her to a booth in the rear of the café. She looked like a teenager in a black leather jacket over black workout pants, her hair pulled back into a ponytail.

He slid in beside her and grinned. "So, you took Chaim up on his Krav Maga lessons?"

Her gaze snapped to his face. "How did you know?"

"Simple, my dear Watson. Your outfit, the ponytail, and you were slightly winded at the station. Either that, or you're a cat burglar, in which case I'll have to search you."

She quirked a smile at him. "That might be fun. I must remember your amazing powers of observation if I decide to hide anything from you. Today was my first lesson with Chaim. He certainly knows his stuff."

"How did it go?"

She ran her arm through his and snuggled closer. "To be honest, I wasn't sure I would like it, but it was fun. Tomorrow I'll probably find muscles I didn't know I had, but I'm good for now. Chaim says I'm a natural. I'm sure he says that to all his students to keep them paying the big bucks for his classes."

Matt shook his head. "I can assure you he doesn't.

I've heard him tell students they're wasting their money."

"That's a great boost to my ego."

"Chaim explained this is serious training, that he'll teach you to kill if your life is in danger, right?"

Her expression sobered. "He did. I'm not real comfortable with that. I'd prefer to disarm an attacker."

"That's a decision you'll have to make when, and if, the time comes."

"I know. I hope to avoid ever having to make that choice."

She opted to change the subject. She had a big heart. He also hoped she'd never have to choose.

She asked, "Are you coming home early tonight? I've missed you."

"Me too," he said and scanned the restaurant for onlookers. When no one was paying attention to them, he bent down and placed a slow kiss on her lips. He raised his head and looked into her eyes. "No promises about tonight, but, when this case is finished, I intend to devote at least one entire week to making up for my absence."

Sara rested her head on his shoulder. "I'm going to hold you to that promise, mister."

Twin Falls Police Station
Twin Falls, Texas

Gabe Morrison, Twin Falls' District Attorney, rapped on the door-facing of Matt's door, and stuck his head in. "You busy, Foley?"

"I always have time for you, Gabe. Come on in and grab a chair."

The DA tossed his overcoat and hat on the tree by the door then pulled a chair close to Matt's desk, sending a slight woodsy fragrance of his cologne wafting across the space between them.

"What brings you out of hibernation, my friend?" Matt asked.

"Obviously not to play golf. Man, I wish I was in Florida." He rubbed his hands over his completely bald pate. "Every time I step outside, my head turns blue."

Matt chuckled. "The Smurf look works for you."

"Not funny, Foley. Anything new on the Davenport case?"

"Not since the last time we spoke," Matt said. "We're closing in on Bauer, but not fast enough to suit me. Looks like he murdered another couple since the Davenports. I want to stop this guy before he does any more damage."

Gabe gave a solemn nod. "You could hold him for seventy-two hours without charges. But, without the gun, all we have is circumstantial; not enough for a conviction."

"I know. When I pick him up, I want to ensure the charges will stick. I've got a tail on him in the interim."

Gabe crossed his legs and leaned back in the chair. "What's this I hear that you may be leaving?"

"Is Doug's office bugged?" Matt asked.

"Not that I know of; is it true?"

Matt didn't want to answer. The last thing he needed to have happen was for this to get back to his people before he resigned. However, he trusted Gabe and he couldn't lie to him. "Looks like it. But not immediately. Probably not for six weeks or more."

Gabe looked at him quizzically. "I don't like that, Matt. Want to tell me why?"

Matt shuffled the paperwork on his desk to the side and shook his head. "Not now; maybe later, after the deed is done."

Gabe stood and retrieved his coat, then stuck the hat on the back of his head. "For the record, it's easier to replace a city manager than to find a good police chief."

Matt shook his head. "I don't want to go there, Gabe."

The Foley Residence
Twin Falls, Texas

Matt turned over and pulled Sara close. He pushed up on one elbow and gazed down at her face, her countenance serene in the bright sun streaming through the window. "You awake?"

"Uh-huh. What time is it?"

"Nine-fifteen. You ready to get up and face the world?"

"Do I have to?"

"Well, the kids have been quiet, but I'll bet they're getting hungry."

She sprang upright and tossed off the covers. "Of course they are. What am I thinking? Or, more appropriately, not thinking? You made me forget all about them."

"So it's my fault?"

She beamed and tossed a throw-pillow at him. "Of course it is. You make my mind go blank."

He grabbed her arm and pulled her back onto the bed against the pillows.

She pealed with laughter. "What are you doing?"

He leaned in and pressed a deep kiss on her smiling lips, then trailed kisses down her neck and murmured, "How am I doing?"

"I don't know; my brain is mush." She took his face in both hands, kissed him soundly, and then gave him a gentle shove. "Enough. We have to spend family time with Poppy and Danny. We were away on our honeymoon, I got the flu, and you've been working insane hours."

He slid out of bed on his side. "True. We'll discuss this memory problem of yours in more detail later. What's your game plan for today?"

"I'd like to take Poppy shopping. We haven't done that in a while. She's a girly-girl and she loves clothes."

"Okay, I'll take Danny rock-climbing. We'll meet at the Galleria afterwards, go ice-skating, and finish the evening off at the Magic Time Machine in Addison. The kids will love it. They get to dine with their favorite action movie and cartoon characters." He slipped into grey sweats. "Want to go out to breakfast, or shall we cook?"

"You did say we, right?"

"Yep. As you're aware, I know my way around a kitchen. How does bacon and pancakes sound?"

She shrugged into her robe and slippers. "Sounds great; you're in charge of the bacon."

Breakfast was ready in record time. As they joined hands at the table, and he blessed the food, he was reminded of the many missed meals lately with this family of his. That needed to be fixed.

The meal wound down and Matt made eye-contact with both children. "So, how's school?"

Poppy brightened. "Danny gots a girlfriend."

"Danny has a girlfriend, Poppy," Sara said. "Not gots."

Face flushed, Danny glared at his little sister. "I do not."

She giggled and leaned forward. "Yes, you do. Her name's Holly and she told me." A pixie grin spread across the little girl's face. "She thinks you're cute."

Danny scowled and pushed away from the table. "Poppy, you are such a *girl!*"

Her cheeks turned pink and she shook her finger at him. "I am not."

Hands on her hips, Sara bit the inside of her jaw to hide a smile. "And exactly what's wrong with being a girl?"

Matt rose and placed his napkin on the table, leaned down, and whispered to Danny. "You just stepped in a hornet's nest, Champ. Come help me put out the deer feed before you hurt yourself."

CHAPTER 18

Twin Falls Country Club
Twin Falls, Texas

Matt and Sara greeted wave after wave of tuxedoed men and beautifully-gowned women there to attend the Annual Policeman's Ball.

The newlyweds were easily the most handsome couple in the room, and that was saying a lot. Matt was much too good looking for his own good, and in a tux he was devastating. Sara stood beautiful and elegant at his side, in a shimmering green gown that flowed over her curves like a liquid sea.

Shannon Connelly made her way to the ballroom entrance and smiled at Matt. "Is anyone protecting our fair city tonight?"

"This is half my crew." Matt kept his face straight. "But if an emergency arises, I can always give you a gun and put you in a squad car."

In a theatrical whisper, Sara said, "I don't think that would be a good idea, darling. You do know this woman, don't you?"

Shannon narrowed her eyes at Sara. "And you're supposed to be my best friend." She patted Matt's chest. "That's a great idea. It wouldn't take me long to put this town right."

Colin joined the group. "Yes, my love, but would there be any citizens left?"

Tonight wasn't a sit-down affair, although a full course menu was provided on buffet tables. Matt would say a few brief words, as would the mayor and city manager. Matt had limited them to ten minutes each. These people weren't here to listen to campaign speeches. They were here to enjoy themselves, since they could only attend every other year. The other half of the force would be here next year.

When the crowd thinned at the entrance, the four

friends moved deeper into the ballroom, just as a stir behind them drew their attention.

Mayor Hall, Doug Anderson, and a man Shannon had never seen before merged into the sea of people, with handshakes, painted-on smiles, and insincere murmurs of, "Thank you for your service."

When the muscles in Matt's jaw tightened, Shannon felt the undercurrent in the room. Everyone knew of Matt's ongoing conflict with the Mayor, but this was something different.

<<>>

Matt immediately recognized the uninvited guest. He had never met Luther Donnell, but he'd seen the man's photo on the resume personnel had forwarded to him. By rights, Donnell shouldn't be here. He wouldn't be on the force until April. However, since he'd arrived with Doug and Hall, Matt couldn't toss him out.

Bringing his brother-in-law to this purely police-department affair smacked of Hall flaunting his power. As the group made their way toward him, Matt whispered to Shannon, "As soon as the speeches end, get the band started."

She gave him a discreet thumbs-up and moved toward the bandstand.

In his designer tuxedo, the mayor cut a dashing figure. Hall was barely five-six, and Matt often wondered how such a small man carried his enormous ego. The most frightening aspect about Hall was that his political ambitions went way beyond his current office.

Hall greeted Matt and Sara with a weak handshake and introduced his relative. "I understand Luther will be working for you soon, Foley. You're getting a good man."

Since he wouldn't be there when Donnell joined the force, there didn't seem to be an appropriate response, so Matt just nodded.

His immediate impression of Luther Donnell was that of a crane. Slender with unnaturally long legs and a large head on a spindly neck, Donnell's thinning brown hair was combed straight back off his brow, emphasizing his elongated nose. Gold wire-rim glasses magnified his heavy-lidded brown eyes, and he was greatly in need of Hall's fashion advice.

Donnell stuck out his hand. "I'm looking forward to working for you, Chief. I have some great ideas I installed in the Cincinnati CPD union. It saved the union budget fifty percent."

Matt had read the confidential report the Ohio police chief sent to the city's human resources director. One of Donnell's *improvements* included that cops under investigation pay their own attorney fees. When the CPD officer's threatened to leave the union, the amendment was revoked and Donnell lost his job.

The buffet lines opened, saving Matt from having to respond. Matt and Sara ate at a table with the beat cops and their wives.

When the meal ended, Hall made his way to Matt's table and asked, "Any suspects in the Davenport murders?"

Determine to keep his cool, Matt shook his head. "Nothing I can talk about at present." Then he added, "Excuse me, I need to say a few words and get this shindig rolling. You and Doug will speak after me."

He guided Sara to a table near the lectern. When he stepped on the dais, the crowd whooped, whistled, and applauded. He made a show of looking behind him. "From your reception, I thought my lovely wife had stepped on stage."

One of the guys called out, "Let her make your speech, Matt. We'd rather look at her than listen to you."

He turned and gave a slight bow to Sara. "I couldn't agree with you more, so I'm going to make it short. Thank you all for your contributions to making Twin Falls a safer place for residents to live and raise their families. Because of your efforts, crimes of all types were down fifteen percent last year. You are the finest group of law enforcement officers it's ever been my privilege to command. My final word is enjoy your evening and take it easy on the booze. There are not enough taxis in town to take you all home. Maybe I should have chartered a few buses."

Laughter followed his exit from the stage.

Doug stood at the back of the room and gave an approving nod, before coming to the podium to take Matt's place.

Doug's speech was short, and Hall's too long. As Hall made his first step off the platform, the band hit the first refrains of Billy Joel's "Just the Way You Are"

Matt drew Sara onto the dance floor and whispered in her ear. "Have I told you how dazzling you look tonight?"

"Yes, but it's always nice to hear. May I tell you how proud I am of you? You struck just the right note of sincere praise, short and sweet, and they love you for it. I can see why Blain thinks you would make a good senator. Not just because people adore you, but you have ethics that are sorely needed in Washington."

He squeezed her waist. "You're prejudice."

"Of course, I am, but I'm also right."

When the song ended, Miles Davis tapped Matt on the shoulder and smiled down at Sara. "I may not have your husband's silver tongue, but I'm better-looking and a much better dancer."

"In your dreams, Davis." Matt held out a hand to Sierra, Davis' elegant date, and they danced away. Next, Ben Stein claimed a dance with Sara.

Matt glanced down at Lucy Turner. "Shall we?" He asked her permission because their relationship had always been a little rocky.

She inclined her head and stepped into his arms.

"You look lovely, Turner. How are you doing after your recent episode?"

"Almost good as new, Chief."

Silence ticked off the seconds. She'd always seemed nervous around him. "You and Davis doing okay?"

She grinned and nodded. "I really hate to admit it, but you were right about making the change in partners."

He threw back his head and laughed. "Well that's a first. Are we friends yet, Turner?"

"We're getting there, Chief."

DOWNFALL

Indian Casino
Durant, Oklahoma

Rain met Davis and his partner as they neared the Oklahoma border, their second visit to the Indian casino. Vicious winds and rain pummeled the car's roof, the wipers beating a steady rhythm, scarcely keeping up with the wall of water in front of them. Ten minutes later, the winds ceased and the rain slowed to a fine drizzle. Temperatures hovered a little above freezing. God help them if the precipitation turned into sleet. If so, they'd have to reserve two rooms at the casino for an overnight stay.

He mumbled under his breath when he discovered there were no umbrellas in the car. When they pulled onto the gambling casino grounds, Davis did the gentlemanly thing and let Turner out at the entrance. He found a spot half a block away and dashed inside. Icy liquid had seeped down his coat collar and he shivered like a wet dog. Warm Bermuda beaches were calling his name about now.

His partner waited for him just inside and they wended their way to the reception desk. He'd called ahead, and Waya Mann stood behind the counter, resplendent in another dark suit.

"Welcome back. I have already had the security tapes you wanted set up. These are different dates and times than the ones you requested on your last visit, correct?"

"That's right. Thank you for your cooperation. We won't tie up your people too long."

Mann smiled. "You are most welcome, and my people are at your disposal." He led the way down the corridor into the casino's security office. "You must come back and enjoy our facilities when you are off duty."

"I've been here many times," Davis said. He inclined his head at Turner, "but my partner is not a gambler."

He laughed. "We can't have that." He slipped Turner a chit for twenty free chips. "In case you change your mind."

Turner didn't accept the gift. She shook her head. "Thank you, but I can't accept gratuities. It's against company policy."

He shrugged and led them to the same room as their last visit, then left them alone with the tech who had helped them on their last visit. Same chairs. Same monitor.

The scrolling images revealed twelve trucks fitting their description, but the drivers all left the casino during the designated timeframe and none of them were Bauer.

"Is this the only outside area covered by security cameras?" Davis asked.

"Except for employee parking; I didn't think you would want to see those."

"Cue that up for me, if you would." Davis cast a sideways glance at Turner. "He could have parked a second car there, figuring there were no cameras in that area."

The tech scrolled slowly through the digital file for ten minutes. The camera was dialed back to a wide angle to show the entire parking lot, for insurance purposes, no doubt. The field of view was wide enough to show all vehicles entering and leaving, with a fair image of the license plates.

About ten minutes into the film, a five-year-old black Dodge Ram pulled into the lot, and a Hispanic man got out. Davis jerked up straight in the chair. The man exited the truck and hurried to the employee entrance then disappeared inside. It was the waiter, Antonio Perez, they'd interviewed previously. That could explain the man's nervousness when they first met. "Keep the video rolling."

At twelve o'clock Saturday, the night before the Davenports were murdered, Bauer walked out the back door, climbed into the Ram, and drove away.

"Bingo," Davis said.

The tape continued to roll, and Bauer returned Sunday morning at ten-thirty. Plenty of time to get to Twin Falls, murder Eden's parents, and return to cement his alibi.

They asked the tech to pull up the employee parking lot video for the weekend the Russells were killed.

Exactly the same scenario occurred. Bauer had driven away in the black Ram.

Davis rubbed his hands together. "I love to see the scales of justice balanced. Now we need to put some pressure on our waiter friend."

Twenty minutes later, the door to the tech room opened. Waya Mann stepped inside with the waiter. Davis waved a hand at a chair in front of the monitor. "Have a seat, Antonio. We have some digital film we want you to see."

Antonio grabbed the chair arms and lowered himself with shaking hands. "Why?"

Davis pointed to the screen. "Just watch."

The tape paused at the point Bauer left the casino in Antonio's truck. Davis leaned against the wall, his arms crossed. "Can you tell me why Mr. Bauer left the casino in your truck?" Davis asked.

Antonio's gaze darted between Davis and Turner, and then settled on his boss. "The man, he gave me five hundred dollars to use my truck for a few hours. He say he doesn't want his friend to know he is leaving."

"And he used your truck the weekend we interviewed you?" Davis asked.

Antonio swallowed hard before he responded. "*Si.*"

"Why did you lie to us the last time we spoke?" Turner asked.

"I was afraid but I didn't lie. I just didn't tell you everything. I didn't want to get into trouble."

"It amounts to the same thing. And you *are* in trouble," she said.

Davis left the room with his partner and closed the door behind him.

"What do you want to do?" Turner asked.

"Get his statement on video. He's probably illegal, and he'll run when we let him go. I doubt the casino checks E-Verify before they hire waiters and housekeepers. The casino tapes and his statement will stand up in court." Davis opened the door and held it for Turner to enter first. "Antonio, you're going to be the star in a video we're going to make."

<<>>

The weather had cleared as they made the drive back to Twin Falls. Ten miles from their destination, Davis' cell phone chimed. It was Matt.

"Where are you?" he asked.

"Ten miles out. What's up?"

"You might want to take a detour to Amy Bauer's place. There's a fire. Emergency equipment is on the scene. I just got here."

Davis switched on the emergency lights. "We're headed your way."

Smoke was visible miles before they reached the Bauer property. Inside the cattle guard, blue and white lights flashed under the gray sky. One police cruiser and two fire trucks formed a line in front of the soot-stained red barn, while thick hoses from the fire engine blasted water onto the roaring flames.

Davis parked on the grass near the fence. He and Turner joined Matt, standing with Amy Bauer a safe distance from the blaze. Matt made the introductions.

"Was anyone inside?" Davis asked.

The woman shook her head.

"How did it start?" Davis directed the question at Amy Bauer.

She raised a hand to her brow, a worried frown on her face. "I have no idea. I was putting up jars of green beans when I saw the flames from the kitchen window."

"Were you here alone?" Turner asked.

Amy chewed her bottom lip and nodded, avoiding Lucy's gaze.

It was another thirty minutes before the blaze was extinguished. Firefighters lingered around the perimeter, jackets open, hats pushed back off their brows, making sure no hot spots remained. The fire crew began to roll up their hoses and store the equipment away.

Turner stayed with Mrs. Bauer, while Matt and Davis looked for the fire marshal, Blake Dennis. They found him in the center of the burned-out shell. He was moving charred pieces of metal around in the smoldering ruins with his steel-toed boot.

Matt said, "I was surprised to see you here, Blake. You don't usually cover barn fires."

"The fire chief called me. His men thought there was something suspicious."

"Any idea how the fire started?" Matt asked.

"Too early to say for sure. It started in this area, and it appears some kind of accelerant was used. Can't tell what kind until we run the tests."

"So someone torched it?" Davis asked.

"Looks that way." He pointed at the metal pieces. "These are gun parts, but no sign of ammo."

Davis exchanged a glance with Matt. The fire had started in the room where Bauer kept his guns. "And, obviously, no sign of explosives."

"He probably moved them. That's not good." Matt turned to Blake. "Let me know as soon as you have the results."

The fire marshal gave a vague nod, making notes in his iPhone.

They made their way back to the two women, and Matt laid his hand on Amy's shoulder. "According to the fire marshal, the blaze started in the gun room. Were all Jim's guns stored in that room?"

"No," she said, "he moved a lot of them last week. Perhaps he knocked something over that started the fire."

"That's possible," Matt said. He gave her shoulder a pat. "I'm going to head back to the station. I'm sorry about the loss of your property. The fire marshal will be in touch with you."

They walked out of ear-shot from the woman, towards Matt's car. "You guys had lunch?"

"We were going to stop in town before we returned to the station," Davis said.

Matt paused by the door of his Escalade. "Follow me. We'll eat, and you can fill me in on what you discovered in Oklahoma."

CHAPTER 19

Chick-fil-A
Twin Falls, Texas

The restaurant had a crowd for mid-afternoon, but Matt found a table for four in a corner. He gave their order at the cash register and returned with a packed tray, and passed out the meals.

Davis placed the paper napkin on his lap and looked at the tray. "What, no cutlery?"

"It's finger food, Davis," Turner said, shaking her head.

"Maybe for you, Turner, but few foods in my estimation should be eaten with your fingers. This is not one of them."

Matt rose, went to the counter, and brought back a cellophane pack of plastic ware. "Now tell me what you found out in Oklahoma."

"Basically, we destroyed Bauer's alibi. He used the truck of one of the casino waiters both times." Davis rubbed his hands together. "And we have the entire episode on tape."

"Okay, let's pull him in for questioning and get the alibi on record." Matt chewed his food thoughtfully before he continued. "Then when we get the gun, if it's the murder weapon, we get an arrest warrant and pick him up."

"What about Eden?" Turner asked.

Matt wiped his mouth with a paper napkin and leaned back in the chair. "Leave her alone for the time being. Once we arrest Bauer, we'll play them off against each other."

"You think Bauer set the fire in his mother's barn?" Turner asked.

"I don't see how it could be anyone else. He's the only one with a reason to destroy those guns." Matt wadded up the napkin and stuffed it on the food tray. "Plus,

Bauer lost the tail we put on him last night. He didn't return to the condo until after the fire was reported."

"I got the impression Amy knows he's responsible," Davis said.

"She at least suspects, that's what I gathered from her body language today," Matt said.

Turner sent a questioning glance at Matt and Davis. "I don't understand why he wanted to destroy the weapons. Seems risky, unless I'm missing something."

"My guess is they may have been used in other crimes, and maybe he didn't want to dump a load on his gun dealer all at once. I think he knows the net is tightening, so he's destroying evidence. My fear is that he's getting ready to run or to make a stand. And I really don't like the fact that he moved the explosives, provided they were there to begin with. We only have Dr. Russell's word they existed."

Davis gave a solemn nod. "And we don't know for certain he kept them in the barn. I would hope he's not storing dynamite, or whatever else goes boom, in that condo."

"Now there's a scary thought," Turner said.

Matt grabbed the tray and headed for the trash receptacle. "Put our best people on stakeout. We can't afford to lose him again."

The Foley Residence
Twin Falls, Texas

Sara threw on her sweats, laced up her running shoes, and headed for the deck. Disliking running in extreme cold, she had let her martial arts classes take care of her exercise, but today she needed extreme physical exertion. A heavy profusion of sweat was required to work out her frustrations with Stella.

After a few limbering stretches, she headed for the path that ran to the lake through the woods. Rowdy at her side, Sara moved along the trail at a steady pace. The day was sunny but cold, especially along the shaded path, and seemed to grow colder as the lake came into view.

Rather than her usual smooth glide, her feet pounded the hard-packed earth in a steady jog as thoughts of the woman's disapproving attitude flooded her mind, adding tension she didn't need or want in her life.

She picked up her pace and slipped on her headphones. The beautiful sounds of Andrea Bocelli's "The Lord's Prayer" seemed to fill the forest with its purity. How could anyone remain uptight listening to that wonderful voice? The tension melted away, and she was reminded how puny her problems were compared to those of so many others. She found her stride and headed back.

Fifteen minutes later, she rounded the turn for home, her tight muscles relaxed and her mood mellowed. She loved the openness and solitude of the big redwood and glass structure with the wildlife outside the back door, happy she and Matt had decided to make this their permanent home.

Matt had encouraged her to make whatever changes she wished in the home's decor, and she'd started to draw up plans to redecorate as soon as the weather improved.

After a shower, she returned to the game room, and spread material and paint swatches out on the desk, putting together a color scheme.

The area was a wide-open combination of many things, library, media room, game room, and a computer alcove in the corner. The various sections were divided into individual rooms by seating and area rugs.

Stella entered, running the vacuum cleaner over the Oriental rugs. She stopped behind Sara and looked over her shoulder. "What are you doing?"

Sara glanced back and smiled. "Selecting colors and fabric for redecorating as soon as the weather turns warmer."

Stella huffed. "I don't see why you would want to change anything. The house is beautiful. Mary had great taste."

"That she did," Sara said and returned to her task.

"Then why change it?" Stella shut off the machine and stomped from the room.

Resting her chin in her hand, Sara released a breath, long and slow, to quell the rising flash of anger that rolled over her. The woman was trying to lay a guilt trip on Sara, and she had succeeded.

In many respects, she understood Stella's resentment. The housekeeper had loved Mary, and apparently felt Sara had usurped her former employer's place in Matt's affection and in his home. What Stella failed to grasp was that Sara had also loved Mary, and would always cherish her friend's memory.

But it was Sara and Matt's life now, and none of Stella's affair. The woman would have to get over her resentment, or leave.

Unable to concentrate, Sara pushed away from the desk and went upstairs. So much for a mellow mood.

She walked into the closet, put on her workout clothes, and headed to the Krav Maga studio.

Twin Falls Police Station
Twin Falls, Texas

Matt strode into his office and stopped short in the doorway. Sara sat on the corner of his desk, her attention directed at the antics of two squirrels playing tag outside the window. She looked lovely in jeans, a lambskin vest, and boots. Her long dark hair flowed around her shoulders. Her jacket hung on the coat tree by the door.

He cleared his throat and opened his arms.

Sara slid off the desk and stepped into his embrace.

"I'm going to have to speak to the desk sergeant about letting beautiful women into my office unannounced."

"Don't blame Chuck. I bribed him."

"Before I asked what the payoff was, you do know it's illegal to corrupt a police officer with payment of any kind?"

"Mmmm, but a girl has to use all the assets in her arsenal to get some attention around here. We can discuss my punishment later."

He chuckled. "Okay, what was the inducement that made Chuck break the rules?"

She picked up a large brown sack from the desk bearing the logo of a local deli, and laughed. "A Ruben sandwich. The man has no willpower. All I had to do was make the offer and, before I finished the question, he said yes."

She held the paper bag in one hand and slipped the other around his neck. "The wonderful smells wafting in your office are from our lunch. If Mohammed won't come to the mountain, the mountain must come to Mohammed."

"I love a woman who knows what she wants. Come, let's take this impromptu feast to the break-room. I'll have to fight off the entire department once they get a whiff of these sandwiches."

They found seats in the lunch area, picked up drinks from the bar, and unpacked the food. Instead of tables, the room had booths of hunter-green, and the floor was covered in green and tan mosaic tile. A large picture window overlooked a small garden. "Did you know Mary donated all the fixtures, and designed everything in this room?" Matt asked.

"Yes," Sara said. "She told me about it while she was drawing up the plans. She wanted your people to have a restful place to get away from the day-to-day pressures of their profession while they ate. She did a wonderful job. It's more like an intimate café than a lunch room."

Matt nodded and bit into loaded pastrami on an onion roll. "How did you know what I liked?"

She gave him a cocky grin. "You're not the only crack investigator in the family." She eyed him.

He eyed her back. "Okay, I give."

"It was really quite simple. When I told the deli manager the sandwich was for you, he told me what you usually ordered."

"That's good sleuthing anyway, Mrs. Foley. How's your day going so far?"

She wagged her hand in a so-so gesture. "I went to Chaim's class before I came here. He says I have the fighting heart of Penthesilea. In case you've forgotten your Greek mythology, she was an Amazon warrior who participated in the Trojan Wars." She bent her arms and tried to form a muscle.

"Amazon warrior, huh? I'm going to have to watch you go through your paces. Maybe even join you on the mat after this case is resolved."

The corner of her mouth tilted up. "I'd love that. We could work out together."

He leaned back in the seat and grinned. "Not sure about that. I'd never live it down if you beat me, and you would have the advantage. It would be hard to keep my mind on the match."

She leaned across the table and kissed him. "I'd go easy on you."

Chris Hunter slid into the booth beside Sara. "When are you going to tell this man we're in love?"

Sara winked at Matt. "I've just been waiting for you to tell your wife first. After all, I don't want to lose a good thing if you're not available."

Chris dropped his head and shook it from side to side. "I guess we'll have to call off the affair, because, if I tell my wife, next thing I know, I'll wake up in the morgue."

Matt's grin spread into a wide smile. "If you don't stop flirting with my wife, you may find yourself in the morgue sooner than expected."

Chris slid out of the booth and saluted, "Roger that, Chief."

<<>>

Later that afternoon, Turner stuck her head in Matt's office door. "We've got James Bauer in Room One, if you want to listen in." She slapped her hand over her mouth when she saw he was on the phone.

Matt lifted the receiver away from his mouth and whispered, "I'll be right there."

When she left, he returned to his conversation with Sheriff Joe Wilson. "Just wanted to know if you would like to meet me in town for dinner; Sara and the kids are going to Maddie's, since I'm working late."

"Where?" he asked.

"You pick, then text me the time and place." He

disconnected and strode down the hallway to the interview room assigned to Bauer.

In the viewing area next door, Matt turned on the big-screen monitor and increased the volume. Bauer sat at the table against the wall, with Davis and Turner on the opposite side. Turner was doing the interview.

Bauer smoothed his tie down over his crisp white shirt, and crossed his legs. "Am I under arrest?"

Turner placed a thick file on the table and adjusted her chair. They had info on the man, but not that much. She had padded the file with blank sheets of paper. It was a common ploy to intimidate a suspect. "No, we just need to confirm some things. This is being recorded, in case you want an attorney."

"I *am* an attorney," Bauer replied.

"Your choice, but you know the saying: A lawyer who defends himself has a fool for a client."

"Very funny."

"I wasn't trying to be funny, just giving you the opportunity to change your mind."

"Unless I'm under arrest, I'll represent myself."

She placed a yellow legal pad on the desk. "Tell us where you were Sunday, January 11th, between 6:00 and 8:00 AM."

Matt sat amazed at the competent attorney persona Bauer presented to the world, totally inconsistent with what Matt knew of the man. No wonder Bauer had flown under the radar for so long.

Bauer huffed a deep breath. "We've been over this, but, for the record, I was at the casino in Durant, Oklahoma."

"Were you there alone?"

"As I told you previously, I was there with a friend, Earl Locke."

"Did you leave the casino at any time during your stay until your departure on Monday?"

"No."

Turner ran through the same questions on the weekend the Russells were murdered. Bauer's answers were the same, except he had been there with Eden Russell. "Do you know anything about the barn fire at your mother's yesterday?"

If looks could kill, Turner would have been a dead woman. "No, why would I?"

"It's a reasonable question, Mr. Bauer. The fire started in your gun room, and it was arson." Turner said. "Why would anyone want to destroy your property?"

The attorney gave her a my-patience-is-wearing-thin glower. "I haven't the foggiest idea, Detective," he hissed. "That's what they pay you to find out."

Turner had nailed him. She thanked him for coming in, and he left.

Matt met the two detectives outside after the interview. "I don't like being lied to, but we've got him. Let's hope our nefarious gun dealer locates that weapon soon."

<<>>

Jim Bauer climbed into his SUV and gripped the wheel to keep his hands from shaking. Violent anger surged blood through his veins, filling him with rage. The AK-15 in the back called to him—to storm through the station's doors and take out everyone in sight. It would be as easy as shooting plastic ducks at the fairgrounds.

He pounded the dash with his fist until the pain brought him back into the moment. This wasn't the time. He wanted more. He wanted to go down in the history books of this city, teach these arrogant cops to be careful who they messed with.

Killing people like Miles Davis and Lucy Turner wouldn't be easy. They were always armed, and would shoot back. Catching them with their guard down would take time, time he didn't have. He couldn't make them go away, but he could make them sit up and take notice. He would leave a legacy greater than the University of Texas tower shooter, Charles Whitman.

Those who survived would remember the name of James Bauer

CHAPTER 20

The Steak Out
Twin Falls, Texas

Matt saw Joe's county SUV in the parking lot of his favorite steak house. Joseph Dawson Wilson had been his best friend since Matt was a skinny kid of nine with a nose too big for his face. Fortunately, he had grown to fit the nose. Joe had been there for Matt through the many trials in his life.

He was always moved by Joe's concern for his safety. More times than Matt could count, Joe had taken that young boy under his wing, protecting him from his abusive guardian after his family was murdered by drug dealers who picked the wrong house. Joe had opened his parents' home, letting Matt spend the night to prevent beatings from his alcoholic uncle. Not for the first time, he realized how blessed he had been to have Joe Wilson in his life.

Matt found Joe at a table in the rear next to the kitchen, his favorite spot. He inhaled a deep breath. If the sizzling smell of mesquite-grilled steaks didn't make a man hungry, then his sense of smell was dead. "Sorry I'm a little late. Things are hopping at the station. Have you ordered?"

Joe gave him a lopsided grin. "Nope. I figured, since you were buying, I'd wait for you, but I did order an appetizer to hold me over until our food arrives." He picked up a potato skin, put half in his mouth, and pushed the platter towards Matt.

They placed their orders and Joe shot him a quizzical look. "Any reason you're treating me to dinner?"

"Nothing in particular," Matt said. "Haven't talked to you since we found Lucy, so I thought we'd catch up." He grinned and reached for a potato skin. "And, I thought I'd run some of the Davenport case details by you. Get your take."

Joe stopped munching. "Okay, what have you got so far?"

"We have an A-1 suspect. We've broken his alibi, but we have no solid proof. Although we haven't found the murder weapon, we do have a good lead on where it might be. The downside is there's no solid motive we've found. A motive isn't necessary for a conviction, but it helps convince a jury."

"Sounds like you're on the right track, and killers usually have a motive, even if it's a stupid one."

"Yeah," Matt said. "My big concern is that this character is unpredictable, has a well-stocked arsenal, and we're pretty sure he has a cache of explosives somewhere. If he decides to hole up, people could get killed. "

"You think he's unstable?"

"No question about it. Turner uncovered some old complaints from his neighbors and people he went to college with. He was involved in altercations with lots of folks. Odd, perhaps even criminal behavior, but nothing they could prove."

"Odd how?"

"Claims to women that he worked in government intelligence. Playing the national hero— keeping the country safe and all that, trying to impress them. When he had a disagreement with someone, their pets went missing. Nothing the victims could prove Bauer was responsible for. He's a lawyer, so he had all the answers. Everyone we interviewed seemed to think he's a loose cannon. My take is he's an IED with his finger on the detonator."

"When you decide to make the arrest, give me a call. I'll provide backup."

"I hoped you'd say that."

The Foley Residence
Twin Falls, Texas

After a pleasant dinner with Maddie and Don Tompkins, Sara drove home and let the children play with Rowdy in the game room. She liked to give them

175

time to relax before getting to their homework.

When they were settled, she returned to the computer desk to continue working on her decorating plans, still unsure whether to recover the furniture or replace it. It seemed a waste to discard the beautiful pieces. They were still in good condition, and of excellent quality.

The downside of reupholstering was they would have to do without the furniture while the pieces were at the decorator's. Of course, they could always rent furniture if it came to that, but she hated the idea.

The soft glow of the monitor welcomed her back to the computer alcove. When she reached the desk where she'd left her decorating folder, it wasn't there. She searched the drawers, but the file folder was gone.

She went looking for Stella, and found her in the laundry room. "Have you seen the tan file folder I left on the desk before I went to dinner?"

Stella turned away from the washer, her face stoic. "Yes, I thought it was trash. I threw it away."

"Why would I leave trash out when there's a receptacle beside the desk? Where did you put it?"

Stella shrugged. "Sorry, I tossed it in the big trash can outside."

Sara's cheeks heated as she watched the housekeeper's face. Stella averted her gaze, a tell-tale sign she was lying.

Hurrying out into the cold evening air, Sara lifted the lid on the large container. There was her folder, its contents loose on top of the trash bags, with wet food clinging to everything. Totally destroyed.

She felt sick. A mixture of fury and frustration churned her stomach. All that work, and now she'd have to start again from the beginning. That was probably Stella's purpose in destroying the file—to delay or stop her redecorating plans. How asinine was that?

This was unfamiliar territory. Sara had never dealt with anything remotely close to this, anywhere, much less in her home. Beatrice and Pete were like family. They had worked for her parents before their deaths. They helped make her home a warm, comfortable place to unwind. Stella was exactly the opposite.

She needed to speak to Matt. Accepting such malice was out of the question.

Later that evening, while Sara prepared baths for the kids and laid out their pajamas, Poppy and Danny settled into a game of checkers, the little girl with her ever-present cup of apple juice at her fingertips. Always the loving brother, Danny let Poppy win every other game.

As Sara came downstairs, Poppy jumped up from the game table. "Oops, I spilled."

"Don't worry," Danny said, "I'll get a paper towel from the kitchen and clean it up."

Stella stood in the game room entrance, her purse on her arm, headed home. "No, you won't." Stella dropped her handbag and rushed over to Poppy, jerked her off the chair by her arm, and gave the child a violent shake. "She'll clean it up. She spilled it."

Danny screamed, "Leave her alone!" He ran forward and shoved Stella away from his sister.

The woman drew back her hand, but, before she could follow through, Sara grabbed her arm.

Sara glared at the woman. She was so angry she couldn't speak for a moment. She inhaled a quick, deep breath. "Pick up your things and leave immediately, or I'll have you arrested."

The housekeeper whirled around, her face flushed red with fury. "You can't fire me. I work for Matt."

"That's where you're wrong. You *worked* for *me*, but you are no longer employed here."

Stella snatched up her purse and stomped towards the front door. "I wonder what Blain and Grace Stanton will say when I tell them how you're desecrating their daughter's memory in her own home."

The front door closed with a crash.

Sara gathered Poppy in her arms. "You okay, kitten?"

The child's big blue eyes welled with tears. "I don't like Stella."

"At the moment, I don't like her much myself. But you don't have to worry about her anymore." She pulled Danny close. "I'm proud of you for defending your sister, Danny. Very proud."

"Can Beatrice and Pete come work here?" Poppy asked. "They're nice."

"I know, kitten, but they want to retire, so we're going to have to find a new, very nice, housekeeper. We won't settle for anything less."

Sara's Home
Twin Falls, Texas

Sara dropped the children off at school, and then drove to see Maddie. She pulled under the portico of her old home. She'd decided to wait until Maddie and Don were married to put the house on the market. And she wanted to give Pete and Beatrice plenty of time to settle their affairs here before moving to South Texas.

She'd been asleep when Matt came home last night, and he left early, before she could tell him about her confrontation with Stella. Truth was she hated to bother him with domestic problems when he had so much going on at the station. But he had to know soon. She'd wait up for him tonight if needed.

She stepped into the entryway and called, "Hello, anybody home?"

Maddie hurried from the kitchen and caught her in a long hug. "I wasn't expecting to see you again so soon. Beatrice and I are having coffee in the kitchen. Come join us."

Sara smiled down at her diminutive aunt. "Have I told you that you look wonderful? Love agrees with you."

Beatrice hurried across the kitchen tile to envelop her with both ample arms. "Welcome, *chica;* I made strudel this morning, just the way you like it with the crispy crust."

Unable to speak, Sara returned the hug, suddenly coming to grips with the fact that she would soon lose contact with this amazing woman. The four of them, she, Maddie, Bea, and Pete had melded into a family after the death of Sara's parents. "Thank you, Bea. I've missed you."

She grabbed a cup from the cupboard, filled it with coffee, and joined them at the island.

Maddie reached across and squeezed her hand. "We had so little time last evening, since the children had school today. Tell us all about what's happening with you and Matt. I've missed our morning breakfasts together," she said.

"Matt and I couldn't be better, except I don't see much of him." Then she blurted, "I had to fire Stella yesterday."

The two women widened their eyes in surprise.

Still upset about the conflict with the housekeeper, Sara closed her eyes for a moment, and then explained what had happened.

"I hope you're not feeling bad about letting the woman go. You absolutely did the right thing," Maddie said, her cheeks flushed with anger. "I can't believe anyone would deliberately abuse Poppy. I've never met better behaved children."

Beatrice muttered in Spanish, her brown eyes flashing. "I will keep house for you. Pete and I will stay close to care for you, *mi hija*."

"Oh, Bea, I would love that, but I couldn't let you cancel your retirement. You and Pete deserve to live your own lives in leisure. You've been loving and loyal for so many years . . ." Sara caught her breath, unable to finish the sentence. She wrapped her arms around the beloved woman. "I can never replace you, but I can find someone who will do a good job and will be kind to my children."

She glanced across at Maddie. "I haven't told Matt, yet."

"He's the last person for you to worry about," Maddie assured her. "He is the most level-headed man I've ever known. He was like that when I taught him in high school. He wouldn't expect you to condone that kind of behavior from anyone. Let me put out the word to some of my friends. They might know of a good replacement for Stella."

"You're both wonderful, and I feel better," Sara said. "I didn't mean to dump my problems on you." She refilled her cup. "Tell me about your wedding plans, Maddie. How are they coming?"

"As you know, it will be a small affair, so everything is set except my wedding dress. I'm having trouble finding something suitable. I don't want a traditional, long, formal dress," Maddie replied.

"At a size two, you should be able to find tons of dresses," Sara said.

"It isn't the size that's an issue, it's the styles," Maddie said. "Bridal shops don't cater to wedding dresses for older women. However, I found a designer in Oklahoma City, online, who will design and make whatever I want. She seems to be my best option at present."

"Let me know when you're ready, and I'll go with you."

"I'd hoped you would," Maddie laughed. "You know, with my vision problems, I might come home with a chartreuse wedding gown."

The Foley Residence
Twin Falls, Texas

Matt had called to say he would be home by seven. Using Beatrice's recipes, Sara made a full-course Mexican dinner and set the table with flowers and candles. Poppy and Danny were spending the night with her old boss's children.

She switched on the stereo system and put on a Carpenters album. She'd always loved the lovely voice of Karen Carpenter.

The sound of a car pulling into the garage made her turn, then the door opened and Matt entered. "Mmmm, something smells good," he said and strode across the kitchen, swept her into his arms, and placed a lingering kiss on her lips. He lifted his head. "And the food doesn't smell bad either. Did you do all this for me?"

"I did, with my own two little hands. Come, let's eat while it's hot. I have something I need to tell you."

"It must be serious if you're enticing me with one of my favorite meals. Want to talk before we eat?"

She nodded and gazed into his eyes. "I know she's been with you for a long time, but...I let Stella go yesterday." Then she told him why.

"That's probably why she'd been trying to reach me at work. I didn't return her calls. I figured if she had a problem, she could work it out with you."

He took her hand and led her over to the dining room chair, sat, and pulled her into his lap. "Sara Louise, you can be assured I will always back whatever you decide. I know you, I know your heart. The only one I'm disappointed in is Stella. I thought she was a better person."

Sara slipped both arms around his neck and whispered in his ear, "I'm so glad I married you."

He laughed. "Not half as glad as I am. If Stella still wants to talk to me, I'll be happy to listen, but I don't think she'll like what I have to say. Now, let's eat. I'm starving."

The Foley Residence
Twin Falls, Texas

The day was bright and fifty degrees, much warmer than it had been in weeks as Sara returned home from her martial arts class. She showered and changed, then went to the office alcove in the game room to check the Internet for temporary maids to use until she found a full- time housekeeper. It was a job she'd never had to do, and she wasn't looking forward to the long, drawn-out process of replacing the housekeeper.

She jotted down a list of cleaning services and scheduled cleaners for twice a week, then created an ad to go to an employment agency and the local newspaper.

Before settling in to make the calls for the ads, she went into the kitchen to make tea. As the brew was steeping, the doorbell rang.

The elegant figure of Grace Stanton stood in the doorway. Nerves skittered up Sara's backbone. She was pretty sure she knew why Grace had come calling. "Please come in. It's so good to see you. I was just about to have some tea. Come on in and join me."

"Thank you. Tea sounds wonderful. I've had my quota of coffee today. How are you? I've been meaning to visit since your marriage, and finally found time today. I hope I'm not intruding. I should have called, but took the chance you would be home."

Sara poured the tea and set a cup in front of Grace, adding milk and sugar to the tea tray. While Mary was alive, Sara spent many weekends at the Stanton ranch outside of Austin, and at their home in North Dallas. They had always treated her like a second daughter.

"We are doing very well. Matt is busy, of course, but I'm learning to cope with that."

"I know that isn't easy. But he's worth the effort. Matt told Blain you adopted two children since we last met. Matt raves about them to Blain. You must bring them out to the ranch so we can meet them."

"I'd love to, and they would adore the animals." Sara smiled. "Poppy and Danny are sweet- natured and totally unspoiled, for which I deserve none of the credit."

Grace took a sip of tea and set the cup down. A shadow passed over her face. "I received a phone call from Stella."

"I wondered if that's why you came. Grace . . ."

The older woman reached across the table and placed her hand over Sara's. "You don't need to defend yourself. I came to tell you not to worry about anything Stella might say." She gave Sara's hand a pat. "Mary loved you, Sara. She would be thrilled that you and Matt found each other. You were the sister she never had, and it was obvious you felt the same way about her. I can't explain Stella's misguided vindictiveness. Mary would have been the first to condemn her actions. I just wanted to reassure you that Blain and I didn't believe her accusations."

"Thank you, Grace. Your understanding means a lot to me." She stood and took her cup and saucer to the sink, and cast a solemn glance at her guest. "Stella took her disapproval out on Danny and Poppy. I couldn't allow that. Please know that I would never do anything to tarnish Mary's memory."

Grace rose, crossed the distance between them, and took Sara in her arms with a motherly squeeze. "I know that. Would you like to see the latest pictures of my granddaughter, Mary? She just turned two."

They shared photos, Sara of Poppy and Danny, and Grace of her latest grandchild.

Grace finished her tea, picked up her handbag, and started to the door. "Don't forget to bring the children to see me. I'd love to meet them."

Standing in the doorway, Sara watched Grace's limousine pull away and disappear into the distance. She smiled and went back inside. It was clear where Mary's classy genes came from.

CHAPTER 21

Twin Falls Police Station
Twin Falls, Texas

A commotion in the corridor outside Matt's office brought him out of his chair and into the hallway.

Chris Hunter, almost at a run, held a rifle in one hand and a Beretta in the other. Cole Allen was about two steps behind him.

A smile beamed on Chris's face from one ear to the other as he stopped next to Matt. "We've got him, Matt. The dealer located the handgun and Bauer brought a rifle to the dealer yesterday. Now we can nail that son of a gun."

Matt slapped him on the shoulder. "Give them to Mac, and let's see if the ballistics match. Tell him to put a rush on it."

He strode back to his desk, picked up the phone, and called Sheriff Gates in Oklahoma. "Hey, Walt, we may have the rifle used in the Russell murders. Can you send me the bullet markings for comparison?"

"You bet. The photos will be on their way in five minutes. If this pans out, I'm going to buy you the biggest steak in Oklahoma City the next time you're in my neck of the woods."

"Thanks, Walt. If this is the gun, you may want to tell Dr. Russell to stand by. He might need to take custody of his children. I'll keep you posted."

The Foley Residence
Twin Falls, Texas

Sara dressed quickly after Matt left for the station. She had a housekeeper interview at eight o'clock, and then she had errands to run. The two applicants she'd spoken to yesterday had proven a waste of her time.

The woman coming today was a licensed nurse, overqualified for sure and certainly not a requirement, but it was worth talking to the woman.

She'd just moved the wet laundry over to the dryer when the doorbell rang, and she hurried to answer the summons.

A woman stood on the threshold, dressed in a navy blue pants suit. She looked to be around five-feet-two, about fifty, with tightly-curled auburn hair. She offered her hand. "Hi, I'm Agnes Welford, but most people call me 'Aggie'." Her friendly blue eyes gleamed.

Sara shook her hand and led her inside. "I'm Sara Foley. Come in. Let me take your coat for you, and we can talk in the kitchen over coffee."

"You're a woman after my own heart. I like informal interviews, although I haven't been on one in quite a while."

Sara took a plate of blueberry muffins and a carafe to the bar, poured two mugs of coffee, and placed it in front of her guest, along with cream and sugar, which Aggie liberally applied to her cup.

She sat across from Aggie. "Your resume said you just finished an assignment with an invalid patient. Why did you leave?"

"My patient, Judge Harland, passed away. I'd been with him six years." She gave a vague smile. "He was grouchy as an old bear, but he was in a lot of pain and, despite his illness, he had a great sense of humor. I'm going to miss him."

"I guess my biggest question, Aggie, is why a licensed nurse would want to work as a housekeeper. You could make more money working in your field."

"Truthfully, Mrs. Foley, I'm burned out on caring for the sick and dying. That may sound harsh, but when you live with someone for a long period of time, they tend to confide in you, all their worries, fears, and problems. They soon become family. It takes a great emotional toll when they pass away, like losing a relative or a good friend. I decided that when I went to work again, I wanted to be with young healthy people who I wouldn't have to worry about dying."

Sara nodded "I can understand that."

Aggie stirred her coffee, a solemn expression on her face. "I could retire, but my husband passed away ten years ago, and we never had children. I'd go crazy sitting around with nothing to do." She chuckled. "I'm what my mother used to call antsy, which today would be diagnosed as hyperactive. Can you tell me why your last housekeeper left?"

Sara looked directly into Aggie's eyes. "I let her go." Sara gave her a shortened version of what had happened.

The woman gave a thoughtful nod. "Is this a live-in position?"

"Is that a requirement?" Sara asked.

Aggie lifted one shoulder. "It's a preference. I don't like to drive, and the job of private nurse, as a rule, required my living in the home. What would my duties be?"

"Light housekeeping, laundry, and supervising a quarterly deep cleaning."

"No cooking?"

"Only if you want to, and we would pay extra for that."

Aggie laughed. "You might not after you taste my cooking." She rose, added coffee to her cup, and topped off Sara's. "Would you consider a live-in housekeeper?"

"It's something I hadn't thought about," Sara smiled. "We do have two extra bedrooms, but I'd have to clear that with my husband. He's the police chief, and sometimes things get pretty hectic here. You might not like it."

Reaching into her handbag she handed Sara an envelope. "I could use a little excitement in my life. This is a letter of reference from Judge Harland's attorney. Obviously, I couldn't get one from the judge himself. The attorney's number is on the reference letter. Feel free to call him. If you're satisfied, and think I meet your qualifications, give me a call. Then, I'd like to meet the children."

Sara smiled as the woman drove away. She liked Aggie's take charge personality. She would give the attorney a call. But first she had an errand to run.

Eden Russell's Condo
Twin Falls, Texas

Chris Hunter and Cole Allen sat in their unmarked car down the street from the Russell condo, awaiting instructions to move in. Chris had supervised the quiet evacuation of the neighborhood via phone calls, with the dispatchers telling them not to panic, but to leave their homes quickly and get to a safe place. If Bauer came out shooting or detonated explosives, the authorities would have plenty to worry about without trying to protect citizens.

Eden left to take the twins to school and Chris huffed out a breath of relief. He looked over at his partner. "At least those kids are out of danger. If all goes as planned, this will be over before school is out." He punched Davis's number into his iPhone and told him the kids were out of harm's way. A policewoman would take custody of them as soon as their mother drove away from the school.

"What do you suppose is holding up the Bauer arrest warrant?" Cole asked.

"Matt is waiting on McCulloch to verify the gun as the murder weapon. He'll have the warrant issued as soon as that happens and give us the go-ahead. Sheriff Wilson is standing by in case we need additional backup."

"You worried?" Cole said.

"I am, and you should be, too. I have a bad feeling about this guy. He's not going down easy."

Cole nodded. That spoke volumes. The young detective had seen a lot of action in Afghanistan, but this was his first non-combat siege as a cop.

He and Cole both wore the latest edition of Kevlar vests, but that didn't make Chris feel comfortable. They needed a Kevlar suit and a bulletproof helmet. Bauer was a madman, with a stock pile of God only knows what in that condo. For all they knew, the nutcase could have a .50 cal. and a box of armor-piercing rounds. Nothing would stop those babies.

Eden Russell returned from school and Cole glanced over at Chris. "You think the warrant will include Eden?"

"I'm not sure. In my book she was a willing accomplice. She had to know what he was doing—knew he left the casino the night the Russells were murdered." He hesitated. A young girl on a bike rounded the corner of the block and headed towards them. "What is that kid doing here? Find some excuse to send her away. I'll call and have the streets cordoned off."

Cole stepped from the car and hurried towards the dark-haired girl. Before he could intercept her, she parked the bike and knocked on Eden Russell's door.

Snatching his cell phone from the dash, Chris called Davis. "Any news on the warrant?"

"We're still waiting on McCulloch. He has to make sure we have the right gun."

"Tell Mac to stop fooling around. It's getting tense out here. We've got pedestrians in the area. Send the black and whites to close down this street and keep traffic away before we have a hot mess here."

Davis said, "Chris, go ahead and arrest Bauer. We can hold him without a warrant until Mac finishes his tests. I don't want things to get out of control while we sit and wait."

"I think that's the right move," Chris said. "We'll get right on it. I'll call the sheriff to move in behind us."

<<>>

Despite the bright early morning sunlight that seeped through the parted curtains, dread overwhelmed Eden as she accepted the reality of her situation. Her expectations of being free of her ex-husband had been dashed with the deaths of Stephen's parents. Instead of being free of him, she faced death or life in prison.

Stephen should have died with his parents, but he failed to show for their anniversary party. Jim had messed up royally. Instead of solving a problem with Stephen's death, he now had unlimited funds to fight her in court.

She stood at the bar and made a face as she downed a half-glass of straight bourbon. She hated liquor, but she needed the false courage today.

She'd debated about sending the boys to school, but finally decided it was still too early for the authorities to come for Jim, and the kids were already gone when Jim spotted the unmarked car down the street.

She reread the suicide note she'd written on the computer, for the hundredth time. The e-mail was addressed to her Aunt Judith. She would never understand the motivation behind what Eden planned to do. Even she had trouble remembering how and why this all began. Had she really wanted Jim to kill her parents? At the time, it seemed the only way to keep Stephen from gaining more time with the twins. She reread the note, then erased it, and shut down the computer.

With her own alibi secured by Jack McKinnon, she never considered Jim would fall under suspicion. Too late, she realized they had both underestimated the authorities.

Eden bit her lip and gazed around the room, momentarily distracted by the clutter. The remodeling project they'd started was still unfinished, and now it seemed it never would be. But that was the least of her worries.

Was she ready to die?

It had always been Jim's master plan. If the authorities started to close in, and they were definitely closing in, the two of them would die together, along with her two sons, rather than face the death penalty or life in prison. She couldn't bear the shame, and had agreed. Whatever it took, she would ensure Stephen Russell never got custody of the boys. At least that's the way things were supposed to unfold.

With the children at school, if she went through with the suicide plans, Stephen would get full custody. She couldn't bear the thought of that happening.

Jim was insane. She should have realized it sooner. The apartment was rigged with explosives, to detonate when the police stormed the building. He planned to take as many of them with him as possible.

Eden reached for the whiskey bottle again and splashed a large portion into the glass. It had seemed so simple in the beginning. Her parents were going to testify against her, help Stephen get extended custody. She had to stop them. Didn't she? And Jim had offered to help.

She paced as she sipped the foul-tasting liquid, her thoughts racing. There must be a way out of this mess. Suicide was a big step. One she no longer wanted to consider. She drained the glass and weaved her way towards the stairs when someone knocked on the door.

Police already?

No, Jim would be shooting.

"Who is it?" Jim bellowed from the landing.

"Give me a minute and I'll find out." The words stumbled over her tongue. She looked through the peephole and blinked rapidly, trying to focus. Finally Taylor's face came into view. "It's Taylor."

"Well, let her in. The more the merrier," he said.

No, Taylor wasn't part of this. Their parents were dead. Eden accepted responsibility for that, but she wouldn't take her little sister down with her.

Eden opened the door, leaving the chain in place. "Why are you here, Taylor? Why aren't you in school?"

"Teacher's in-service day. I thought Nash and Nicolas would be home."

"No, they had school today. How did you get here?"

"My bike."

Eden huffed an exasperated breath. "Go home. I'm too busy for company."

"You're not busy, you're drunk. I can smell you from here." Taylor whirled and stalked toward her bike.

When she was sure her sister had gone, Eden climbed the stairs, her feet like cement weights.

She had made her decision

CHAPTER 22

Eden Russell's Condo
Twin Falls, Texas

Cole uttered his favorite curse word under his breath and stopped, unsure what to do next. If he walked to the door, Eden would see him, and would know why they were there. But if he let the girl go inside, she could be a hostage, or get killed when they came to arrest Bauer.

He turned back to Chris and gave him a what-do-I-do-now shrug. Chris pointed, and when Cole turned back, the girl had gotten on her bike and hurried away. He heaved a deep sigh and returned to the unmarked Charger.

"Davis told me to go ahead with the arrest without the warrant. If we don't get this taken care of soon," Chris said, "I'm going to have a heart attack. We would have been in deep poop if that kid had gone inside. You ready to roll?"

"Tell me about it." Cole pulled his gun and chambered a bullet. "Ready when you are."

A red Jeep pulled to the curb in front of the Russell condo. As the woman exited the SUV, Chris almost choked. "Good lord, what is she doing here?"

"Who?" Cole asked.

But Chris was already out of the door, rushing to intercept her, yelling to Cole as he ran, "It's Matt's wife. Get us some backup. Now!"

<<>>

Eden stepped into the bedroom. Jim Bauer stood at the front window, scoped rifle clutched in his hand, his eyes bright and excited. She suddenly realized he was enjoying this.

"You ready, Eden? Ready to pull the plug?"

She stopped in her tracks, her voice cracked. "Why?

191

W-What's happening?"

"Nothing at the moment. Looks like they're waiting for something. Maybe just keeping us under surveillance. Could also mean they're waiting on an arrest warrant and back-up."

She sat on the bed, eyes focused on her demented lover, and considered her options. Perhaps she could find a way out after all.

The authorities had no evidence against her, there couldn't be. After all, she hadn't killed anyone. She could claim it was all Jim's idea; that he had acted alone without her knowledge.

Jim would have to die. He was an attorney, and he wouldn't take the fall alone. She couldn't have a long, drawn-out trial; she'd lose against him in court, and she'd lose the boys. She'd rather die first than see Stephen win.

Jim was determined to go out in a hail of bullets and brimstone. To implement her change in plans, she had to have a weapon to stop him. She scanned the bedroom and spotted the nail gun on the dresser. Would that work, or just irritate him into killing her with his bare hands?

Bauer gave a quick peek outside around the curtain. A deep laugh swelled in his chest. "Well, look who's coming to pay you a visit. Looks like we have our first victim."

Eden lifted a corner of the drape and sucked in a breath. Sara Foley was crossing the street, a pastry box in her hand.

"No!" Eden shouted, but, before she could stop him, Jim aimed and fired.

<<>>

Cole snatched the radio from the dashboard and made the call for help.

At a full run, Chris Hunter launched into the air and brought Sara Foley to the ground as a shot from the condo broke the still morning silence. Chris grunted and crumpled, covering Sara with his body.

"Mrs. Foley, get behind the retaining wall!" Cole yelled, firing three quick shots at the second- floor window as he covered the distance between Chris and Sara. He lifted his partner across his shoulders, and transported his limp body behind the barrier, while bullets pinged off the bricks, sending tiny cement projectiles raining down.

With Sara safely behind the wall, Cole sneaked a look around the façade, and winced. He was pinned down. The sniper had the high ground, and there was no way to move without the risk of getting hit. He had known since the police academy that his job was dangerous, more so as a street cop than as a detective. But he'd never let himself fixate on it. That could cause him to freeze in a crisis. He just let his Marine training kick in. Take out the enemy, protect your buddies, and pray you and your team survived the encounter.

He'd practiced this scenario a thousand times on maneuvers and in combat, and he knew what to do without thinking about it. But his objective today wasn't to take the building; it was to take care of Chris until backup arrived.

Without taking his eyes off the condo, he asked, "You okay, Mrs. Foley?"

"Y-Yes. Just a few skinned elbows, thanks to Chris. Is h-he okay?"

Cole glanced down at his partner and swallowed twice to get control. Chris was losing blood rapidly from the bullet that shattered his shoulder. "He's hit pretty bad."

Removing her cashmere scarf from around her neck, Sara pressed it against Chris's shoulder to staunch the blood flow. "Thank heavens he's unconscious, or the pain would be unbearable."

Fear weighed heavily in Cole's chest with each breath he drew. "I phoned for back-up. Help is on the way."

But would it be in time to save Chris's life?

<<>>

From outside the condo, three bullets shattered the window, and Jim ducked and cursed. He set the rifle on automatic, looked above the window sill, and sent a hail of bullets through the broken glass.

"Why did you do that?" Eden screamed and shoved him.

"Get down before you get your head blown off. Can't you see someone is shooting at us?" He sat on the floor, below the window, reloading the rifle. "Besides, I didn't hit your friend. Some Good Samaritan stepped in front of her. Probably a cop."

While he was distracted by the scene outside, Eden lifted the nail gun from the smooth surface. She hesitated only a moment before placing it close to his temple and pulling the trigger.

Bauer turned a disbelieving gaze on her, a look of horror on his face.

Her lip trembled and remorse curdled like lead in her stomach. She reached out to him, failing to notice his right hand inching towards a black button on the window sill.

Seconds before the fireball rushed at her, Eden understood.

Panic clutched her throat and she tried to cover her face. She'd been right. Jim wasn't going alone.

As his last act before dying, he detonated the bombs.

<<>>

An explosion rocked the earth beneath Sara's feet. Percussion waves stripped limbs off the trees above her. She pressed close to the wall, and she and Cole tried to shield Chris from the fallout.

Sara peeked over the ledge, at the condominium now consumed in flames. Roaring heat poured from the shell that remained of the once beautiful building. Tornado-like winds rocked the Jeep, and it burst into flames. Smoke and dust enveloped them, and large chunks of cement and wood soared through the air and fell like artillery and just as deadly. Waves of intense heat from the burning building wrapped around them; lessened somewhat by the chilled morning air.

She closed her eyes and said a fervent prayer for

protection. They were out in the open, with no protection from the deadly rubble falling like hail around them. Her palms stung and her elbows throbbed from the fall after Chris tackled her. She pressed the scarf tighter over Chris's bullet wound and smoothed the hair away from his face. His breathing was shallow, his skin clammy. He'd lost too much blood.

She stroked his brow. "I'm sorry my good intentions put you in danger, Chris. Please, please hold on."

Where was that ambulance?

A dark cloud seemed to cover them, and Sara lost track of time, trying to make Chris as comfortable as possible as they waited for the fallout to end. Shrill sirens promised the imminent arrival of emergency responders rushing to their aid. It couldn't arrive too soon for her. Chris needed help, now.

As the smoke began to dissipate, through the haze and dust the street became utter chaos, looking like TV footage of Beirut bombings. Fire trucks, police cruisers, and cops shuffled through the rubble, and someone lifted away a large piece of the building's roof that had shielded the three of them—miraculously shielded them from the explosion's aftermath.

Visible through the smoke and dust, two ambulance units slid to the curb, and emergency techs ran towards them. One of the EMTs helped Sara to her feet. "Are you hurt?"

"Nothing important." She steadied her balance and moved away to make a clear path to Chris. Her injuries were of no consequence compared to his. He was fighting for his life. "Please," she pointed at Chris, "take care of him. He's a police officer with a gunshot wound in his shoulder. He's lost a lot of blood."

Two techs immediately surrounded Chris and soon had him on a stretcher and inside the emergency unit, with oxygen and an IV going. When he was secured inside, the rear doors slammed shut and the vehicle careened out of sight, sirens wailing.

Once her heart rate slowed, Sara sucked oxygen into her lungs. The coppery taste of blood touched her tongue from a busted lip she just realized she had.

<<>>

Matt hung up from briefing Doug Anderson on the latest developments in the Davenport case when his phone rang.

The desk sergeant's breathless voice sounded through the phone line. "Chief, shots have been fired at Eden Russell's residence. Chris Hunter is down and your wife's at the scene."

"Sara?" Matt asked. "What's she doing there?"

"I don't know, Chief. Cole didn't say."

"Cole is with Chris and Sara? Are they okay?"

"I don't know, Chief. Davis and Turner are on their way now."

Fear choked off his air passage and Matt concentrated on breathing. It felt like a Texas longhorn was sitting on his chest. He speed-dialed Davis as he hit his office back door at a full run.

Davis's voice crackled through cell phone static on the line and he didn't wait for Matt to ask a question. "We're about a block away. There's been an explosion. Smoke and dust is so thick we can barely see. I'm going to give my phone to Turner so I don't smash into something or someone. She'll stay on the line and let you know what's happening."

Five minutes later, Matt's SUV slammed into the curb. He jumped out, leaving the door ajar. Smoke curled around Matt, burning his nose as he frantically searched for Sara. A too-familiar fear crawled up his spine and left him trembling. *Please, she has to be alright.*

"Chief," Turner's voice came through his cell phone. "Chris is alive. He's on his way to Twin Falls Memorial."

Matt hissed out a relieved breath. He caught a glimpse of Cole Allen through the smoke and mist, and strode towards him. The young detective pointed to an ambulance parked kitty-corner to the street. Matt's heart almost stopped. Fearing what he might find, he ran to the emergency unit and stepped to the open back doors. "I'm looking for my . . ."

He stopped when he saw Sara sitting inside while a tech applied a bandage to her elbows, an icepack held to her mouth.

She spotted him and dropped the icepack, then leaped into his arms, burying her face in his chest. "Oh, Matt...Chris is . . ."

He took a deep breath and let the adrenaline dissipate through his body, put his hands around her waist, and pulled her against him. "I know. He's on his way to the hospital. Still holding on." He held her even tighter. His throat clenched as he shuddered out a long breath. "Thank God you're alright. What were you doing here?"

Face smeared with soot and dirt, her lower lip swollen, she squeezed her eyes shut, her voice a warm wisp against his cheek. "I hadn't visited Eden after the death of her parents. I stopped by to offer my condolences. I...I think she and the boys . . ."

Matt shook his head. "The twins are safe. They were at school."

"Then, Eden . . ." Her gaze clouded.

He nodded. "I think so. She was apparently inside."

His cell phone signaled a text message. He pulled it from his pocket, read the message, and returned it to his pocket.

Sara pulled back and gazed up at him. "Why would someone shoot at me from her condo?"

He cupped her face in his hands and felt his jaw muscles tighten. "Shots were fired at you?"

She nodded, and he felt a tremor run through her body. "Just before the building exploded. That's the shot that hit Chris."

"I'm sure it was James Bauer, but we won't know for sure until all the pieces are put together. If you're up to it, you need to give Davis or Turner a statement of what happened." He paused. "We can postpone it if you like. I want to check on Chris. Feel like going with me?"

She nodded. "I'll talk to Miles later. I couldn't bear waiting any place else for news on Chris. Does his wife know?"

"Turner just texted me. Cole and Stein are picking her

up. Both her boys are in school, and we don't want her driving under that kind of stress."

Twin Falls Memorial Hospital
Twin Falls, Texas

The emergency waiting room was crowded with the entire detective staff, the Hunter family, and friends. The media arrived right behind Matt and Sara, but he stopped them in the parking lot.

The mayor pushed through the reporters and photographers, never one to miss a photo op.

Matt held up his hand. "You'll have to wait here. The detective's family needs privacy." He tilted his head at Mayor Hall. "The mayor will give you an update when there's any news."

Hall smiled and stepped in front of the cameras, and Matt went inside.

In the ER waiting room, Doris Hunter, Chris's wife, sat on a turquoise leather sofa, Miles Davis beside her, holding her hand. When Matt and Sara entered, Doris stood and gave him a tight hug, her eyes red, face muscles taut, holding it together as thousands of law enforcement wives had done forever. He returned the embrace and introduced Sara, then went to the desk and asked the receptionist to find Gaye Bishop, head nurse in ER. If there was any news, Gaye would know. She came from a family of police officers and made sure any LEOs were taken care of when they passed through her ER.

It took the receptionist a few minutes to find Gaye, but soon she stood in front of him, her face strained with concern. He didn't have to ask. She knew what he wanted. "Chris is still in surgery. Last I heard, he was stable. The surgeon will contact Chris's wife as soon as he's finished."

Matt thanked her and returned to the waiting room.

Doug Anderson entered behind him, bypassing the mayor who was shaking hands with Doris, and proceeded to join Matt in a nearby alcove.

"Any news?" Doug asked.

"Not yet. He's still in surgery."

"Do they think he's going to make it?"

Matt gave a solemn shake of his head. "We haven't spoken to a doctor. We're just waiting and praying."

<<>>

Doug Anderson stepped away, stopped, and then turned back. "I have to go back to the office. Call me when you hear anything. And, Matt," he paused, "forget about Luther Donnell. He withdrew his application."

Matt raised an eyebrow.

Doug could feel the pink flush creeping from his collar and over his face. "He took a job in the governor's office."

"Doing what?" Matt asked.

"I didn't ask. He didn't say. And if you send me your resignation, I'll tear it up."

Doug left through the emergency room entrance and plodded to his car. He opened the door and slid behind the wheel, but didn't start the engine. A short rap on the passenger side window startled him.

He glanced over to see Mayor Terrence Hall—the man responsible for Doug almost losing the best police chief in the state. And there was no guarantee Matt wouldn't leave anyway.

Hall gave a wave, walked to his car, and drove away.

Doug had known Matt Foley for ten years. He was an outstanding law enforcement officer, and even finer human being. He'd had a stellar military career. Eight years in the U.S. Army 75th Brigade, a Ranger special mission unit sharpshooter. He'd done two tours of duty, one in Iraq, the last in Afghanistan.

And because of Terry Hall, Doug had decided to serve his own selfish interest, rather than listen to Matt's sound counsel of why Luther Donnell was a bad fit for Internal Affairs. He'd tried to force Matt's hand. It only took one meeting with Donnell to know Matt's analysis had been spot-on. The man was a clown.

Hall had forced Doug to make a choice between doing the right thing and the happiness of his youngest daughter.

Allie's dream had always been to attend the same college her parents and her siblings had gone to. She wasn't a scholar, but Doug had thought her grades were good enough for her to be accepted. Somehow, Hall had learned Allie had applied to the college.

And, like Satan in the Garden of Eden, Hall came to him one afternoon and offered to guarantee Allie's admittance to the college, provided Doug would ensure Donnell was hired in the IAD spot. He alluded to having inside connections at the university that could assure her admittance or denial. Doug capitulated.

He gazed through the windshield at the sky filled with millions of stars, and knew he deserved no credit for Hall's inept brother-in-law withdrawing his resume. Doug had been granted a reprieve he didn't deserve, and it had cost him the respect of a man he admired. Turning the key in the ignition, Doug made himself a promise.

He would do everything in his power to see that Hall was not re-elected next term.

<<>>

While Matt was gone, Sara called her aunt and asked if she would have Don pick up the children at school. Her aunt assured her it wouldn't be a problem. With the children taken care of, Sara slipped into the restroom to wash her face and try to straighten her hair. Her purse had been in the Jeep, and was probably now melted to the chassis.

She gazed at her reflection in the mirror and groaned. Her hair was mussed and littered with cement dust, her face streaked with dark smudges, and her bottom lip looked as though she was pouting.

There were no face cloths, so she pulled one of the brown paper towels from the dispenser. The texture felt like sandpaper and left her face red and raw, but it did the job.

When she returned to her seat, Matt was back, an expression on his face somewhere between concern and amazement. "Is there news about Chris?"

He gave his head a shake as if to clear it. "No, not yet."

"Then what?"

He nodded toward the entrance. "Doug just told me my Luther Donnell problem had gone away."

"Did he say why?" she asked.

His lips tilted upward. "Nope, just that Donnell had taken another job." The corner of his mouth gave an almost indiscernible twitch. "But I have a good idea who might have brokered the deal."

Chris Hunter was in surgery for four hours, and, as the time passed, the number of people in the waiting room diminished. Outside, the media was the first to leave. They had deadlines to meet. And Doug and Mayor Hall had both left earlier. Finally, only Matt, Sara, the three detectives, and the immediate family remained.

When the doctor came through the double doors, they all stood. He walked over to Doris, but spoke in a voice that all could here. "Your husband is well. He's resting in recovery. The damage was extensive, but he won't lose the use of his arm. However, he will need therapy for a long time. He's still under sedation and will be for a while. You can visit him after he's moved to ICU."

Relief flooded over Sara. She couldn't have lived with the reality that the funny, sweet man had died saving her life.

She leaned close to Matt, drawing strength from his nearness. "If you're ready, I think I would like to go home now."

The Foley Residence
Twin Falls, Texas

Matt took Sara's hand as they stepped into the kitchen.

"Sorry about your Jeep, Matt," she said, her voice just above a whisper.

"Nothing for you to be sorry about. It wasn't your fault. Besides, it's covered by insurance."

He understood she was making conversation to hold

back the day's trauma. He wanted to hold her, to erase all that she had experienced today. "Come; let's get you in the shower to get rid of the dust and smoke. You'll feel better."

Like an exhausted child, she let him lead her upstairs, and stood in the bathroom while he turned on the shower and set the temperature.

As she showered, he made a fire in the hearth and turned back the covers, then returned to the kitchen and made her a cup of chamomile tea with honey. He went back into the bedroom and found her already in bed, with Rowdy's head on her shoulder. The Yorkie watched her with big, sad eyes, as though he understood her exhaustion and pain.

She winced when the cup touched her tender lip, but Matt coaxed her to drink the tea, and then gave her a melatonin tablet to help her sleep.

He sat by her bedside, watching her troubled slumber, and asked himself if there was anything he could have done to spare her the horror of what happened today. He could have warned her to stay away from Eden Russell, but that would have been premature. Finally, he accepted he could never cover all contingencies. He climbed into bed and thanked God for His mercy in keeping her safe.

CHAPTER 23

The Foley Residence
Twin Falls, Texas

A week later, things were getting back to normal, and Sara invited Agnes Welford back to meet Matt and the children. The attorney, whose name Aggie provided, gave the nurse a raving reference. As an extra precaution, Sara had saved the coffee cup the nurse drank from on the first interview, and had Matt run her prints through police files. They came back clean. With her children, she couldn't afford to take chances.

Matt had gone a step farther and checked her references at hospitals she worked for in the past. They only had nice things to say about her.

He had no problem with a live-in housekeeper, as long as Sara was comfortable with the arrangement. He'd pointed out, however, that, if Aggie didn't work out, it would be more difficult to let her go.

That was an issue Sara had considered, but finally decided other people dealt with that all the time and she could handle it if the problem arose.

When the doorbell rang, Sara invited her in and led the petite woman into the game room. She wanted to keep the meeting as informal as possible. Sara introduced Matt and the children. Poppy and Danny rose from playing with Rowdy to meet her.

When Matt shook her hand, Aggie looked up at him and grinned. "I'll bet all the women at the station are in love with you."

Matt blushed and looked a little uncomfortable. "If so, I assure you they're keeping it to themselves."

Sara laughed. "Only about two thirds swoon when he passes; the older ones try to mother him."

Aggie walked over to the little girl. "Now, let me guess, you must be Danny, and the handsome lad standing next to you would be Poppy. Right?"

Poppy giggled. "Noooo, I'm Poppy and he's Danny."

"Well, I'm glad you straightened me out," Aggie said. "Do you have any questions for me?"

Never the bashful type, Poppy asked, "Can you cook? I can. Miss B'trice teached me how."

"Taught me," Sara corrected.

"I'm probably going to need your help." Aggie knelt down to the little girl's eye level. "You see, I've been cooking for sick people and, to be honest, it didn't taste very good."

"I can show you how." Poppy nodded her head enthusiastically. "Want to see the kitchen?"

Sara placed her hand on Poppy's blonde curls. "Let's wait until Aggie starts to work, then you can show her around. How would you like some coffee, Aggie?"

"Sounds good to me," Aggie said.

<<>>

Sara left to make the coffee, and Matt took the chair next to Aggie. "Where did you grow up, Aggie?"

She laughed. "I was a preacher's kid, so I lived a lot of places before we settled in Tyler. Born and raised in East Texas. My dad was a full time preacher and rose farmer. The farm was beautiful and smelled wonderful when they were in bloom, but you couldn't eat them. Like other businesses, a recession kills the need for most folks to buy flowers and, of course, preaching didn't pay that well either. There were some hard times."

Matt nodded, his eyes full of understanding, and she wondered if he'd had a rough childhood.

She'd always felt those hard times made her stronger, made her appreciate things more. Her theory on what was wrong with kids today was they had too many toys and too much time on their hands. For sure, you didn't have the problem with gangs back when she was growing up.

"I remember a deacon in the church where my dad preached. Before he gave my father his monthly check, he would critique dad's sermons for the whole month. I always thought that was humiliating for my dad, but, you know, he took it and never complained. My dad was the sweetest, most humble man I ever knew."

Sara returned with a tray and cups. She filled them and handed the first one to Aggie. She was impressed that Sara remembered how she took it.

"My, just listen to me run on," she winked at Matt. "I'll bet you're great at interrogating crooks."

Sara took a seat by her husband and curled her feet up on the sofa. "So what do you think, Aggie? You ready to go to work?"

"Give me a week to get things wound up at the judge's place and I'm all yours."

The night air was cold as Aggie made her way to her Honda Civic and headed home. With her eye on the speed limit, Aggie felt good about the decision she'd made to work for the Foleys. They were down to earth, no airs about them.

She was good at reading people, and hoped she wouldn't be disappointed. People didn't always show their true character to strangers. But she liked Sara and Matt and, from news reports, they'd been through a rough spot recently. In her nursing career, Aggie had witnessed strong people in tough times, and their inner strength, born of faith and courage, always saw them through. A truth she'd learned at her father's knee and had been reinforced throughout her personal and professional life.

Twin Falls Police Station
Twin Falls, Texas

Matt prepared for his final wrap-up meeting with the detectives on the Davenport and Russell murders. His cell phone rang before he made it to his office door.

Caller ID flashed Blain Stanton's name. "Are you and Sara okay? The media reports had us worried, but I knew you'd call if there was any real trouble."

Matt closed his office door behind him and ascended the stairway leading to the detective bureau. "Great. Things are back to normal, thank heavens."

"Glad to hear it. I think you need to find a safer

occupation. I won't even ask what Sara was doing there. I think she's a magnet for trouble."

Matt laughed. "I wondered about that myself. But the job isn't always this bad."

"Don't kid me. I'm keeping score."

Matt could almost see the big grin on Blain's face through the phone. "Hey, I understand you lost an opportunity to employ an outstanding officer. True or false?"

"You wouldn't know anything about Luther Donnell finding a job in the governor's office, would you?"

"Rumor has it that he has a job with a big title, no responsibility, and is primarily a gofer." Blain roared with laughter, and disconnected.

Matt shook his head and couldn't keep the smile off his face. Having a guardian angel sometimes came in handy. But he still had issues to resolve with Doug Anderson.

When he entered the bureau, the three detectives were already seated around the conference table. Chris's smiling face was sorely missed.

"Okay, guys, let's get this case report on its way to all the need-to-know folks. Stop me if I say something you don't understand or you think is wrong.

"Jim Bauer was the actual shooter in both the Davenport and Russell murders. Ballistics confirmed the gun and rifle used were his, and bore his fingerprints. He set the fire in his mother's barn and rigged the explosion in Eden's condo, apparently a murder/suicide plot.

"I'm confident he fired the shot that hit Chris, although we have no proof since the rifle was destroyed."

Davis nodded. "Chris's evacuation of the homes in that area saved a lot of lives. He deserves a medal."

"You're absolutely right, Miles. And Doug Anderson is preparing to do just that, as we speak," Matt laughed. "If I know Mayor Hall, he'll claim it was his idea. Chris just carried out his instructions."

"There are still a lot of unanswered questions. With Eden dead, there is no way to determine how deeply she was involved," Turner said.

Matt shrugged, feeling more relaxed than he'd felt since returning from his honeymoon. "Had she survived, she would have been charged as an accessory. But it's a moot point now. Only she would have benefited from the murders. Stephen Russell believes he was supposed to be killed the night his parents were murdered. The emergency call from his patient may have saved his life. As for Bauer, he had no reason to kill any of those people, although I think he probably enjoyed it. He was a warped individual."

"Did we ever find a reason for the empty briefcase?" Cole asked.

Davis shook his head. "It's only conjecture on my part, but I think Bauer destroyed the attaché contents to get rid of the custody papers and maybe Art's notes of what his testimony would be. Perhaps Bauer didn't want to leave any evidence that might point to Eden."

Turner shook her head. "You know, I don't understand how someone like Eden Russell can fall that far. She had looks, money, intelligence, yet she did something so monumentally stupid it defies description. How could she think for a minute she could get away with four murders? I'm glad her boys have a stable life with their father."

"That is the only good thing to come out of this mess," Matt said. "However, you left out one item in your list of her attributes," Matt said, and passed out copies of the report to each of them. "Arrogance, or, as it's also known, pride. It's the first deadly sin."

Christensen Memorial Park
Twin Falls, Texas

Wind flapped and tugged at Matt's overcoat as he and the small group of mourners trekked through a gusty, fine mist to the gravesite. Except for Matt, and the lone media crew, there were only five people in attendance at the double funeral for Eden Russell and James Bauer, Judith Bittermann, Claire and Taylor Davenport, Winston Seymour, and Amy Bauer.

The family opted for a graveside service, and the pastor's words were short and simple. He could hardly extoll the virtues of the deceased.

The minister recited the familiar words of The Lord's Prayer, "Our Father, which art in Heaven, hallowed be Thy name . . ." and the caskets was lowered into the ground.

Matt met Judith under the covered awning provided by the memorial park. He sat down beside her, took her hands in his, and said the only thing he could say. There were no words suited to this occasion. "I'm sorry, Judge."

She patted his hand. "You know, it's inconceivable that the child I watched grow up is largely responsible for such heinous acts. I hope my sister didn't realize before she died that Eden sent Jim there to kill her and Art. It would have been worse for her than dying. They gave that girl everything she ever wanted, loved her unconditionally, despite her treatment of them. It's just so...so wrong."

"You never suspected she might be involved?" he asked.

It seemed she started to shake her head, but then stopped. Her words came out as a gentle exhale. "Yes, I think we all suspected, but it was so extraordinary. We couldn't believe it and ignored our intuition, even knowing that Eden's reactions to everyday events were always a little off. Anytime anyone offended her, no matter how trivial, she never forgave them. I should have told you that early on. Perhaps we might have avoided how this tragedy ended."

"It's no good blaming yourself, Judge. Hindsight is a wonderful thing. We can learn from it, but it doesn't change the past. Unfortunately, there are no crystal balls around when we need one."

She turned her head away, and Matt understood she tried to hide the tears welling in her eyes.

Taylor walked over and put her arms around the judge. Judith wiped her eyes and smiled. "Matt, Taylor is coming to live with me. She felt she would be more comfortable in my home than with Claire, and I love having her. She'll be a breath of fresh air in my life."

The young girl's eyes were clear, but sad, as she gazed up at Matt, and she sounded much too old for her twelve years. "Thank you, Chief. You did what you promised. You caught my parents' killer."

"I don't deserve the credit, Taylor. More people than you could possibly know were involved in bringing Jim Bauer and your sister to justice. And one good man was seriously injured."

"Taylor and I sent him flowers and a card. I'm so sorry he got caught up in this tragedy," Judith said, and smiled. "Taylor convinced me that our lives would not be complete without Sugar, and the Connellys graciously agreed to give her back."

Matt gave Judith and Taylor one last hug, pushed his hands into his overcoat pockets, and strolled back down the hill to his car.

So much pain. Such a senseless waste.

He looked up at the overcast sky, but he didn't ask 'Why, Lord'. He knew there was no answer.

CHAPTER 24

Twin Falls Memorial Hospital
Twin Falls, Texas

A week later, Matt held Sara's hand as they entered Chris Hunter's room on the hospital's fourth floor. The small area was filled with flowers of every description, as well as Matt's other three detectives.

Chris sat up in bed, his left shoulder heavily bandaged, holding court with a huge grin on his face.

Sara crossed the room, leaned over, and kissed his cheek. "I owe you one, Chris."

Chris beamed up at her. "You might need to do that again, my shoulder hurts."

Sara came back and kissed both cheeks.

The wounded detective put his one good arm behind his head and heaved a deep sigh.

"Have you seen the newspapers?" Matt asked.

Chris grinned. "No, I've been busy fighting off the attention of all the nurses."

Matt passed Chris the newspaper he'd brought with him. "You made the front page. You're a bona fide hero, my friend."

Cole Allen stood against the wall near the bedside, and chuckled. "Mrs. Foley, less you think Chris was trying to save your life, I must tell you he knocked you down to take the pie away from you."

Davis chortled and bumped knuckles with Cole.

"Go ahead and yuk it up you two," Chris gloated. "I'm getting kisses from beautiful women. And while you guys are dodging bullets and chasing killers, I'm going to be soaking up rays on a Florida beach."

Lucy Turner winked at Chris. "That's right. These guys are just jealous of your good looks and sparkling personality, not to mention all the attention you're getting."

Chris nodded and his brow creased in twin furrows.

"Yeah, but it was a waste of a beautiful pie."

Sara laughed, "I'll bring you as many pies as you can eat, Chris."

Davis walked over and took Chris's hand with a firm squeeze, his face suddenly solemn. "Guess we'd better get back on the desk, keep the city safe." He cleared his throat. "It will be a lot harder without you, bud."

The three detectives filed out, with handshakes and a hug from Lucy Turner.

Matt stood beside the bed. "You know, Chris, you don't have to retire. I'll find a spot for you. I'm looking for someone in IAD, as one of the guys is leaving in April. You'd be a big asset there."

"I appreciate that, Chief, but the doc says this arm is only gonna be about fifty percent. I've always heard you know when it's time to pull the pin. And, for me, it's time." He laughed. "I can get a tan while I turn my wife's hair white and harass my kids until they move away for good. But, if I get bored after a few months, I reserve the right to change my mind."

"Any time you're ready, just let me know. And, Chris, if you ever need anything, anything at all, you know where to find me. I owe you a debt I can never repay."

Twin Falls Police Station
Twin Falls, Texas

Matt glanced up when Ben Stein rapped on the open door of Matt's office. "You wanted to see me, Chief?"

"I did. Come in and have a seat." Matt reached for a folder on his desk while Stein settled into a chair. "You know Chris Hunter isn't coming back, right?"

Ben nodded. "He's going to be missed."

"That he will," Matt said. "His retirement leaves us short one detective. Would you be interested in the position?"

Stein's eyes widened. "Yes, of course I would. I didn't think you would consider me because of Lucy . . . uh . . . we . . ."

Matt held up his hand. "I know, and I gave it a lot of thought before I decided to offer you the job. I finally decided that you and Lucy were adult enough to handle it. So don't make me regret my decision. You will be partnered with Davis. He recommended you for the job."

"I'm flattered, Chief. I don't know what to say except, when do I start?"

"Next Monday," Matt said and passed him a gold shield. "This belonged to Chris. Make him proud."

Stein rose and shook Matt's hand. The new detective stopped in the doorway. "I will. Thanks, Chief, and you won't be sorry."

The Foley Residence
Twin Falls, Texas

Matt poured a cup of coffee and stepped out on the deck to join Sara and the kids. Bright rays of sunlight met him as he joined his family, who were taking full advantage of the early-spring-like day.

Sara sat in a recliner, reading the small brown book in her hand.

"Good novel?" he asked.

She looked up and turned the front cover towards him, revealing the title, *The Hiding Place* by Corrie ten Boom. "My favorite book on faith and miracles. I try to read it once a year to remind myself that, no matter how bad things get, and whether we feel His presence or not, God is always there."

He leaned back in the chair, wanting to capture this day in his thoughts, reminding himself he had everything in life he'd ever wanted, a woman he adored, who could match him in strength of character and force of purpose. He loved her humor and intelligence, her warmth, her passion for life and those she loved. She was the second chance he didn't deserve.

He had been blessed with children who were smart and, above all, kind, despite the trials they'd endured.

It frightened him a little. But he wasn't looking for things to worry about. God wanted him to live by faith, and he was good with that.

The doorbell rang, and he rose reluctantly, not wanting to have this rare family day interrupted. "I'll get it."

A solemn-faced man stood in the doorway. He was medium height, with light brown hair worn a little long. Steel rimmed glasses covered his brown eyes. "Chief Foley, my name is John Landers."

It took Matt a moment to put the name together with a memory, and then he knew why the man had come.

"Come in, Mr. Landers. I've got coffee in the kitchen."

"Please, call me 'John'."

"Okay, John. I'm Matt."

Matt handed him a cup of coffee, and they stood in the kitchen and watched Matt's family through the window.

And Matt recounted for John Landers the last thirty minutes of his wife's life.

THANKS . . .

Thank you so much for reading **Downfall.** I hope you enjoyed the experience. My objective is to write suspense novels that will engage your mind in the lives of the characters and solving the mystery. I write novels that I would like to read, absent of violence, brutality, and erotic content, but with shining characters, settings, and exciting plots readers can't put down. It is my sincere hope that my reader come away feeling delighted with the reading experience—honoring God in the process.

If you enjoyed this novel please do me a favor and go to Amazon and leave an honest review at: http://www.amazon.com/dp/B00YG5J9AW

Indie authors depend on reviews and word-of-mouth advertising.

I'd also like to ask that if you find any errors or typos that you contact me directly at my email address: www.vbhtenery@aol.com

Even though all my novels are edited by others, we are all only human and mistakes occur. It is my goal to produce the most perfect product possible.

I love to hear from my readers and have made many friends from the comments on my website and through emails. Please feel free to contact me at any of the following:

Website: www.vbtenery.com
Twitter: www.twitter.com
FB Author Page: www.facebook.com/vbtenery
eMail Address: vbhtenery@aol.com

Newsletter Invitation

My Thank You gift to you . . . a Free copy of

Broken Vows

Prequel to the Matt Foley Series

Available only to my newsletter subscribers. Get your free copy when you sign up at:

www.vbtenery.com

BROKEN VOWS
A Prequel to
The Matt Foley/Sara Bradford Series
A Novella

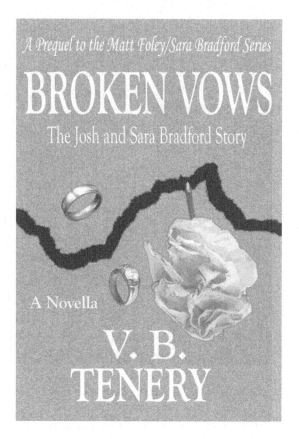

Attorney Josh Bradford can resist anything but temptation. A serial
philanderer who, despite his failings, is still deeply in love with his wife.

He has vowed to change, but when his most recent lover is murdered, he and Sara find themselves at the top of the authorities list of suspects.

The murder is his wakeup call . . . his only hope . . . that the police will find the killer before his marriage and career are shattered beyond repair.

http://www.amazon.co.uk/gp/product/B01557SABS

WORKS OF DARKNESS
Book 1 in the Matt Foley/Sara Bradford Series

Some secrets just won't stay buried.

A construction site provides a horrific discovery when a worker uncovers the skeleton of a small child wrapped in a sleeping bag. Police Chief Matt Foley soon links the murder to another cold case, the hit-and-run death of Attorney Josh Bradford.

The long-suppressed memory of the young victim's childhood friend, Sara Bradford may hold the key to both crimes. But Matt has mixed emotions about Sara—his prime suspect in her husband's murder.

Matt soon discovers the twenty-five-year-old mystery has the power to stretch across decades to kill again.

Purchase WORKS OF DARKNESS on Amazon

THEN THERE WERE NONE
Matt Foley/Sara Bradford Series
Book 2

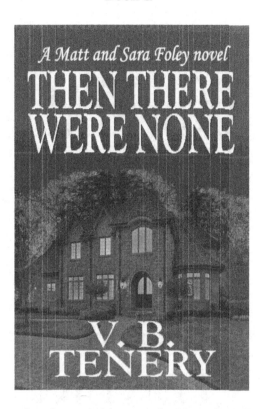

Mass murder doesn't happen in Matt Foley's town . . . it doesn't happen to his friends. Someone is going to pay.

Disturbing crime scenes are nothing new to the Twin Falls Police Chief. But this one is different. The victims are friends. In their Tudor mansion just inside the city limits, a family is dead—husband, wife, two kids, and the family cook.

The killer made one mistake. He left a survivor.

The husband is one of the big three in the microchip industry. The family lived a quiet modest life. It doesn't make sense.

Until . . .

Purchase <u>THEN THERE WERE NONE</u> on <u>Amazon</u>

DOWNFALL
Matt Foley/Sara Bradford Series
Book 3

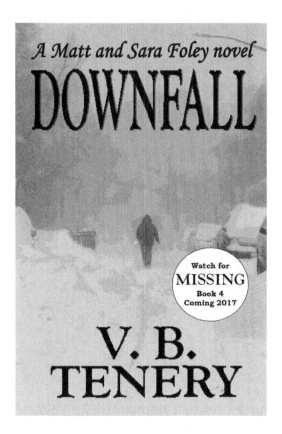

A Matt and Sara Foley novel

DOWNFALL

Watch for
MISSING
Book 4
Coming 2017

V. B.
TENERY

Police Chief Matt Foley has a new bride and the most complex case of his career.

A prominent couple prepares to retire, when an assassin's bullets retires them permanently. And he doesn't stop there.

As the investigation pushes forward, layers of deceit, greed, and bitterness are peeled away, and two families, connected by marriage and murder, face the exposure of their darkest secrets. It's just another case until Matt finds his wife caught in the killer's crosshairs.

http://www.amazon.com/dp/B00YG5J9AW

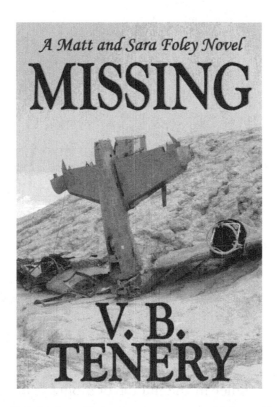

Police Chief Matt Foley's secure world is collapsing on multiple fronts.

A shadowy figure from his past seeks vengeance in its simplest form. A life for a perceived injustice.

The ex-convict-father of Matt's children has re-emerged into their lives.

While Matt's life hangs in the balance, Sara Foley is missing on the wrong side of the Mexican border in the clutches of a Mexican drug lord.

Their restoration lies in the hands of an old nemesis.

Coming Winter 2017

DEATHWATCH
WWII Historical Suspense

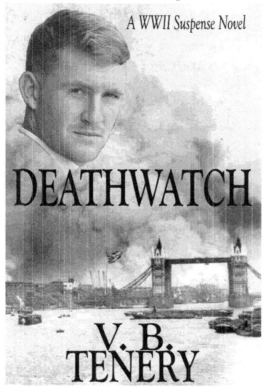

Finding a killer in the middle of a blitz is murder.

When a cryptanalyst in Britain's top-secret Code and Cypher School is murdered, alarms sound in the highest echelons of Parliament. Was it merely a lover's quarrel that ended her life, or was she killed after telling the Germans everything they wanted to know? That's what MI6 Agent, Commander Grey Hamilton must find out.

He is joined in the chase by an old university friend from Scotland Yard, and a young American genius who has been singled out by the killer as his next victim.

As the Luftwaffe escalates its reign of terror over London, the unlikely team dodges bombs while searchingthe Underground and London docks knowing failure is not an option. The lives of English soldiers and perhaps the fate of the British Empire itself, is at stake.

http://www.amazon.com/dp/B01BVXDXAI

Against the Odds
A Novel

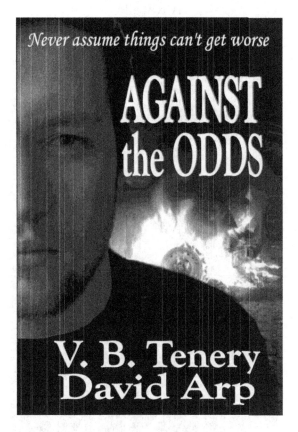

It was the mother of all bad days.

The date, September 11, 2012. The place, Benghazi, Libya.

While a brave band of warrior's fight for their lives in the consulate and CIA annex, outside, a Mossad Agent, a missionary, and a Mississippi giant fight a different battle.

Caught between terrorist and an enraged Russian arms dealer, they must complete the mission and manage to stay alive until they can escape or the cavalry arrives.

Never assume things can't get worse.

http://www.amazon.com/dp/B01N0W687Q

Angels Among Us
Matt Foley Series
A Novella

    In the season of Love, Peace and Joy, a chance meeting with a young woman in a supermarket sets Detective Cole Allen on an urgent quest to save the lives of three young women.
    It will take the combined skill and dedication of the Twin Falls Homicide Bureau, and a helping hand from God, to locate and end the nightmare of the helpless victims.

http://www.amazon.com/dp/B074T97D96

Last Chance
The Matt Foley Series
A Novella

LAST CHANCE

V. B. TENERY

Chance Crawford is back in Afghanistan.

A place he swore never return to.

No longer the team leader of a Marine Recon unit. He's now a CIA agent, searching the mountains of the Hindu Kush for a Taliban chief who wants to defect.

While tracking his objective he encounters two children in need of a protector. And he's the only one available.

It's mission impossible but he has never run from trouble.

Coming Winter 2017

DEAD RINGER
From the Pelican Book Group

Mercy Lawrence is terrified.

Bermuda airport facial recognition software has identified her as missing runway star, Traci Wallace. Despite Mercy's protests, Traci's husband, ex-CIA agent Thomas Wallace, is convinced Mercy is the mother of his ill six-year-old son. With only his son's welfare in mind, he abducts Mercy and takes her to a private island to care for the boy.

But Mercy soon discovers there are men much more dangerous than a father desperate to save his son. Her doppelganger has made deadly enemies—a relentless team of killers who now want her dead.

When Thomas is lured into a covert mission to rescue a CIA asset and uncover a government mole, Mercy is left isolated and alone—and Thomas finds himself stranded on foreign soil with a compromised mission and a wounded agent. Fighting against a rogue nation's timetable for launching a nuclear strike, he must escape Saudi Arabia alive and rescue Mercy and his son before assassins finish the job they started.

Purchase <u>DEAD RINGER on Amazon</u>

THE WATCHMAN
From the Pelican Book Group

Gifted with supernatural abilities, he'll protect the innocent and avenge the abused, he is . . .   The Watchman

When Detective Noah Adams meets the abused son of a powerful judge, he knows he must intervene, and fast. The violence is escalating, and even Noah's special gifts may not prevent the unthinkable from happening.

Relentlessly pursuing two cases, Noah receives a chilling message: Cody's deranged father has taken his son and it's up to Noah to follow the judge's twisted trail to find the boy before it's too late.

Corrupt city officials, a missing socialite, an attempted murder, and a rescue in the middle of a blizzard entangle Noah in the most complicated case of his career. A case that will mean his ultimate redemption or will take him back into the dark history that haunts him.

Purchase THE WATCHMAN on Amazon

A Matt Foley/Sara Bradford novel

WORKS OF DARKNESS

V. B. TENERY

Turn the page to read an excerpt of the first four chapters of: WORKS OF DARKNESS.

"The night is far spent; the day is at hand, let us therefore *cast off the works of darkness."*
—Romans 13:12

Chapter 1

Bay Harbor Development

Construction foreman Jason Watts stood by his truck and gazed across the job site. Heavy equipment cleared the prime lakefront property of stumps and rubble as machinery shifted sand from one place to another. The smell of damp earth permeated the air around him. An early morning chill crept under his coat collar making him shiver.

Across the way, his backhoe operator scooped up a load of sand, lowered the bucket, and stopped the machine. Isaac Hummingbird, the Native American operator, stepped off the front-end loader and tossed something to the ground.

"Hey, Jason, you'd better come take a look at this." Hummingbird stood next to what looked like a large, white trash bag.

Jason shoved his clipboard onto the truck's bench seat and trotted across the field, the dirt still sticky from the recent storms. He noted the heavy, dark clouds hovering overhead as he crossed the field. Fierce October rain that pummeled the area had thrown him behind schedule, forcing him to play catch-up. Big time. The moneymen who financed the project were popping Xanax by the handful.

Those clouds would dump any minute, and he'd have to send the crew home. Again. And lose another day's work. "Whatcha got, Hummingbird?"

The machine operator didn't reply. He stepped back and pointed at the open bag, the side folded back. It was the tattered remnants of a sleeping bag. Cold sweat broke out on Jason's brow, and a tight knot clutched at his gut, his breath shallow as he gazed into the opening.

1

Inside, were the skeletal remains of a child, the bones white and clean.

Pink overalls hung on the shoulder bones of the wasted frame. Tennis shoes had slipped from the feet. A small birthstone ring hung loosely on the right ring finger.

Jason rubbed his hand over his face and drew in a lung full of moist air. He removed a cell phone from his jacket pocket. "I'll call it in."

Home of Police Chief Matt Foley

After finishing an eighteen-hour shift Wednesday, Matt Foley hadn't made it to bed until after two o'clock. He'd finished a full day at the station and then spent the evening at a political dinner with his boss.

Matt's Yorkie awakened him at six o'clock before the alarm went off. Rowdy's whines predicted storms better than *The Weather Channel* and he stuck to Matt's side like a burr under a saddle until the sky cleared.

The dog shivered and tried to nose his way under the covers. Matt lifted the blanket and allowed the frightened animal to snuggle close. Otherwise, he would keep whining and neither of them would sleep. With luck, they'd both catch a few winks before it was time to get up.

Half-awake, Matt reached over to touch Mary, to hold her close. But the sheet was cold and empty, her pillow undisturbed. He closed his eyes and turned over, refusing to revisit the dark memories.

In his state between drowsiness and slumber, the phone rang.

He waited. The caller might give up and the message go to voicemail. Didn't happen.

Whoever it was kept redialing.

Fumbling for the bedside lamp switch, he snatched up the phone, and pressed it to his ear. "Foley."

Static filled the line before Sheriff Joe Wilson's voice came through, strong and clear. He chuckled. "It's me, Matt. Did I wake you?"

His friend was persistent, if nothing else. "No, I always let the phone ring fifteen times before I answer.

I'm awake now. What's up?"

The cell phone connection faded for a second before it came back. "Construction workers turned up the remains of a child at Bay Harbor. It's about a mile past the bridge on the reservoir road. You know the place?"

Matt tossed the cover back and slid his feet into slippers beside the bed. "What are you doing out there?"

Lightning filled the bedroom with flashbulb brightness, followed by a bass roll of thunder. Rowdy whimpered and moved closer.

"The foreman called me, but this one's your baby. It's within the city limits."

"Yeah, I know." Matt tossed the cover back and headed towards the shower. "I'll find it. Anything else?"

Joe paused for a second. "I spoke to the desk sergeant at the station. Your people are already rolling on it. Since it's a kid, I thought you might want to get involved."

"Thanks, Joe. I'm on my way."

"Wear your rain gear. It's coming down out here."

Matt rubbed his eyes and yawned. "Don't remind me."

"I'll keep the scene clear of tourists and media until you get your lazy behind out here."

In twenty minutes, Matt had showered, dressed, and headed downstairs, the Yorkie whimpering at his heels. Matt picked Rowdy up. "I hate to leave you here alone in a storm, buddy, but I can't take you with me."

Rowdy still in his arms, Matt snatched a Benadryl tablet from the medicine cabinet. He stopped in the kitchen, wrapped the pill in a hunk of bologna, and fed it to the dog. That would calm him until Stella came in at ten.

He didn't have time for a pet. Keeping Rowdy wasn't good for either of them. But Matt had never been able to consider finding the dog another home. They both missed Mary. The Yorkie was the only reason he came home at night.

Home had become an insidious adversary he didn't want to face. Everywhere he looked, there were reminders of his wife. Even Rowdy had been her dog.

Mary hadn't been a morning person, but she had insisted on seeing him off each morning. A cup of coffee in her hand, eyes half-closed, she'd leaned into him for a lingering goodbye kiss, saying, "Something to remind you to come home."

He recalled the first time he'd kissed her. They'd met at a political fund raiser and afterward he'd walked her to her car. She'd opened the door then turned to thank him. He'd leaned down and placed a light touch on her lips. A nice-meeting-you acknowledgement of his attraction to her. When he turned to walk away, she'd said, "Call me, Matt."

His job and his friend Joe had saved him. Kept him from falling into the abyss of grief. He couldn't think of his own sorrow while helping others with theirs.

Perhaps he should sell the house, find the dog a good home. But that was a decision for another time and another day.

He strapped on his nylon holster, stuffed the 9mm Glock in the pocket, then retrieved his slicker and rain boots from the closet. With the galoshes securely snapped over his shoes, he strode through the kitchen to the garage and climbed into his Expedition. He backed out of the driveway and headed towards the city. Coffee would have to wait until the Starbucks drive-through.

Bay Harbor Development

An ocean of gray mist greeted Matt's turn onto the aqueduct roadway. The downpour had stopped, but a steady drizzle persisted. In the distance, a flock of geese honked their way farther south for the winter. The fresh smell of wet pine needles drifted through the SUV's window.

Ahead, blue-and-white strobe bars of two sheriff's cruisers pierced the gloom. The vehicles formed a roadblock just before the bridge. Uniformed deputies, in canary-yellow ponchos, stood in the road and turned back a press van and onlookers. The grim set of the officers' jaws spoke volumes.

One of the deputies recognized Matt and waved him through the maze.

Matt made a right turn after the bridge. A mile down

the gravel road, he swung his SUV in beside the sheriff's vehicle. The mire clung to his rubber boots as he trudged up the muddy incline. At the top of the knoll, the land leveled out for fifty yards where construction trucks, sheriff's patrol cars, black and whites, and a coroner's van formed a half-moon around a muddy, yellow backhoe. The worksite lay about a hundred yards off the lake's beachfront.

Matt's detectives had beaten him to the crime scene. Lead detective, Miles Davis, waited near the mud-splattered machine. He stood six-feet tall, with a tight, muscular frame. No ordinary slicker for Miles. In his belted London Fog coat and Denzel Washington good looks, he appeared more at home on the cover of a men's fashion magazine than at a grubby crime scene.

Within the cordoned-off area, Davis motioned for the Crime Scene Unit Chief, Dale McCulloch, to join him. Dale's people set up two portable lights to dispel the morning gloom while he recorded video and pointed his assistant to locations where he wanted still shots. Camera flashes added sporadic brilliance to the gray morning.

To the untutored eye, a murder scene looked chaotic as people moved in different directions. But to a cop, the investigation progressed like a synchronized ballet, a symphony of precise motion. The company missed nothing. Cataloged everything.

Matt stood out of the way as the detective squatted like a catcher behind home plate beside the remains of a sleeping bag. Davis pulled the flaps aside and exposed the contents. He straightened and called the photographer to move in for close-ups.

Sheriff Joe Wilson caught Matt's eye and lifted a coffee cup in a salute. Joe's fullback physique and chiseled features lent authority to his slicker-covered uniform. At six-foot-three, he could never meld into the background, and the Stetson he wore negated Matt's one-inch height advantage.

Joe saluted Matt with the foam cup in his hand. "It's about time you showed up, Foley. I'm tired of standing in the rain, babysitting your crime scene."

"And a good morning to you, too," Matt said and

reached to shake hands.

Joe scowled at him.

County medical examiner, Lisa Martinez's petite frame looked smaller than usual standing next to the sheriff's bulk. The usual cigarette between her fingers was missing. Probably difficult to smoke in the rain. Her thick, dark hair was pulled into a ponytail under a navy blue cap—strikingly beautiful, despite the miserable weather.

"Hi, Lisa," Matt said. "Is he always this grumpy in the morning?"

She laughed. "Only when he misses his fiber."

Matt inclined his head towards the taped-off area. "Who found the body?"

Joe pointed to a group of men near the backhoe with his coffee cup. "One of the workers uncovered it before the rain started. He unzipped the bag—found the skeleton. I haven't talked to him. Detective Hunter is doing that now."

Matt followed his gaze to the crowd of construction workers. Detective Chris Hunter stood in their midst, notebook and pen in hand.

A hole yawned in front of the machine. Dale had stretched a tarp over the grave, but it hadn't stopped the storm's runoff from seeping into the hole.

Lisa left to join the CSU team, and Joe put his hand on Matt's shoulder. "So, how are you doing?"

Matt shrugged. They'd been friends too long for him to lie.

"That doesn't tell me much." Joe released the grip, giving Matt some space.

"I don't know what you're looking for, Joe. Why do you ask?"

"Because I've seen you in the valley, my friend."

Matt knew Joe cared. Really cared. But his questions brought back emotions Matt didn't want to deal with. Not here. Not now.

Matt hesitated. He needed to change the subject. "Lisa been out here long enough to reach any conclusions?"

"She arrived shortly after I did." Joe nodded towards the group headed their way. "You can ask her."

Lisa, Miles, and Dale caught up with them.

"Anything so far, Lisa?"

She gave a slight shrug. "The articles we found, as well as the skeletal remains, are those of a child. Can't be sure, but the age appears to be about six or seven. Two front teeth are missing, which is consistent with a child that age. I'll have to have DNA tests done, but based on the clothing, it's a girl."

"Any idea how long ago?" Matt asked.

She turned and scanned the gravesite. "A very long time. My best guess is twenty years or more. The skeleton is intact. The depth of the grave and the sleeping bag kept animals from scattering bones across the countryside."

Davis handed Matt a plastic bag that contained a small piece of red plaid fabric "We found this still inside the bag with the manufacturer's label attached. The plastic liner is intact. Lucky for us, vinyl doesn't decompose quickly. One reason landfills keep piling up."

"Any thoughts on cause of death?" Matt asked.

Lisa shook her head. "Too soon to make a prediction. I'll let you know more after I get back to the morgue."

"Anything to help with identification?"

"Relatives, if and when we find them, should be able to make a positive ID of the clothing and a birthstone ring that were inside the bag."

A construction worker near the backhoe skirted around the crime scene tape and stopped in front of Davis. He held out his hand. "Jason Watts, job foreman. We're packing up. How long you guys gonna hold on to the worksite?"

The detective turned to the grim-faced supervisor. "As long as it takes, but just this area. You guys can work the other sections, weather permitting." He shoved his rain hat off his brow. "Look, it's a moot point. You can't work today in this mess anyhow. We'll have to sift through every shovelful of dirt inside that hole before I can let you guys back in."

Watts punched his hands into his pockets. "The developer will not be happy. We're working on a tight schedule."

"I understand," Davis said. "Nevertheless, I have to

secure the scene, big and messy as it is. Homicide 101."

The man shook his head and turned to leave.

Matt stopped him. "Those buildings over there, are they part of the Bay Harbor project?"

Watts turned back and faced Matt. "Yeah, they'll come down though. The plan is to clear the lakefront property first. That's where we'll start putting up homes as soon as it's ready."

"Are they safe for us to go inside?"

"They're structurally sound," Watts said. "But they're a mess. A bunch of drunks and druggies have used them as crash pads."

"We'd like to take a look. Is that a problem?" Matt asked.

"Knock yourself out." He waved as if to say 'They don't pay me enough to do this job," and walked back to his crew.

Davis shook his head. "He thinks he has problems. Years of weather, people, and animals have erased any evidence there might have been here. You want to check out those buildings now?"

"Yeah. It shouldn't take long."

They trekked fifty yards uphill to the two structures. Davis moved up beside Matt as they stepped around the mud puddles that dotted the path. "What were they used for?"

"For more than fifty years, twenty acres of this property belonged to the Twin Falls First Baptist Church. They sold it when the developer bought all the land around them. These buildings were a retreat. The two-story structure was a housing complex for guests, and the one-story was used as a fellowship hall for meetings and meals."

Davis raised an eyebrow. "What's a retreat?"

Matt's gaze swept the property. The grass came up to his knees, most of the windows were broken, and a tree had fallen against the roof. "It was a place for people to get away from telephones and televisions, to reconnect with each other and God. As a kid, I used to come here for summer camp. It looked a lot different then."

The apartment's outer door clung to its upright position by a single loose hinge. Matt shoved the door open and kicked trash out of the way. Inside, a wide hallway ended at the stairs that led to the second floor. There were eight bedrooms on each side of the corridor, all with built-in bunk beds. The same upstairs, six bunks per room.

He and Davis checked the downstairs. The foreman was right. Empty wine bottles and drug paraphernalia were scattered on the bare wood floors.

Deep down, it squeezed Matt's gut to see the place in such disrepair. He'd spent some of the happiest times of his childhood here. At the last upstairs bedroom on the west side, he stepped to the window and stopped. "Davis, come look at this."

The detective's footsteps sounded in the hallway. "You find something, Chief?"

"Take a look."

Davis entered and stepped to the window. "What?"

Matt moved aside so Davis could get a closer look. "That's a perfect view of the burial site from here. Have Mac get some pictures. When we find out who our victim was, someone may have seen something. It's worth a shot."

After a baleful glance at the debris on the floor, Davis rubbed both hands down his face. "McCulloch will have to bag and catalog all this stuff just in case we get a suspect."

Matt grinned. "It's a long shot, but if it was easy..."

"I know, I know...anybody could do it."

Matt slapped his shoulder. "You're learning."

The CSU Chief met them as they came back down the hill. "We're outta here. The weather forecast looks better tomorrow, and it'll give this place some time to dry out. I'll bring some extra help from the lab, maybe some college kids I know, and we'll do a grid search. We'll be here by first light." He glanced at Davis. "You gonna leave people to guard the site until we return in the morning?"

"Yeah. Probably not necessary but I'd rather be safe. Mac, before you leave, I have a job you're gonna love." He led Mac towards the retreat.

Joe Wilson came forward as Matt reached the crime scene. The sheriff stopped, removed his hat, and smacked it against his leg before replacing it. "I'm heading out. I'll give you a hand with the authorities in surrounding areas. Ask them to check old files for missing children."

"Thanks. That'll save us some time."

"Tell that housekeeper of yours to throw an extra potato in the pot, and I'll come to dinner one night." He took two steps then turned back. "Even better, you can buy me a steak at Ruth's Chris."

Joe crunched a foam cup in his big fist and handed the trash to Hunter who had just joined them. "Here, hold this."

Hunter took it then stood there, glanced at the crumpled cup in his hand, and shook his head.

Matt grinned. "I'll give you a ring."

The lab techs began to pack away their gear, and Matt plodded back to his vehicle.

When he reached the truck, Lisa leaned against the door. She backed away with slow, easy grace. "I didn't expect to see you today, Matt. You haven't been around much lately."

"I've been busy. How's Paul?"

"He's fine." Her tone held a slight edge. "He asks about you often. The other kids were impressed the police chief came to watch his games."

Matt attended a few of Paul's little league games in the summer, but stopped when Lisa's attraction to him became apparent. Divorced from Paul's father only a few months, she was vulnerable. Not a situation he could handle right now. Besides, involvement with someone he worked with was asking for trouble.

His hand closed around the door handle. "Tell Paul I'll try to catch a game soon."

Davis shouted Lisa's name. She gave him a wave of acknowledgment and called back to Matt as she departed, "Better hurry. There's only one left on the fall schedule."

He started the ignition and watched Lisa walk away.

Joe came into view as Matt backed out. The sheriff stood beside his cruiser. His gaze followed Lisa Martinez with an expression Matt hadn't noticed before. Joe and Lisa? Funny, he'd never have put those two together.

Joe, laid back and easy going. Lisa, volatile as a firecracker. Another reason to avoid the woman. He didn't want to get in his old friend's way.

Matt pushed the hood of his slicker back and stared at the horizon. The deaths of children haunted his dreams long after the cases ended—ghosts that took up permanent residence.

Mist swallowed the scene behind him as he drove back across the aqueduct. The last sound that drifted through the open vent was a chorus of katydids—singing a requiem for a fallen child.

Chapter 2

Twin Falls Police Station

At ten o'clock, Matt turned onto the county road that passed the site from which the city had taken its name. The falls had lain dormant for fifty years after an upstream dam diverted the tributary that fed them. Embarrassed by the poor condition of the town's namesake, city leaders took action six months ago, starting a water re-circulation project now hidden behind a white construction fence. Friday, water would once again flow freely over the historic site. The unveiling would take place tomorrow, with a full-scale celebration banquet at the country club Saturday.

Matt merged with the traffic on I-75, the expressway that separated the haves from the have-nots in his town. The courthouse and police station sat in the older, less-affluent side of the city.

Traffic around the square brought him to a standstill. The somber scene at Bay Harbor claimed his thoughts, triggering a memory. When his life spiraled out of control two years ago, he'd spent many nights at the station unable to be alone at home with the memories. He'd brought Rowdy's bed to the office to keep him company. The job kept him focused—gave him a reason to keep going. Despair had led him to the cold case files.

Not many murders in his town. Domestic violence accounted for the four or five annual homicides. The old files had turned up two unsolved cases.

The most recent, Joshua Bradford. Killed four years ago in a hit-and-run accident. That happened on his watch. His only contribution to the cold case files. The second, a six-year-old girl who'd disappeared twenty-five years ago, long before he'd become chief.

He'd spent a lot of time playing "what if" with those cases, especially the Bradford accident. It wouldn't be ignored, like a fever blister he kept running his tongue over.

Matt hated loose ends. Even more, he hated that a killer still walked the streets.

He parked behind the station at his private entrance. Still early, the station looked almost empty. Administrative help had arrived but the day watch officers had already hit the streets.

In route to his office he stopped for a cup of coffee, and got lucky. Someone had brought in a box of donuts. He tossed a five dollar bill in the kitty and took two.

Seated at his desk, he ran a finger under his shirt collar, wiggled his tie loose, and sipped coffee while he waited for the computer to accept his password. After a moment, the unsolved case files flashed on the screen. He found the Pryor file in the database then strode down the corridor to pick up the casebook.

It took twenty minutes to find the notebook on a dusty, bottom shelf. He wiped the cover with his handkerchief and returned to his office. He put the book down on his desk, then checked his voicemail for messages. He was clear.

Matt flipped through the familiar pages. The book held all the notes from the original investigation, complete with the child's grade-school photo and a list of the witnesses interviewed the night she'd vanished. The timeframe was right. And the age and sex were consistent with the evidence from the gravesite. Including descriptions of the clothing she wore. Looked like their victim was Penny Pryor, but the dental records could confirm or dismiss it.

Thumbing through the witness list, two names caught his attention. Brandt Michael Ferrell, Texas' newly elected governor, and Sara Taylor, widow of Joshua Bradford. Taylor was Sara's maiden name.

Sara Taylor was six at the time the girl vanished, and now the primary suspect in the hit-and-run death of her husband. Matt just hadn't been able to prove it.

Book in hand, he carried it upstairs to the Detective Bureau on the second floor. The room was large, furnished with desks for the four investigators, three males and one female.

Even though most crimes happened at night, detectives worked days, and rotated for night call-outs. They worked days as support branches, such as the coroner, technicians, and labs were on eight to five schedules.

He found Miles Davis and Chris Hunter at their desks, and handed the book to Davis. Matt tapped the cover. "Looks like this is our victim."

Davis's eyebrows rose almost to his hairline. "How'd you find it so fast?"

"The crime scene rang a bell and I know the cold case files like the back of my hand. When do you want to speak to the parents?"

"Hunter and I can handle it, Chief, unless you just want to be there."

"I need to be involved in this one, Miles. Penny was the niece of Brandt Ferrell, our esteemed governor."

Home of Sam and Lily Pryor

Matt dreaded next-of-kin notifications. It was the most difficult part of being a cop. No matter how many times he'd tackled them, they never got easier. And those involving children were the worst of the worst.

He and Davis parked on the street in front of the Pryor's two-story brick home in an older, but still exclusive, part of town. Tall pointed cedars formed privacy walls on both sides of the property. Thick Bermuda grass lay across the lawn like a soft green carpet.

Matt glanced at his watch. Past six in the evening. They had waited to give Sam Pryor time to get home so his wife wouldn't be alone to get the bad news.

They got out of the car, Davis carrying his briefcase with the items for identification. When they reached the door, Matt rang the bell. The photo image of Penny's pert face flashed before him. A pretty little girl with red hair and a sprinkle of freckles across her nose—an innocent upward tilt of her lips revealed a gap-toothed smile. The face of a future unfulfilled.

What had it been like for Sam and Lily Pryor to lose this child, have her disappear for a quarter century? To always wonder what happened, hoping she was alive somewhere? To wonder what kind of woman she might have become? He couldn't imagine the pain that must have caused.

He started to ring the bell again when the door opened. The woman in the entryway was too thin, but attractive in a fragile kind of way, with curly red hair and blue eyes. Eyes the same color as Penny's.

"Mrs. Pryor?"

"Yes. May I help you?"

"Mrs. Pryor, I'm Chief of Police Matthew Foley, and this is Detective Miles Davis. We'd like to speak to you and your husband for a moment. May we come in?"

He held out his badge wallet.

She stood in the doorway, not moving, eyes wide and unfocused. She stepped back and gripped the door handle, her voice almost a whisper. "You've found Penny."

The view through the door revealed an open floor plan of the kitchen, dining room, and living room. A slender man with glasses and receding dark hair stepped away from the kitchen sink and came towards them. "Lily, what's wrong?"

"Sam—"

Sam Pryor quick-stepped to the door, and Matt reintroduced himself and Davis. "May we come in, sir? It would be better if we discuss the purpose of our visit inside."

She moved farther back into the entrance and cast an imploring glance at her husband. "Sam...it's about Penny."

Sam Pryor moved closer to his wife and put his arm around her. "Please, come in. My wife seems to be in shock. Is it true? Have you found Penny?"

He led his wife to the sofa and offered them a seat with a wave of his hand. "Is she... alive?"

Lily's eyes welled with tears, her face flush with emotion. Her shaken husband embraced her and tried to maintain a brave face for his wife. "We haven't heard from the police in years...it might not be Penny."

"I'm sorry. We think the remains found this morning may be your daughter." Davis opened the attaché lid

15

and brought out the three color photograph of the victims clothing and ring. "I know this is difficult, but can you identify these items? Did they belong to your daughter?"

Sam took the photo of the ring. He stood and walked to the window. He cleared his throat, his voice husky, but didn't turn around when he spoke. "This is her ring. We bought it for her sixth birthday."

Lily had taken the other shots. She clutched them to her chest and rocked back and forth, tears rolling down her cheeks.

As gently as possible, Matt asked, "Are those Penny's?"

She nodded.

Sam seemed to realize he'd left Lily alone. He came back to her side and lifted his gaze. "Where—"

"The Bay Harbor construction site," Davis said. "You know where that is?"

"Yes. It used to be a church retreat." Sam pulled his wife close. "I'd heard they sold the property."

Davis collected the photographs and placed them back in the briefcase. "We'll return the ring to you as soon as we can, but for the present, it's evidence. This is the home you lived in when your daughter disappeared?"

Lily wrapped thin fingers around her husband's arm and spoke in a near whisper. "We decided not to sell. Afraid Penny would return someday...and be unable to find us."

"We have just a few more things to cover before we're finished," Matt said. "Can you get us the name of Penny's dentist, and the names of any neighbors who lived here when your daughter disappeared? You can email it to Detective Davis when you have the information."

Davis handed Sam his business card.

He took the card, glanced at Davis, then back at Matt. "When can we claim the...her?"

"As soon as the coroner is finished." Matt shook his hand. "I'll give you a call."

He and Davis stood. Matt reached in his jacket pocket and handed Sam his business card. "I'm sorry for your loss. This is my personal cell phone number. Please call me if there's anything we can do to help."

Sam nodded and placed the cards on the coffee table.

"We'll let ourselves out."

Penny's parents sat huddled together on the sofa, as Matt closed the door softly behind him. Lily's soft sobs followed them out.

He and Davis drove back to the station in silence.

Chapter 3

Global Optics

Cloaked by the downpour, the man sat in the car and sipped his black Starbuck's Pike Place. While he watched Sara Bradford enter the building, people went in and out of the Global lobby.

Discovery of the child's body yesterday had forced him into a decision he'd hoped never to make. Sara held his future in her hands though she wasn't aware of the knowledge tucked inside her head. Too bad. Really. He'd grown fond of her. She had matured into an intelligent, beautiful woman.

Safe for so long, he'd been lulled into believing no one would ever know—the secret would go to the grave with him. But the gods of fate decided otherwise.

He rotated his neck to ease the tight muscles, stiff from his painstaking work last night, and the job he'd assigned himself today. Taking a human life was never easy, but it wouldn't be his first time. He'd do what must be done to protect the life he'd built.

Lightning flashed across the dark sky, illuminating the interior of the car. In the brief glare, he caught sight of his reflection in the rearview mirror and realized he no longer knew the stone, gray face that stared back at him.

Chapter 4

Global, Optics

Sara Bradford shook her head. Some days you get roses, some days you get thorns. No roses today.

Traffic routed around the wreck on the rain-slicked freeway made her twenty minutes late to work. She hated being tardy. Punctuality was encoded into her genes at birth. A gift from her father.

She hurried through the lobby and into the skywalk separating the distribution center from the home office complex. Rain misted the walkway's windows but didn't conceal the threatening sky that hovered outside.

Inside the warehouse, the corridor split. One way led to the production area, the other to management offices. A waist-high counter ran across a reception area for greeting salesmen and visitors. Her secretary, Jane Haskell, whose desk was just outside Sara's office, glanced at her watch when Sara entered. "Better grab a fast cup of coffee. Things are happening. There's a veep meeting in the boardroom in ten minutes. I thought you weren't going to make it. Want me to get your coffee?"

"No, thanks. I'll get a cup upstairs." Sara unlocked the door, placed her handbag and briefcase inside, and grabbed a leather legal pad holder from the desk drawer.

On her way out, she stopped at Jane's desk. "Any idea what the meeting's about?"

Jane's ebony eyes crinkled with mirth and the corners of her mouth tilted upward. "Who, me? No, no. I just work here."

Arms crossed, Sara grinned. Her secretary had the inside track on the company grapevine. "Don't kid a kidder. You know more about what goes on here than the CEO. So give it up."

White teeth flashed in Jane's pretty, dark face. "Well, if I were to guess, I'd say it's about the buyout rumor that's circulated all week."

Jane had nailed it. Sara expected an official announcement from the front office before the end of the day. "I guess we'll know after the meeting."

She hurried back through the skywalk. Time was short, so she took the elevator to the fourth floor rather than her usual route via the stairs. Corporate life offered few chances for physical activity, and she took advantage of the stairway whenever possible. At thirty-two, she attributed her healthy glow to a commitment to avoid the easy path.

The elevator's one glass wall offered a rain-splattered view of tall oaks and a rippling pond in the park next to Global's property. A ding announced the top floor, and the silver doors slid open.

The welcome aroma of roasting coffee beans exuded from a high-tech coffee maker in the butler's pantry adjacent to the executive boardroom. Sara ducked inside, filled a foam cup and stepped next door.

Orange oil mixed with the scent of leather, greeted her as she entered. An impressive mahogany conference table flanked by fourteen plush leather chairs held center stage. Original oil paintings, highlighted by hidden ceiling lights, adorned the fabric-covered walls.

She scanned the table's occupants, recognizing the faces of her counterparts on the executive staff. With a good morning nod, she eased into the closest vacant chair.

Senior Vice-President Charles Edwards entered and sat beside her. He checked the time on his Rolex and leaned close. "It must be something important. Roger called in the big guns."

Hiding a smile behind the cup in her hand, she glanced at him. In his early to mid-fifties, Charles was tall, well-tanned, with short-cropped gray hair. He wore an immaculate dark-blue suit, always elegant and touchingly gallant. Jane called him *GQ* Man. He could be a bit arrogant, but Sara liked him. Perhaps because he reminded her of her father.

Before she could comment, Global's CEO Roger Reynolds strode into the room and stood behind his chair. The first thing she noticed when she'd first met

Roger was his charisma, packaged in a thin frame with perfect teeth and short blond hair. The second impression had been to stay on her toes. His reputation for ruthlessness preceded him. And in short order she understood why.

He placed a well-manicured hand on the back of his chair and scanned the faces around the room. His gaze stopped at Sara for a fraction of a second, then moved on. "People, this will be a short meeting. I'm aware rumors have been floating around about a Global buyout. The rumors are true. Yesterday, Millennium Ventures, a large investment firm, acquired Global Optics. The public announcement will hit newspapers this morning."

Fragmented conversations erupted, filling the room with an audible buzz.

Roger held up his hand. "Two weeks from Monday, the new owners will arrive here at nine o'clock to meet with department heads and to tour the facility."

Charles Edwards sat back in his chair, a furrowed frown on his face, clicking his Mont Blanc pen. He asked the question on everyone's mind. "Will they bring in their own management team?"

Roger shrugged. "You know as much about that as I do, Charles. However, it's always a possibility. I think we can expect some changes. A word of caution. Make sure your departments are spotless when the management team arrives for the tour." He glanced around the table. "Any other questions?" Signaling that the meeting was over.

Sara remained in her seat for a moment.

Amazing. No rallying encouragement for the troops. Roger left them with the impression some or all of them could lose their jobs. Not a model of good leadership.

She retrieved her folder from the table and fell in behind the solemn group exiting the conference room. As she stepped into the corridor, Roger touched her elbow and guided her away from the crowd. "Come back to my office. We need to talk."

A summons to Reynolds' realm was a rare occurrence for her. Although one of Global's eight vice presidents, she'd never been part of Roger's inner circle. He liked yes-men, and she didn't fit that mold.

She eased into step beside him. They moved without speaking into the executive suite. As they entered, Roger's phone rang. He waved her to a seat and stepped behind his desk to take the call.

Sara sat on one of the earth-toned sofas grouped near the windows. Her gaze roamed to Roger's massive desk clear of everything, except a pen set, computer, and telephone. No family pictures, nothing personal.

She studied the bookshelves above his credenza. Books said more about a man than his clothes or bearing. For a moment, her father's study flashed into her mind. The classics found a home there, as well as his light reading collections by Zane Grey and Louis L'Amour. The King James Bible held a prominent spot within easy reach.

Roger's books consisted of business management best sellers. Nothing to give insight into the man. Perhaps that in itself, said something. She mentally shook herself—being too critical. After all, this wasn't his home library.

The call ended, and Roger crossed the room. He sat on the sofa across from her and sucked in a deep breath. "I need you to clean out your office. Pack your files and personal items. Leave the cartons there until further notice."

Shock must have registered on her face. Heat warmed her cheeks, an event always followed by red splotches on her neck. A curse she'd lived with through every emotional crisis in her life. "I...don't understand. Are you letting me go?"

He laid one arm across the sofa back, his face void of expression. "That's not what I said."

"Then what...?"

"The new owner hasn't given any specifics, except to say you would be leaving your current position. There were no instructions to let you go." He winced as though trying to show compassion. "I assume these people have other plans for you. Details have been vague, to say the least."

She didn't buy his lack of knowledge. How much input Roger had in the decision to move her out, she didn't know. However, she felt certain he hadn't gone to bat for her. Whatever happened when the new firm took over, she couldn't expect any support from Roger.

No point in pursuing it now. Difficult as it was, she had to keep it together. Stay professional.

Roger asked, "Do you understand what I need from you?"

Of course, she understood. "The part about cleaning out my office came through crystal clear."

He leaned back and crossed his legs. "Take the rest of the day off, if you like."

She shook her head. "I'd rather pack after the warehouse staff leaves at noon. I've scheduled two weeks of vacation to start Monday."

Roger nodded. "That's probably best. The time off will do you good. I'm confident you'll be offered another position, either here or in one of their other divisions."

He stood and walked her to the door. "You will, of course, need to be here for the meeting Monday after your vacation. You should get answers to any concerns you have then."

She released the breath she'd been holding and lifted her chin. Roger wouldn't get the satisfaction of seeing her angst. She felt his gaze linger until she disappeared around the corner.

<<>>

The rest of the morning passed in a blur. Warehouse personnel left at noon on Friday, so she had the place to herself. She sorted through the desk drawers, packed the files in cartons, and labeled them.

Jane would be curious when she saw the boxes. If she asked, Sara would have to tell her the truth.

Leaning back in her chair, Sara stretched tense muscles in her neck and shoulders. She'd packed, everything except a picture of Josh she'd kept in the desk drawer after his death. Misty eyed, she lifted the silver-framed photograph and ran a finger over the glass, smoothing back the lock of hair that always fell across her husband's brow. A motion performed so many times in private before the relationship took a left turn.

The marriage had been anything but ideal, but she

missed his dry sense of humor and his gentleness. She hadn't had a chance to say goodbye, to say she was sorry she'd failed him—to say she loved him. He'd left for work that morning and never returned. She blinked back the moisture that stung her eyelids, and slipped the picture into her handbag.

Financially, she would be okay if she lost her job. At least for a while. She still had most of Josh's insurance money. Aunt Maddie also insisted on contributing to the household expenses. But in a job market flooded with laid-off executives, finding another position that paid as well as Global could take a long time.

From the doorway, her gaze roamed over the office that had been hers for five years. Her chest tightened and she inhaled a deep breath. This might be her last walk-through inspection.

<<>>

Security guard Don Tompkins, glanced at the monitor as Sara Bradford left her office. His gaze shifted to the next screen as the warehouse camera clicked on, activated by motion sensors. Cameras followed her progress. With shoulder-length dark hair and olive complexion, she stood out in a crowd. In a quiet way. Large hazel eyes and a generous mouth took her looks to the next level, from just pretty to beautiful.

She stopped before a bank of high-rise forklifts plugged into battery chargers. A lone machine sat apart, unconnected.

Unusual.

Don leaned in for a closer look.

Warehouse supervisors routinely connected the machines before leaving at the end of a shift. Dead batteries meant lost productivity the next day.

Sara stopped and glanced around, then dropped her handbag on the lift platform.

A bright flash filled the monitor. The floor quaked, and a loud *boom* sounded from the distribution center.

The video screen went dark. Emergency lights immediately snapped on, casting an eerie glow over the scene.

Don dashed towards the skywalk and shouted at the young guard behind the counter. "Call 911. There's been an explosion in the warehouse. Sound the fire alarm and evacuate this building. Now!"

A rush of adrenaline made the blood pound in his ears as he broke into a full run. In the dim lighting, the camera showed the forklift, mangled and enveloped in flames.

Purchase WORKS OF DARKNESS on Amazon

V. B. Tenery is the author of the award-winning Matt Foley suspense series and other novels, including, Deathwatch, Against the Odds, The Watchman, Dead Ringer, Last Chance and Angels Among Us. She lives in East Texas with her family, three dogs and one lone cat.

Her love of reading blossomed at a very young age. Quickly bored with television, she devoured books, impatient for the next visit to the library.

After finishing school she went to work for one of the country's largest optical firms. Writing took a back seat to her career when she became director of service for the firm's national warehouse. Marriage, a young daughter, and active involvement in church turned her into an occasional weekend writer.

When the company she worked for downsized, she jumped at the opportunity to retire and write full time. Since then she has written multiple Christian suspense novels in an on-going series and stand-alone novels.

Sign up for her newsletter on her website: www.vbtenery.com

Follow her on FaceBook and Twitter!